LOVE
& LIKE

LOVE & LIKE

BY HERBERT GOLD

Meridian Fiction
THE WORLD PUBLISHING COMPANY
Cleveland and New York

HERBERT GOLD

Herbert Gold was born in Cleveland, Ohio, in 1924. He has
received a number of important literary prizes, including a
Ford Foundation grant, Guggenheim and Hudson Review
fellowships, an award from the National Institute of Arts and
Letters, and an O. Henry Prize. His stories and articles
appear regularly in leading periodicals. In addition to
Love & Like, Mr. Gold is the author of five novels: *Birth of a
Hero, The Prospect Before Us, The Man Who Was Not
With It, The Optimist,* and *Therefore Be Bold.*

MERIDIAN FICTION

Published by The World Publishing Company
2231 West 110 Street, Cleveland 2, Ohio
First Meridian printing March 1961

for my mother and father;
for Ann and Judy;
for Isaac Green and his wife

Acknowledgements

Acknowledgement is made to the original publishers of the stories in this collection which appeared in the magazines below: To *Atlantic Monthly* for SUSANNA AT THE BEACH; To *Antioch Review,* Fall 1954, for A CELEBRATION FOR JOE; To *Commentary,* July 1957, for ARISTOTLE AND THE HIRED THUGS; To *The Dial,* Fall 1959, for SELLO; To *Discovery,* No. 3, © 1954 by Pocket Books, Inc., for THE BURGLARS AND THE BOY; To *The Hudson Review,* Vol. IV, No. 3, Autumn for THE HEART OF THE ARTICHOKE, Vol. X, No. 1, Spring 1957, for PARIS AND CLEVELAND ARE VOYAGES, Vol. XI, No. 3, Autumn 1958, for LOVE AND LIKE, Vol. XII, No. 4, Winter 1959-60, for A TALE OF TWO HUSBANDS; To *Midstream,* A Quarterly Jewish Review, for ENCOUNTER IN HAITI; The story TI-MOUNE appeared originally in *The New Yorker;* To *Playboy* for WHAT'S BECOME OF YOUR CREATURE?; To *Vogue* for THE PANIC BUTTON; To *New Directions* for the five stories which appeared in FIFTEEN BY THREE.

Contents

The Heart of the Artichoke

My father, his horny hands black with sulphur, lit a cigar with a brief, modest, but spectacular one-handed gesture, his thumbnail crr-racking across the blue-headed kitchen match; when he described his first job in America, selling water to the men building the skyscrapers, teetering across the girders for fifteen cents a pail, green flecks fumed and sailed in his yellowish Tartar eyes; he peeled an artichoke with both hands simultaneously, the leaves flying toward his mouth, crossing at the napkin politely tucked at the master juggler's collar, until with a groan that was the trumpet of all satisfaction he attained the heart; he—but he was a man of capabilities, such feats apart.

As my mother said of him before they married, "He's well-off. Lots of personality." Older than the other women of her family, she used the word *well-off* in a primitive sense, to signify a general relationship with the world, not subtracting from the term all but its usual financial refrain: "Well-off very, he's a Buick. . . ." But she took the word from Aunt Sarah and Aunt Ethel; it's important that the vocabulary derives from economic security, to be extended outward only by an exceptional act of vitality. We, my brothers

3

and I, could never eat enough for her. "Don't aggravate me. Eat. Eat," she would say.

"We already ate," I pointed out.

"But look at your father!"

He was eating. He ate with silent respect for food, a great deal, and not out of gluttony but with appreciation for his own labor in it. He knew the cost. In each spoonful of soup carried with music to his mouth I heard the winds whistling through the branches of the knaedloch trees; I saw the farmers' trucks, laden with chopped liver, musing in his crocodile eyes. "Eat," he pronounced at intervals, assuaging his love for us, "eat, eat."

We ate with a hunger in our bellies or in a filial loyalty while his was in his heart. Wearing a sheepskin coat which came as a gift from Mother and Pitkin's with the no-overhead, a silvery-pronged crate-hammer arming his back pocket, he climbed into the cab of his truck before dawn on market days, his wife's lips still parted against their single pillow while he checked off a list measured in gross over a breakfast of liver-and-onions with the other fruitmen in Solly's Market Tearoom. Perhaps at the earlier moment of supper, while we heedlessly digested, carloads of artichokes were coming in at the Food Terminal for the Thursday morning auction. He would get the best for Jack's Food & Vegetable: *The Best is the Best Buy*.

"Always," my mother piously breathed after him. She was proud of his slogan. "He made it up himself one day I remember it, he was by the cooler sorting asparagus. Lots of personality, loads," she informed Aunt Ethel and Aunt Sarah. "Eat," she said to me. "The nice ovenbaked potato."

I once asked the address of the poor hungry man in China who would be glad to finish my potato. "I'll send it to him with Mr. Kennedy the mailman," I suggested.

"I need your backtalk like I need my own brother

Morton's agar-agar oil for his constipation, Henry Ford should take him. A whole tablespoon," she said. "I need it." Repenting of my sarcasm, I never believed in the poor hungry man, although I had recently become convinced of China at least in Geography.

My father had the knowledge of things—how to hoist an orange crate in a movement like a dance, how to tell an honest farmer from one who will hide his bad Pascal or Iceberg under bravado and a show of good ones, whom to trust in the fleet meetings of money at a fruit auction; this is already a great deal. Only once was he famously tricked, and by Uncle Morton, a man who installed automatic sprinkling pipes in his lawn ("For show! for the neighbors!" my mother communicated, outraged) but spent his Sundays tightening the faucets and complaining that his daughters filled the bathtub too full. (How clean can you get?)

Well, this brother-in-law, exalted by cupidity in one federally sponsored moment, suggested a partnership in the property in order to eliminate my father's competition at an auction: Should brothers, or almost-brothers, bid each other up like cats and dogs? No, the answer.

Afterwards, the deal secured, my father approached, tendering a hand-rolled cigar fraternally-in-law and saying, "Nu Mort, now about the partnership I think well we should let Henry there in the Republic Building, not that Hank from 105th Street, Henry a reliable man Hazelton Hotels uses him, draw up the papers—"

"Partners! hah!" Villainous Uncle Morton, performing for some secret inner croak of applause, permitted himself laughter at such innocence. "I'm partners me only with my wife"—and they haven't spoken since, nor have his daughters and I, cousins all.

But this was real estate, not food, which was the true sphere of my father's power; besides, such an error brings

scope and savor to a legend of paternal infallibility. He
could say, or let my mother say, while above the broad
cheekbones his eyes glittered like two long plump lima
beans on sidewalk display in the sun: "The only time Jake
got it but good, it was that time with the Woodward
property, his own brother-in-law my brother, they run a
house in the Heights and two cars—they need it?—a Buick
sure and a Chevie for Yetta and the kids, may his breath
turn sour in his old age—"

And his daughters' too. Amen.

As my mother talked, my father measured us from
under a vast biblical forehead which had sojourned in
Kamenetz-Podolsk; it was a forehead that barely escaped
the scars of reprisal for a tradesman's life given to a man
who needed labor in the open air. He wrestled out this
frozen compression, these knotty ravages, at the cost of an
over-quickening in the work of the store, wielding cases
with a plunging violence and mounting trucks like a burly
fruitstore tomcat. Over-happiness too is a threat, Zara-
thustra said. The yellow flecks of his long narrow eyes
fumed in contemplation. His sons were strange animals,
born in America.

Question-shaped, my belly in advance of my thoughts,
I had unnoticed by all but myself become skinny, pimply,
shrewd, and poetic. I trained myself to wake at dawn, not
for work like my father or to drink formula like my youngest
brother, but because of the possibility that Pattie Donahue
might feel my presence and stir in response to it; I believed
in telepathy, tuning in on no messages because no one sent
me any. I searched her face during Miss Baxter's Reading
and The Library How To Use It for a sign of complicity
(received no answer); I never spoke to her, for reasons of
shyness and reasons of magic. She had aquarium eyes, profoundly green, profoundly empty, and a mouth like a two-

cent Bull's Eye candy, and pale transparent fingers busy as
fins. She powdered her nose in public, no longer picking it;
she touched her ears to make sure of their presence on the
beach of her head; patiently she plucked the angora from her
mittens off the front of her cardigan, with this gesture of
pale-boned fingers exploring herself and me. Together only
abstractly, we were linked by both imagining atrocious ways
to wish her well.

I let her swim again in my memory. She considered the
future by judging it with the deliberate active forgetfulness
of a fish floating asleep under ice: power through patience.
Pattie Donahue wanted more than love, more than strength;
she wanted mastery in denial, divinity in refusal of her own
blood. Up the ladder to godhood or down to fishliness? That
was her one risk in life. Seaweed is good for you! Lots of
iodine! She had a repertory of head-tuckings, wiggles, peeps,
curtseys, suckings, winks, herself charmed by herself; she
was crippled for eternity, condemned to increase by parthe-
nogenesis. She could not laugh with her body because her
body could never move to another's, sway as it might under
the seas of her ambition. Bemused, pious, she granted herself an adoring hand, fingers straddling to squeeze her
sweater at the root of milk and psychology. Recall that
princess who could undress before a slave because she did
not regard him as a human being? We are all sometimes
slaves.

Slavishly I kneeled for her chamois penwiper where
it fell behind her desk in Music and Singing.

"Oh thank you," she said.

"Never mind, never mind"—me melting like March
ice in a spring pool of timidity and chagrin.

"Oh don't stop me, Daniel Berman. Thank you indeed.
My mother says I need practice how to be gracious. Please
let me do thank you. Oh thank you, Daniel Berman. . . ."

This too is a sort of excess!—and I let her take me under the green grasp of her greedy eyes. The fishy princess pouted, ducked, abstractly reached; I worshipped this body shivering and glistening under bracelets like scale. I saw her as age. Age during that time signifies secret power, secret passion, and the death which follows age is known only as the death which follows love. Girls, born queens, are always older than boys, ten-thousand-eyed drones, living for love, empty-headed, precariously housebroken. "Oh thank you really," said Princess Pattie Donahue, her royal sardine, queen of the hive.

She was gracious on me.

One day, the talk of the Horace Greeley Junior High playground, a pride for events beyond me took her; she wore a shiny black brassiere which hung in lank splendor beneath the faintly distended yarn of her sweater and the morning's accretion of pink angora. She plucked, she pinched; in my poems I never found a rhyme for Donahue. Desire for a girl with nipples like tapioca spots! She went out, it was alleged, with high school seniors.

It was at this era of sudden sweat and pubic rancor that the issue of working in the store afternoons or at least Saturdays became prominent. "To help out," my father said.

"To learn the value of a dollar," my mother said.

"To know what's what in life," my father said.

"To learn the value of a dollar," my mother said.

"To find out it's like something to be a man," my father said.

"To learn the value of a dollar," my mother said.

"To see how people—"

"To learn the value—"

"To help—"

"To learn—"

There always remained another word to propose on the subject. "I have homework to do?" I asked, making this a question because the whole world knew I did no homework.

"Your cousin Bernie works in his father's store," my mother said. "He's learning the value."

"Your cousin Irwin works in his father's store," my father said. "Very mature kit, grown-up. Knows what's what."

No fonder of my cousins, I began to work in the store. At first there were compensations besides learning the value and knowing what's what; for example, I quickly suspected the potentialities of stacking Jello. Its six delicious box colors made possible the development of a penchant toward baroque in counter displays. I gave over to fantasy in exercises of pure structure; I brought art to Dried Desserts (end of the first aisle), evolving from a gothic striving and simplicity to a rococo exuberance, raspberry mounting lemon in commercial embrace. The Jello man beamed and said I had talent. He promised me an autographed photograph of Jack Benny from his sample case, the signature printed as good as original, the *same identical thing.* I stood off, narrow-eyed, architectural, three loose boxes in each hand. While orange buttresses flew and lime vaulted over naves of cherry, my father grew impatient. "Is that all you got on your mind, the playboy?" It was not all, but he was right: there is a limit to what one can do with Jello. And what finally happened to my dream of a celestial engineering? Bananas were sliced into it.

I knew that my friends were playing touch football in the street or perhaps, if it were late afternoon, amorously lobbing rocks onto Pattie Donahue's front porch. Pity the man with an unemployed throwing-arm! Aproned and earth-bound despite my Buster Brown aviator shoes, I stood in exile among the creak of shopping baskets and a cash-register clang, such matters unmusical where a rumor of roller skates on a girl's sidewalk pledges passion eternal and a well-placed rock portends an invitation to Rosalie Fallon's second annual traditional Hallowe'en party; these are suburban verities which held even in the prehistory before Mayor Cassidy's first reign, when I began my studies of how to pee in an enamelled pot. A marksman now, I turned sullen despite my skill, sour as a strawberry plucked too early; my father knew their need to ripen wild in the sun, unfingered by ambitious farmwives. I was a bad crop, green through, lazy for spite.

"Stop slouching," my mother said. "Stand up like a mench. Bernie *likes* the store. He stays and works even when Uncle Abe says go home, here's a quarter."

I learned contempt for my cousins, the submissive ones, who worked so that they could spend dimes like grown-ups instead of nickels in the Chippewa Lake slot machines. No amount of labor could harden their gluey hands. Irwin had flat feet, a moustache at fourteen because his mother did not tell him to shave, the habit of standing too close when he talked, and, as luck would have it, a talent for projecting his bad breath with such accuracy that any customer's sales resistance must have died in the first whiff. Later he learned to brush his tongue, shave his armpits, sprinkle himself with Johnson's Baby Powder, and rinse his mouth with spearmint mouthwash. Anything for a client. He gave up his soul, a pulpy one at that, which resided in the crevices of his teeth.

Bernie, Narcissus Gaynesbargh the Go-getter, developed an artist's pure love for illness, hospitals, and operations. He saved up enough—"All by his lonesome," bragged Aunt Sarah—for an operation which joined his ears more cunningly to his head. "Clark Gable can let him-

self go, he's a big man already, but not my Bernie," his
mother proudly recounted. "Today he looks a million—
stand frontways, Bernie! And how tall is your Daniel?"

Bernie had enough left over in his account to have his
piles removed during the after-Christmas slow spell. *Carpe
Diem:* he obeyed our junior high motto, constantly im-
proving himself, a medically-made man, an expert on
vitamin pills, eye exercises, and local anesthesia. He was
also judicially-made; let us not omit the subtle alterations
in the orthography of his name. Imagine the legal nightmare in which a Ginsberg-into-Gaynesbargh signifies more
rebirth than immolation! The suicide was a complete success. Neither his ears nor his ancestors stuck out, although
the stitching showed.

"*They* will marry nice rich girls from New York City,
you'll see," my mother threatened me. Later both took
Marital Engineering courses, one at Miami University and
the other at Cornell, and it paid, because Bernie married
a nice rich shoe business from Hartford and Irwin married
a wholesale Divan & Studio Couch, a steady thing.

"But," as my mother said, "you can't measure happiness in dollars and cents. There are things more important especially with taxes these days. A sweet little wife,
a nice little family. . . ."

"Have a piece Sanders." Aunt Sarah consoled her
with the Continental assortment. "I got it by Sanders Chocolates when I went downtown to look for my new Person
Lamb yesterday. Purse-and-lamb, I mean. Who knows
maybe I'll settle for a Shirt Beaver, the season's almost
over."

Not even Aunt Sarah can distract my mother when
philosophy comes over her. "You could marry in a low
element, maybe he wouldn't really be rich only pretending,
living high, that kind of a click—"

"My Irwin hm hm, you should know he sent me a this year's pillow direct from the factory to me," Aunt Sarah might remark. "He don't have to put birds in his vest, my Irwin."

"Don't tell me, I know," Mother groaned. "Some people are real type bigshots, some people have to make look big to themselves with escalator heels and Scotch shoelaces, who ever heard?"

"My Irwin—"

"What, you crazy? He's a nice steady boy your Irwin, clean-cut, a neat dresser. I'm mentioning it so happens one of those fast clicks, oh, oh."

"Ho," breathed Aunt Sarah.

They communed in silence over the family shame. They clopped the bitter memory from their outraged palates. They drew the lesson from what befell poor Cousin Bessie, who returned from a vacation—she had a nice job with the government, too—with pierced ears and coral earrings, a pair of chartreuse silk slacks, and a new man to replace the one who broke his head. "My new husband," she announced, indicating a plump individual with oily sunburned pouches under his eyes, Novelty-style shoelaces, and a sky-blue Kalifornia Kravate with a silver-lightning pin, the tie tucked into a Hickock Kowboy-type belt: "Roland, he's in the wholesale business in Los Angeles."

"Wholesale what?" Mother had asked, suspicious already.

"Just wholesale," Cousin Bessie said equably. Roland smiled to show the gap in his teeth bridged by invisible platinum. His little woman spoke for him: "He has the biggest outlet in Los Angeles."

"Ellay," he corrected her.

Later, after Uncle Moish from Indian River Drive

discovered that this Roland was a bad-type thief off the legit, not a dealer in factory-to-you eliminate-the-middleman low-costs, they helped Bessie out again. She promised to be more careful next season. She was pushing thirty-five, although the family loyally counted only the last twenty-seven of them; she had combed the summer time mountains and the winter time seaside since she buried Lester. Mother took three deep breaths and announced, addressing her in the ceremonial third person while Besssie wept wholesale tears: "Next time she should vacate a week ten days in Atlantic City on the Atlantic, the sun, the salt water taffy, she should meet a nice steady New York type fella, she still got her health why not? Knock on wood. Just he shouldn't have the biggest outlet in Ellay."

Still my cousins were generally nice, steady, and successful even at that early time. I was recalcitrant, a failure in affairs.

"The whole world knows. Aunt Ethel and Aunt Sarah know, it should happen to me I try to be a good mama to you. The whole city knows."

Aunt Sarah encouraged my mother in her own way. " 'Mama,' my Bernie tell me,"—and her eyes moistened over such devotion—" 'Mama,' he says, 'you look like sugar in the urine again. What did I tell you about those two-dollar Sanders assortments?' . . . . So thoughtful," she concluded, folding her arms across a high stalwart bone of her *garment,* leaning back, and waiting for my mother to tell something good about me. I couldn't even read an oral thermometer. After a while she sighed for pity, yawned for contentment, and added soothingly, "Your Danny working nice in the store these days maybe? Just tell him about my Bernie, he'll learn, you got to encourage."

"I look in the looking glass I ask myself why, I got no

answer. A son of mine, why? A thirteen-years-old lump,"
she encouraged.

It wasn't laziness. That's a maternal answer. I would
have worked in other ways, and did; if I could have remained at some comprehensible task, delivering orders perhaps, building shelves, loading the truck, or manipulating
the stock in the basement, I might have attained a fulfill-
ment equal in its way to Cousin Bernie's avarice for operations. The constant pouring of commands from a triumphant father shivered and shattered my sense for work: he
wanted me by his side, proud of an eldest son, any eldest
son. For good reasons of his own—he had been poor, he
wanted me to see what he had done for himself and for us
all—he urged me to learn the pleasure of a direct delicious
manipulation of money, its worn old touch of cloth, its
warmth of hands and pockets, its smell of sex and work, its
color of economy or death in our world, signed in those
days by Andrew W. Mellon. "Here! it says right here.
Read it yourself. That's the Secretary of the Treasury of the
United States of America, U. S. A., his own autograph."

"Oh for God's sake. Jake, you can notice such things?"
—my mother discovering new depths, she a modest econo-
mist, my father not.

"Notice notice," he admitted virtuously. Money was
poetry, a symbol of life and power on one side, economy and
death for him with the White House on the other, but only
a symbol—how could I understand such metaphysics, un-
graduate-schooled in that epoch of despair with girls and
ambitions of purity? My agile Tartar-eyed father made the
distinction by enjoying both the earning and the spending,
finding his truth higgledy-piggledy in an exploit of strap-
ping a load-and-a-healthy-half on his 1928 White Motors
truck or in giving himself to a snack of artichoke with
Kraft's dressing, the heart his end but the money-colored
leaves loved for what they were.

He wanted me to clerk, to *wait on trade,* then, to be an aproned catalyst toward the final term. How could I take money from Mrs. Donahue, whose daughter no one but Tom Moss knew I loved, while Pattie herself teased her mouth with an end of lipstick without glancing at me in my feminizing wraparound? My languishing yip should have betrayed me: "That'll be just three sixty-five, please," recited as I had been taught. It did not; no one saw me. The money joined money in the new Serv-a-slip cash register. *O love me, Pattie! look!*—and I feared that she would. I gave the cash to Hannah, the cashier, my father's deputy while he bargained with the Wheaties jobber for bonus Eversharps and an electric fan-flame wood-glow fireplace.

"Okay, Little Jack, you're picking up now. I'll tell your pa. Just keep the hands out of the pockets when you're making a sale. Say thank you to the customer." Hannah had a tongue cracked and ridged, mounds at the meaty sides and fissures among the yellowish scale, betrothed to dyspepsia. These wounds came of a continual talking confused with a continual eating. No one knew a remedy. She suffered unsilently, chewing Baseball Gum. "I said take hands out of pockets that's a boy. I said say thank you to the nice customer."

"Thank you, Mrs. Donahue," I mumbled miserably.

I carried Mrs. Donahue's order to her Hudson. Pattie moved ahead, her rump twitching like a snapdragon delicately pinched. I fled as she fumbled with her purse for a tip. The next Monday, inspecting my approach from her station at the side entrance to Horace Greeley Junior High, without taking her eyes off mine she bent significantly to whisper into her friend Rosalie Fallon's ear. To stifle their laughter the two of them made paws of their silly adored hands at their mouths. This gesture insured politeness and (reward for a suburban virtue) the secret renewal of laughter when the grocery boy had passed. Sober and unblinking, Pattie nonchalantly rubbed her edible kneecap.

"Don't call me Little Jack," I told Hannah once more without hope. "Call me my name."

"Okay. . . . Little Jack," she said, humorously chewing.

Sometimes I carried a book to work, wearing it piously between my shirt and my chest, and then hid with it and a cigarette in the basement among the cases of Libby's Whole Sliced Pineapple and Hinz-zuzz Pork and Beans with Tomato Sauce. The whitewashed walls sweated; the storeroom smelled of dampness, rat poison, cardboard packing cases, and a broken bottle of soy sauce. Here I was happy, the complicated atmosphere making me dizzy as I perched corrupt with one of Andy's Wing butts on a peak of pineapple under the dusty 40-watt bulb. Sometimes I put down the Poe (I had memorized *Ulalume* without being able to pronounce it) and moodily considered my childhood, before Pattie Donahue and before my parents had decided I was a man, when I had sometimes visited this range of cans and bottles to leap like a goat among it in my innocence. I practiced a tragic sigh, inhaling soy.

Always my father roared down the stairway to discover me. "YOU THINK YOU CAN KID ME, HAH? The A & P can't even kid me, I got a list of your tricks—"

I stood up with no answer, understanding that he would forever find me, silent in my wished chagrin. I could not explain to him the disgrace of working in a store in a neighborhood where boys had important unexplainable things to do, secret clubs and fatal loafing, while their fathers managed offices for Standard Machines or handled law cases for insurance companies downtown. I wanted him to commute instead of work, like the others; I could not tell either of us the reason for my stubborn reluctance to follow him to the market, racy and challenging though it was. I felt a justice in his despair with me. A coward, I hid each time.

"Your mother says today you'll be good, I say I'll find you sneaking off with a book."

I studied his boots on the cement and deeply assented. He had looked in the backroom to see if I were filling orders, giving me the benefit of a doubt and profligate hope which is still my debt.

"Nu, what do you say for yourself? I'm going crazy upstairs, it's a big one-cent-sale, the Saturday help's no good these days. . . . Hah?"

I said nothing.

"Why not tell me another lie, you'll be good like you promised I should be happy?"

I stared, Poe sweaty in my hands.

"So why don't you at least say you had to go to the toilet, the mensroom?"—a treble note of exasperation hidden in his bass, wanting an excuse for me, loving his oldest.

I refused this. I was over-moral for a moment, going on thirteen, as he was over-happy; I despised anything but extreme commitments, surrender to his world or defiance of it.

"What's the matter, you constipated? You got stomach trouble?"—pretending that I had given us this excuse, unable to bear our misery together.

He watched the tears silently fill my eyes.

He relented; he appealed to me, trying to preserve his anger by shouting; he betrayed his helplessness by heavily sitting down beside me on the canned pineapple. "What's the matter, you hungry, you want your mother should make you a tomato and balony sandwich with Kraft's Miracle Whip dressing?"

"I want to go upstairs and help out," I whispered at last.

Reconciled, unable to preserve animus, he bumped

against me up the narrow steps. Instead of letting me sink
into the crowd of customers reaching with their lists and
their clippings of advertisements at the counters, he ordered
me to go to lunch with him, knowing that I liked this. To
have the Business Men's special with Dad in a restaurant
was one of the compensations; choosing food is the act of
a god—only gods and business men don't have mothers to
tell them what to eat, filling their plates with it. It was a
pure joy although a bad restaurant; we had to go there because Guy Mallin owed my father two hundred dollars,
which he never paid and we couldn't eat through by the
time he left his wife and ran off to Montreal with Stella, the
waitress, and a week's receipts. (When this happened Dad
tried, although he knew little about the restaurant business,
to help out poor Mrs. Mallin, who had no children but only
a thyroid condition to give her an interest in life.) Both of
us would have preferred an egg roll and hamburger steak
at Louie's, the Chinaman across the street, and our unity
on this—winking across the table as fast-talking Guy
Mallin approached—cleared the hatred of civilizations between father and son. I should insist on this: the storm con-
fined itself to its direct object, my laziness, rising like an
east wind to its peak on the busy day, Saturday or before
holidays, then falling away. "You learn with meet people,"
he only said. "You learn with know their ways."

After we finished our lunch I hid in the basement of
the store to read Edgar Allan Poe.

2

As the months went by, the ruses deepened and the
anger swam like some exiled bull carp in the deepest pools
of the natures of my mother, my father, and me. Pattie
Donahue had definitively given up roller skating in the

street, and not only on bricked Pittsburg Road but also on
the mellifluous asphalt of Chesterton Avenue. We were
freshmen in junior high, seventh graders learning dignity
from a Social Dancing teacher added to the curriculum by
the Board of Education which decided that Grace and Poise
(formerly Comportment) were as essential as geography
and algebra to the Young Men & Women of Tomorrow, be
they bond salesmen like their fathers or *homemakers* like
their mothers. The Real Estate Taxpayers League issued a
protest against educational frills; pioneering virtues that
made our country great, assessment already excessive, it
argued. Artichokes, bulky and hard to handle, were coming
into season again.

Shamefully I pretended to be sleeping Saturday mornings when my father had gotten up at three or earlier.
Mother was more violent, my father more deeply hurt—the
denial, after all, was of him. She nagged constantly; yet on
Saturdays when I stayed motionless slugabed, her pride in
sleep—"It's very healthy"—protected me there. Later, my
father telephoning to ask if I had arisen yet, he fell silent
before her report, pressing the receiver to his ear amid the
mob of shoppers importunate about fork-tongued Hannah's
dais, and he darkly said nothing while Mother repeated,
infuriated with me but stubborn in her allegiance to health:
"Let the kid sleep just one more morning, kids need sleep.
It's good for them."

Having vacuumed, she herself got ready to go to the
store for *relief*. Out of some relic of pride I could not bring
myself to feign until she would safely leave me among my
angry bedclothes in the occult reproach of a house. "I'm
up," I fatally admitted. I reached for a paltry revenge in
wearing yesterday's socks. She edified me in a steady tor-
rent on the streetcar to the store:

"No good! big lump! lazy good-for-nothing! You're thirteen already and look at you!"

"Twelve," I corrected her.

" 'Please Daddy I want to work in the store like a big man,' Bernie always says. Aunt Sarah says. Such a go-getter! But what do you say?—look ma the dog wet the rug I'm twelve years old. Aunt Sarah says I should stop aggravating myself. Please give a look my waricose weins from standing up." She had forgotten that the effect of threatening to telephone Aunt Sarah when I was *bad* had been dissipated years ago with the advent of Unlimited Calls. Sometimes I had even offered to dial the number for her.

"A big lump like you he should give me a rest, take the load off your feet Ma like Bernie, not trouble trouble all the time."

"Why is it you always say I'm thirteen when it's something you want me to do and know I'm twelve?" I asked, a savant without rimless glasses: "And when I want to do something I can't because I'm not old enough, I'm only eleven? My birthday is July twentieth at six o'clock in the morning."

"I remember," she said morosely. "And a fine night I had with you in Mount Sinai all night too, they almost had to use force-its. Dr. Shapiro said my bones were so delicate close together. . . . Thirteen, going on now. Even Uncle Morton knows about you, I'm so ashamed in the family why I told Aunt Ethel I'll never hold my head high again, at least Morton he got daughters they keep themselves clean at least not so much aggravation, all right so worry a tiny bit they should marry nice, but not heartache a no-good like you day in day out—"

Outside the streetcar the first autumn leaves were burning in piles on the street, sending up an odor redolent of freedom in the open air. My friends flamboyantly loitered on the Saturday streets, chalk in their mouths, their hearts unfettered. Pattie Donahue was perhaps walking alone in Rocky River Park, just waiting for me telepathically to find her.

The store opened about us with the intense plushy smell of old vegetables. Hannah was comforting old Mrs. Simmons, a childless widow whose husband had been manager of the Guarantee Trust, Rocky River branch; she generally admitted herself among us with the distant face of someone who disliked the smell of the inside of her own nose, but now she claimed to have seen a spider in a hand of bananas. "It probably wasn't a deadly poisonous banana spider," Hannah said. "Did it have a lot of legs? Furry ones from Costo Rico?"

"A South American banana spider! oh!" Mrs. Simmons, realizing that it was a foreign element, rolled her eyes in search of a pleasant place to faint.

"Probably not deadly poisonous, though. Probably just a sleepy little old banana spider from the deadly jungles of Hatey." Mrs. Simmons fainted. That is, considering her dignity and the aristocratic unpaid bills in the drawer with Hannah's sandwiches, she *swooned*. "Anyway no one else saw it, the thousand-legger bug, the horrible deadly spider," Hannah mused on, rubbing Mrs. Simmons' wrists without taking off her Ovaltine Birthstone & Goodluck Ring.

"Ouch, you're scratching," said Mrs. Simmons.

My father, harried but always expecting the best, greeted me with an order. Stack the oranges, wait on Mrs. Simmons, put on your apron, what's the matter with you? . . . . Could I confess the chief reason for my tardiness, a hope that telepathic pressure concentrated among my bedclothes might compel Mrs. Donahue to buy her Ohio State hothouse tomatoes and Swansdown ready-mix no-sift cake

flour before my surrender to penance in a wraparound?
*Develop Your Will Increase Your Power. Sample Booklet
Fool Your Friends. 25c Coin or Stamps.* No, I could not.
My father's will developed, he spoke a language in which
existed no vocabulary to explain that, among the people
with whom he chose to bring me up, it was more important
to run end in a pick-up touch football game, spinning
craftily about the young trees planted by the Our Street
Beautiful committee, than to fill orders in sour old orange
crates on Saturday afternoons. We all paid, in our various
ways, a price for those trees and for the privilege of overhead doors on our garages and colonial-style magazine
racks for our Saturday Evening Posts. He did not draw the
consequences of his ambition for me; if he judged our
neighborhood to be better than that of his childhood, then
our neighborhood would judge his world. In a develop-
your-will (Fool Your Friends) like my father's, the only
lack was the will to find my will-less longing. He worked!
Mother worked! Like dogs!—They were right, but they
could not see through to my rightness, forgetting a child's
hunger to belong. Ulalume might have been for the ages,
but Rosalie Fallon and Pattie tongued their malicious pencils and wrote my fate in their Slam Books. He knew he was
a foreigner, my father did; I had to discover it in pain,
shame before my parents, and self-judging. "I earned my
own living when I was thirteen, and proud of it," he had
said.

"Your father earned his own living when he was
twelve," Mother remarked contentedly in explanation, "and
he is proud of it. *Proud* of it."

"Thirteen he said," I said.

"Proud he said," she said.

He studied me in sorrow and silence, figuring with his
short black-nailed thick-knuckled hands reaching for the

silvery crating hammer in his back pocket. I was just a kid.
I even looked like him. Hannah said so. Even Guy Mallin
said I was a chip off the. Hey kid? You want a Business
Men's plate with chocolate ice cream instead of the green
peas with butter sauce? It should be easy to figure. . . .
"Gravy on that there ice cream haw-haw yessir, hey kid?
Gravy!" Guy Mallin roared. "A real chip if I ever saw one,
Jake. I'm telling you listen to me now. Your eyes. Your
chin. His mother's, a sweet little woman you got there, nose.
Yessir. Your hair. Off the old block there, Jake. Good
material, hey? It won't be long before it's *Jake & Son,* what-
do-you say? I'm telling you now Jake you heard what I
said."

"Maybe things are different these days," he told me.
"You ain't the way I was."

My father had the gift of listening to the artichokes at
the top of a load in such a way—they informed him in a
language which only he and the artichokes spoke—that he
always knew when their brothers at the bottom were de-
fective, defeated, edged with rust or shriveled from a stingy
soil. Silent in their hampers, they communicated by the
violence of love, all knowing their role on this occasion as
opportunities, each thick-leafed one, for a sociable debating between farmer and merchant, green, crisp, candid,
and nutritive after a pleasant journeying into the hands of
women. They accepted the gift of himself which my father
made, their shoots curly for him, their unbaked hearts shy
in a bra of ticklish felt. Buy us! sell us!—they asked nothing more. Artichokes understood my father, and his sympathy for vegetables arose to meet theirs for him. Devotion
—he gave this freely. He accepted, too, being stuck with
thorns.

Unfortunately I, even in those days, was not an artichoke—perhaps not so rewarding, my heart not luscious

with a dab of miracle-whip, stunted in fact, even hornier, full of bad character and a brooding plant rust. "Lots of personality," my mother had said, feebly defending me when as a child I had refused to shell lima beans for the store with the rest of the family on Friday nights. "Everyone says he takes after your side, Jake. Ethel says, Sarah says."

"Since I was thirteen! I got scars on my back, the bucket cut me, the greenhorn I didn't get a pad cloth. Look at Irwin, look at Bernie born the same week like you in Mount Sinai, you was the first so I got your mother a semi-private. A healthy kid like you, he sleeps all morning Saturday."

"Since he was twelve years old a greenhorn," Mother mournfully intoned. "Who ever heard of it?"

Pattie Donahue plucked at her sweater and pouted with kiss-proof lipstick (maybe) over teeth lucky to serve her. Lewis Snyder, the sheik, told stories about Rosalie Fallon and Pattie. Tom Moss told me. "The liar," we agreed, ferociously believing him.

Such matters flowed in time; the store remained outside time, its claim ripening through the spines but as incredible to me as a heartless artichoke to my father. The store gulped me down. I evaded, I squirmed, I stubbornly bent, receded, and persisted like heartburn, taking all shapes but in fact knowing only itself, which has no shape and a mysterious matter.

"You don't want, what kind of a reason is that?" my mother demanded, fertile as Hera in argument. "No reason, that's what kind."

I couldn't explain to myself or to them, much less to Aunt Sarah or to Aunt Ethel, to Hannah, Guy Mallin, or Cousin Bernie the Smarty. Let him marry a nice rich girl from New York Queens in the clothing business, I don't care, I sacrilegiously insisted. My single purpose was love for Pattie Donahue, whose father carried a portfolio to work in his hairless pink little hands; she would love only the elaborate loungers, the conspicuous consumers—a little Veblenite she was! You Americans all long for the useless, the hymen no proper end; it feathers no beds, it fleshes no bellies—this Mother and Dad might have pointed out if they had argued their philosophy. I sensed, too, that my father's agility and strength and love, moving among the objects all his in the store, were a threat to me, the more dangerous because—one of his few fatal thoughts outside the moment—he was beginning to see Jack's Fruit & Vegetable in terms of immortality for both of us. He asked only a sign of recognition for this gift to me.

I refused his gift daily now. Even the Jello counter fell into ruins. My ultimate denial lay outside morality, essential to character. My father was over-happy, over-moral. I crouched like a troll under a mushroom in the cellar, a troll who read *Ulalume* and murmured, "Pattie Donahue!" with dilated eyes in the shadow of a shipment from Procter & Gamble. Poor Dad!

We can measure his desolation. He left his struggle and joyous head-on combat with farmers, jobbers, salesmen, Saturday help, policemen, wilting lettuce and pears which remained green until they rotted, competitors, the chain stores, the landlord, debtors, creditors, the delivery truck, the account books, the government, insects, rodents, spoilage, wastage, heat, cold, the margin of profit, draw items, push merchandise, merchandise which he could not get, premiums, samplers, one-cent giveaways, Christmas trees on January second and Easter candy in May, children who skated through a display of jars of olives (the olives lined up one by one in bottles shaped like a straw, optically illusive, expensive all the same), Mr. Jenkins who insisted

on Aunt Mary's pancake mix and would not be content
with Aunt Jemimah's or any other Aunt's because he
wanted to honor in this way his poor dead old Aunt Mary
his mother's sister, Mrs. Rawlings the klepto whose chauf-
feur dropped her off at the store every morning to slip a
bottle of vanilla extract into her pink muff (her daughter
paid, but we had to keep score), the charity ladies and the
lottery girls, the kids selling advertisements in their paro-
chial school bulletins, the beggars who claimed to have
had a store just like his in Phoenix, Arizona, until they hit
a run of bad luck back in '29 (he was unanimously elected
to a directory circulated by a syndicate of beggars, Phoenix
& Miami Beach Chapter), the faithful customers who tried
to convert him to their religions, Mrs. Colonel Greenough
who came with tears to tell him that her husband forbade
her to shop at Jack's Fruit & Vegetable any longer because
the colonel himself had given him three months to read a
book on technocracy and he had not yet complied (she
bought a farewell bouquet of cauliflower before she left),
the high school teacher who wanted to pay an overdue bill
in the privacy of her chamber, the judges asking support
both moral and ah financial in the coming primaries, the
tax collectors, the bill collectors, the garbage collectors, the
health inspectors, the housing inspectors, the zoning inspectors, electricians, refrigerator repair men, insurance
which only covered fires begun by safety matches when his
fire had resulted from a cigar butt, illness among his clerks,
jealousies, rivalries, romances, extended lunch hours, female troubles which (a gentleman) he could not publicly
doubt, inventories, lentil soup in cans labelled liver pate,
children who descended like locusts to remove all the tops
from the Ralston boxes to send away as a mark of esteem
for Tom Mix, the electric cash register playing Chopin in
a short circuit, Hannah who had B. O., Andy who left his

hair among the macaroons, Myrna who showed too much of her bosom in order to encourage Mr. Tramme to take an extra cantaloupe, and other problems which I'll not mention because I want to avoid making a list.

My father abandoned his direct response to these issues in order to *use psychology* on me. He appealed in subtle ways. He tried to *get me interested*. His Tartar eyes were made to squint for laughter and appetite, not cunning. My heart contracts with sadness for him now, sadness and regret. He came to me on the porch one Sunday afternoon, his great arms slack at his sides, saying, "Say!" in the way of a good fellow, and asked me to write a paragraph for his weekly advertisement in the neighborhood throwaway. I responded, too, working hard at a composition modelled on The Raven, sharpening three pencils into oblivion before I finished. Proudly I announced to Tom Moss the prospect of publication in the West Side Advertiser.

The work never appeared. Trochees had no place next to bargains in Crisco. The Crisco people paid half and supplied the engraving; the Spry people, not caught napping at the shortening, offered to pay sixty per cent and sent my mother a portable sunlamp for her sinuses. I wasn't even impregnated with Vitamin D or viosterol from Wisconsin, living by Poe and Pattie. Psychology failed; my father came as an alien to such maneuvres. Nevermore!

One day I sneaked out of the store at 4:30, made my own dinner of Laub's rye, Blue Moon pimento cheese with those taste-delightful little chopped-up pieces of real pimento, Krunchy peanut butter (kan't remember the brand), and Thursday's spoiled milk; then I went to an Edward G. Robinson with Tom Moss. The three of us stood off the coppers for a reel and a half, and when they finally got Edward G. the camera noticed a paper boat which sailed down the gutter in the symbolic rain. "Just like The Strange

Case of Monsieur Whatsizname," I pedantically reminded
Tom. We fought back our tears, magnificent to THE END,
ate a dime's worth of evergreen mints, and went divvies on
a Spicy Detective to read under the Jantzen's Swimsuit for
That Lee-*uscious* Look billboard on the way home. I told
him about Pattie and he told me about Rosalie Fallon. Our
patient listening to each other was more than politesse; we
learned through it although the histories remained classi-
cally similar, unmodified in months except for the time
Rosalie kicked Tom in the shins when he complimented her
by rubbing one of the last March snowballs in her face. He
rolled up his pantleg to show me the wound once more. I
accused him of preserving it with salt. He denied this. He
accused me of envy. I lowered my eyes. Tom was a lady-
killer, he was; I'll never understand how he did it.

"Well, goodnight Tom. Good luck with Rosalie."

"Well, goodnight Dan. I'll ask Lewis Snyder about
Pattie. He took Virginia Thompson out on a date and
maybe she knows something. He'll tell me if I ask him because I know something on him."

Goodnight. . . . Goodnight. . . . In that midworld of
childish seriousness and the first adult frivolity of passion
Tom and I needed the sense of banding together, our suffer-
ings held in common while our sense of them remained un-
touchable, pariahs of glandular enthusiasm in a structure
built of economy. He gave me the Spicy to hide in the
garage. I had often dreamed of moving through an atmosphere of glue, invisibly held from my family's home in an
empty night. Empty?—full of unknown excess. Now I
whistled, leaving Tom Moss an hour before midnight, forgetting that I had last seen my parents seven hours earlier
when my father had said, "Wait on trade!" and I had crept
out the back door where Andy was boxing strawberries and
beet greens were blackening in the sun.

The door to our house was locked. The windows were dark. There was no key under the mat. The crickets suddenly deafened me, like in the movies. I thought I knew, then, how Edward G. felt when the boys went over to the South Side mob, but found a basement window open, crawled through the coal chute, and significantly murmured Pattie's name out of the side of my mouth. Ulalume Donahue, Killer Berman's moll. . . . I'd have flipped a quarter with disdain except that it was too dark and I had no quarter. *Dad!* I thought. I worried about the gas stove upstairs. Maybe they were all dead and so I should bang on the door until they let me in to sleep in my own bed. What if there were rats in the basement? Big ones like in the Paris sewers with Gene Valgene? The washing machine opened its mouth at me in the darkness. *Mother!* I thought. If the water pipes broke and I got drowned they'd be sorry. They'd be sorry someday when I spit blood into my monogrammed handkerchief from sleeping all alone in a damp basement. They would be sorry. I was sorry. *Mother and Dad!* I thought.

Without taking off my shoes I slept on the extra kitchen table in the basement, amid dirty laundry (my pillow) and old hatreds (my dreams).

3

Even this passed. The next Saturday I was as faithful as Irwin, as true as Bernie with his eyes like spoiled oysters. I tasted during one evening the delights of approval, staying up with Mother and Dad while we discussed the day's business, counted the receipts, and discussed the pros and cons of tangle displays against neat pyramids of cans or fruit. I spoke for tangle displays, Mother for order; Dad listened to us both, sipping his tea with little Ahs through his lump of sugar, and reserved decision. He tried to lasso

my head as he used to in a ring of cigar smoke. "It's too
big," he complained. "Just like mine, a size seven seven-
eights. So look what needs a hat! You want a Stetson?"

We had a long late supper, and before going to bed
he slipped me three dollar bills in a secret conspiratorial
gesture while Mother stacked the dishes.

"I saw! I saw!" she cried out, her eyes peeping bright
in the mirror over the sink. We all giggled together.

Dad slapped her rump, yawned, and said, "Nothing
like a good day's work, hey?" in his imitation of Guy
Mallin.

"Jake, you crazy?" At peace with each other, we
parted. "And don't forget whose birthday is next month,"
my mother said: "Yours. You'll be thirteen, kiddel."

She had it right this time. It was a real truce; I knew
its joys. But had anything been altered? As aphoristic Aunt
Ethel might say, "A leopard coat can't change its spots."

A few days afterward I received a letter. The envelope
carried my name on the outside, together with the smart-
alecky title *Master,* all printed in green ink. I studied it,
marvelling, my first mail since the revolutionary discovery
of INCREASE YOUR WILL POWER FOOL YOUR FRIENDS,
and for that I had sent away a coupon and a quarter. I
sniffed it. I licked the ink and made a smear of what our
art teacher called *graded area.* I tasted my name in green,
finding it more subtle than black but just as lucid. At last
I decided to open the letter.

It was an invitation from Mr. B. Franklyn Wilkerson
to go on a Nature Walk a week from Saturday. Mr. Wilkerson, who taught General Science to the seventh grade, had
worked out a plan to augment his income during the summer vacation by conveying flower names and leaf shapes
to suburban scholars. Small, swarthy, with three daughters
and thin black hair artfully spaced and glued into place to

cover his scalp, Mr. Wilkerson recited Science (general) with his neck petrified for fear a sudden breeze or emotion might betray his baldness. Zealous, he devoted himself to general science textbooks, turning the pages slowly to avoid drafts. A real scientist would have perforated the pages. He was but a general scientist, however, combining, as he thought, the virtues of the practical and the theoretical in Elevating the Young, an intellectual sort whose pink resentful mouth and clenched neck gave him the expression of someone who had swallowed a banana sideways.

The first walk, a free trial, would take place on a Saturday, and the Saturday before the Fourth, the third-busiest day of the year in the store. I decided not to go.

Tom Moss was going. Lewis Snyder, who had dates alone with girls, was going. I learned that several of them, including Rosalie Fallon and Pattie Donahue, would be botanically present. I decided to go.

We met, everyone carrying lunch but me, at eleven-thirty. Mother didn't know about it; I had run away from the store, taking my cap from under the cash register and, for some last scruple, telling Hannah to tell my father that I had gone. "Where?"—but I disappeared without answering, subtle as a hungry tomcat unable to hide its rut, sneaking around corners with its yellow eyes scheming. Lewis Snyder had a scout canteen filled with near-beer left over after repeal. I suspected him of planning to offer Pattie some.

Pedantic, amorous, shifty-eyed general scientists, we followed Mr. Wilkerson into the Rocky River reservation. He wore a checkered golf cap, its band black with Sta-Neet, and showed how he had taught his wife to wrap his lunch—cellophane insulated the devilled eggs each from each. "Practical. Sanitary, germ-free. Vitamins spoil in the open air," he advised us.

Tom Moss, my friend the sceptic, whispered to me
that he thought it was supposed to be *good* for you to be
out in the fresh-air, and then went to step on Rosalie Fallon's heels.

We penetrated the woods, already hungry. "Now right
here on your left children we find an interesting phenomenon page one hundred and forty-eight in Brenner's figure sixteen that orange growth over there with the black
spots now that's a wild spermaphore," Mr. Wilkerson remarked. "Ess. Pee. Ee. Arrh—"

"Looks like a toadstool to me," I said.

"Spermaphore. Silver spoons unreliable poor quality
silver these days no workmanship. Damp places. Twenty-
four on a picnic without a general scientist. Could have
told them. Whole party dead in eight to ten hours. Horrible.
Too bad. Ess, pee, ee—"

A voice occurred behind me, whispering, "Hello, Daniel Berman." It was Pattie. "Toadstools are very poisonous,"—she leaned sociably. "Do you like are you fond of
mushrooms?"

I soared into paradise at her feet. "My mother cooks
spermaphores with meat loaf," I said, "and stuffed peppers."

"Oh!"—a gasp of scandal. "She does not. You'll all
be dead. . . . Does she?"

"Yes," I lied, death-defying—what could be a better
beginning between lovers? All lies come true in a world of
such supple twelve-year-old facts. It was cool here across
the city from the store. Birds soon to be falsely named
cocked their heads in the trees and lectured us. Someplace
customers swarmed amid the imperatives of telephones and
the distance between my father and me widened past
even the nine-month doubt separating an instant of giving
from the birth of a son. Fatherhood, a metaphysical idea,

was being taken from Dad as Mrs. Rawlings slipped her
daily bottle of vanilla extract into her bosom, no one to distract her, and as Mr. Wilkerson bravely broke the perfidious
spermaphore with a five-foot stick, no academician he, a
man of general action in science. Rosalie Fallon gave her
pressed-lip assent and moral outrage against hypocritical
silver spoons while my thoughts fled back from the store to
recall prepared speeches of passion for Miss Donahue,
known by Killer Berman and Edward G. as Ulalume or
The Lost Lenore.

"Oh-h-h," she was saying.

"Look the bug," I replied.

She pretended to be scared, not. I knew. Death and
complicity—love is not a biological gesture in suburban
children, O Mr. Wilkerson! I had forgotten my speeches
and Ulalume.

Despite this meeting I again felt deserted, lunchless
at lunchtime. Tom Moss pretended not to notice: excuse
him his hunger. "Where's yours?" Pattie asked, her mouth
full.

"Don't have any. My mother didn't. Not hungry anyway."

Girls always have enough to give. Suburban girls
(economical) always have enough to invest. Sweetly she
murmured, "You can have one of my bacon and tomato-
motto sandwiches and a bite of cottage cheese with the
canopy, please do." Smiling, licking her lipstick, her eyes
calculating under the modest fluttering venereal lids, she
whispered intimately: "And a cookie—the one with the
candied cherry in the middle, please do, really."

"Oh!" I protested.

Take take, my mother would have said.

"Really, I don't mind, please do," said dainty Miss
Patricia Donahue.

I did.

Later, when we bid farewell to sporting, big-toothed, intellectual (generally scientific) Mr. Wilkerson, and thanked him for a lovely nice afternoon, and promised to ask our parents to fork over five smackeroos for a Program of Nature Walks, Pattie Donahue allowed it to be known that I was walking her home. Under the circumstances even Lewis Snyder had to count it a date with a girl alone; the evidence whelmed, overwhelmed. I obeyed the protocol. We had a coke and then an ice cream stick. That Snyder must have been eating his heart out, at least aggravated. All right then—I soliloquied with Tom Moss *qua* Conscience & Scorekeeper—half-credit then for a daytime date.

"Did you get a free one?" I asked.

She read her ice cream stick. "No," she said.

"Neither did I. Don't believe in luck anyway"—and I expounded my philosophy of will power concentrate your way to fame and/or fortune. I tried to recite *Ulalume* but forgot it.

My mother's arches were hurting in her Enna Jetticks, but she avoided my father so that he would not order her home. Andy was making off to the vegetable cooler with a bagful of macaroons. Basketwood splintered under orders; customers fidgeted untended; my father wiped his forehead with a paper towel from the pine forests of Maine, leaving crumbs of lint, and mourned me.

"I never knew you were so smart," said Pattie Donahue.

We had fallen silent, sitting on the front steps of her house in the shadow of a bush where her mother could not see us. Up the street someone was hosing his car, an incontinent sound, in preparation for a Fourth of July trip. The afternoon was over. Pattie Donahue, an economical creature, an Indian giver, took back her gift in a way which expressed her genius. Business acumen. Operating costs and turnover. Appraising me with her turtle-round eyes, shrewd to calculate the value of an investment, she first created a bear market by sighing Ohh, rustling her dress, and accidentally touching my arm with her transparent turquoise-veined hands. Cologned and dusted with powder, she breathed on me.

"Yes!" I spilled out, naked in summer smells. "Do you like me, Pattie? I like you."

"Sure I like you"—disappointment and a pout that it had been so easy. Even economy becomes sport with such a housekeeper. "Sure I like you but you're too fat."

"Fat?" I repeated stupidly.

Her laughter tinkled in the July calm by the watered bush. "Fat I mean skinny. I mean you're just a *grocery* boy, you. You just grub around a certain store I could name all the Saturdays *I* ever heard about, except I suppose today—"

She was a sly old creature, that Pattie Donahue. The lips: *grocery boy*. The frozen iris: the same. Her laughter caroled forth, free, enterprising, resolute, the investment paying off in a Saturday afternoon dividend of power. Not all men are men, her laughter told her. This is a profit forever, my face told her.

"Oh but—oh but—oh but—" I said.

She put her little hand to her mouth and delicately closed it. Tee-hee. She looked at me, unblinking. My father, knowing he was a foreigner, could have accepted this in the perspective of history. I had to discover a fact without a past; it leapt out at me like some fierce fish from the glittering shale of Pattie Donahue's economical eyes.

I stood up. "Thank you for the sandwich and the cookie," I said. (The cookie with a preserved cherry on it.)

"Oh me no," she said.

"I was hungry."

"Oh you're welcome really," she said. "Thank you for the coke. Thank you for the ice cream."

"Goodbye, Pattie."

"It was nice, Daniel Berman," she said, "truly very nice."

4

I prowled, growing up fast that afternoon. I climbed a fat hump of a mailbox for packages and, my hands hanging in front, or my elbows on my knees and my fists in my cheeks, I watched the traffic on Parkside Boulevard. I did not choose the sentimental places, the tree by the lake, the woods where the river on which we skated in winter spread out like a sheet. I began to understand how the lost Lenore really got mislaid, without a dark conversational bird, without a tomb, without even a long metrical sigh. A heavy July sky lowered and thickened above me. I perched on the box like an animal in a dream.

But I was no animal in no dream. I was wide-awake, me, itchy, straddling a mailbox. Once someone mailed a book between my legs. I did not stop to wonder whether it were some quaint and curious volume, this being already forgotten lore. I studied the houses squatting like fat-necked bullfrogs along the boulevard, puzzled over the nay-saying mouths and step of the emerging strollers, celebrated and grieved for the crystallizing structure of my judgment (my *complexes*), no longer contained by sad and pretty words—grieved but did not cry.

Long after dark I finally went home. My parents were in the kitchen, talking in low voices, the relieved hawing of Saturday nights absent today. Entering at the street, I went directly to my room and lay down on the bed. I made none of the dramatic flourishes of locking the door or pushing the footstool in front of it.

"Daniel!"

Doltish, I wondered if this were what it felt like to be an adult. It was true that for weeks I had been awakening mornings with my bite clamped, my jaw aching, and my tongue plunged against my teeth. Was that the seeding for Pattie Donahue's educational crop? her economy predicted by my extravagance in sleep?

"Daniel!"—Mother's voice. I went. Mother stood by the kitchen table. Dad sat without looking at me, his head lowered, his hands about a bowl of soup. "You should come when I called you," she said.

"I did come."

"When I called you I said. Not whenever you please." She looked at my father and waited for him to speak. He did not. We all waited for him, the challenged one, amid the summer smell of flypaper in the kitchen and the buzzing of the wily flies.

Resentfully I broke the stillness: "I went on a nature-walk."

"What?—what?"

"I learned what's a toadstool and the names of birds. A naturewalk. Mr. Wilkerson general science from junior high, he—"

"And what about Mr. and Mrs. Slave-their-head-off, I suppose your parents by the store?" my mother asked. The sarcasm gave me hope; it was, after all, only dialectic again. How soon hope returns! We dwell in it even after the exile to which Pattie Donahue's laughter and nibbling teeth send us.

Turning to my father, whose head bent over the table in a way I only remembered afterward—his brother had

died and Mother said he was crying because he was sad and
I didn't believe her because daddies don't cry—I appealed
to him with a manly challenge: "Almost everyone I know
went on the naturewalk."

He did not yet look up.

"It's educational. Mr. Wilkerson says. Tom Moss was
there. Almost everyone in our grade Seven-B Seven-A was
there—"

"Lookit my waricose from standing up all day working like a horse eating my heart out," Mother said. "You
should take a load off my feet, not I should carry you like
a baby you're going on fourteen."

"Thirteen," I said.

"Going on anyway," she insisted, "*going* on. That's
what it means. Big lummox. Look at my waricose go on
look lookit."

She could not know—my cruelty at twelve years, soon
thirteen!—that my only concern was for surgery on the
distended veins, as other women had, instead of wearing
the lumpy corset that bulged about her calves under
webbed brown stockings. My garment, she called it. Like
taxes, Jake says. Teeth too, O! Sarah had the same trouble
after Bernie and she took calcium. You ask me I think
better injections in the arm, injections.

Dad listened watchfully over the soup in the evening
heat. He hunched and studied vegetables in the bowl.

See how I admit the two of them to paper. Put my
refusal of their world, which was their deepest gift to me,
beside a son's longed-for and imagined love for his parents.
Let me call myself a liar, but don't you be quick to do it.
"Want to playboy around all your life dreaming smoke in
the head?" my father used to ask me, and yet he loved me
despite the law that we cannot love someone who refuses
our gifts. I did not see the power and light of his world, in

which the four causes were felt in action with my mother, vegetables, and the Saturday specials; I had looked for light and power in Pattie and Poe while all the Aristotelian potencies and more lay waiting for me with the combustible garbage swept into the backyard at closing time each evening. The backroom, emptied and cleaned, was filled and emptied of carrot tops, beet greens, and the furry blue glow of spoiled oranges. I stalled; my father waited. I looked; my father watched.

A week earlier I had overheard Mother murmuring into the telephone, "So how's your Bernie? My Daniel shouldn't be better, he got a all-A report card and with a B plus in gymnastics, he gained two pounds by the scale but he's full of complexes, still a heart-ache in the store. . . . Yah. . . . I read in the paper it's complexes, Jake says he'll grow out. . . ."

But only the complexes kept growing out. It's because I really like my parents that it costs me so much to speak kindly of them. I remember how my father offered me his entire world and I threw it in his face like a rotten orange because he left out one little lump of an Atlantis, my *own* world.

"Listen to your father he's talking," my mother said. He had not yet spoken, but she knew him well and knew he now would. "You take his fifteen cents for a movie, don't you? Listen to your father."

Still sitting in his washed-out shirt crusted with salt under the armpits, in his old blue serge work pants, once dress-up with the sharpy stripe down the legs, more generous than fathers have a right to be, he tried to help me expiate my sin in a ritual of reprimand. No ceremony could heal him this time, but he waited. This time before the beginning: "At your age I was a man," he said.

He was right.

He swayed over the soup, food breathing back into his body the prayers he had forgotten in leaving his own father. His swaying shoulders heavily sloped and remembered. His father had forbidden him to go to godless America, better to die than to be unfaithful. This too he had forgotten, his father struck down by a Cossack's rifle, but the chant in his voice and the dance of his shoulders remembered.

"Look at you"—he could not. "Are you a man?"

No. Right again.

"A playboy. A nature-walker. A eater of ice cream."

All true. I still like ice cream, especially with Hershey's chocolate syrup. He taught me quality in food, my father. I waited for him to force me to make myself what we both agreed I should be; no ceremony could compel it though only ceremony could confirm it. Still I had to choose. Untheological, without brand names, we improvised ritual.

"A lollypop!" my mother shrilled, thinking she was on her husband's side. Here she was wrong. I was not a lollypop.

"Let me tell it, Rose," my father said softly, as if this were an incident on their trip to South Haven. "It's my turn to tell it, Rose."

"I don't care"—me turning in my pointed shoes perforated for ventilation and sweet beauty's sake under the eyes of Pattie. I mourned her now, blaming my birth. "I don't care about you." I lowered my gaze to my father's stubby foreign feet in steel-backed boots. "None of the kids have to do it. I don't care about you and your store."

He needed an instant for this. I gave it to him overflowing. "And—your—store."

His hand floated up like a speck fuming on the eyes; his fist crashed down on the enamelled table like the plung-

ing claw of a crate-hammer. "Oh! Oh!"—Mother. Soup
splashed out on his pants and ran weeping with little red
carrot eyes.

His gaze was prophetic in mine. "*Some kits help out
in the store*," he said.

"We were practically supposed to go," I said, neither
retreating nor regretting, gaining time and learning patience. "Mr. Wilkerson is a teacher."

"*Some kits remember their father and mother.*"

Everyone knows where it hurts when you begin to
cry—that place at the back of the throat. Pins jabbed under
my eyelids. My palate ached. The tears hurt most in that
instant before they break out. . . . And then I imagined
cologned Pattie's cool laughter at my father's pronunciation
of the *d* in *kits* ("—remember their father and mother"),
and then drunk with the idea of the murder of someone I
loved, my belly awash at the thought, I screamed him to
his feet:

"I won't, I *won't* work in your store. I don't want it.
It's not my life. I hate it. I hate it!"

He stood huge over me, smelling of leafy vegetables
and sweat, smelling of his strength and his terror because he
would have to beat me. This is the reek of power, what the
men at the Food Terminal understood when Ollie the Agent
tried to shake down him first of the West Side men. . . .
The opponents were uneven. He had wise muscles, protected by years of work and good eating, the skills of use,
the satisfactions of his time of life. He had three sons, only
one of those baby brothers of mine lying awake to listen.
His swaying body knew it loved me as his father had loved
him, the woman carrying her child on a belly or breast, the
man taking his son only at the eye or the fist. There must
have been a great satisfaction in his fear and love at that
moment.

My sole weapon was exactly my dissatisfaction. My
father's arms swam with veins among the curled oily hairs
on his light bluish freckled flesh. No bow-straight shoulders
like Atlas the World's Most Perfect Develop It! No Culver
Academy athlete calling for Pattie Donahue in his uniform
at Christmastime! It was a body which had worked well
and been used with pleasure, a happy body, soup on the
pants, making its own purpose and content with this.

Mine, as I have said: discontented. I looked for a use
for it. I said:

"And you and your grocery boys and everyone! *I hate
you!*"

Mother was crying and stacking the dishes in the sink
when his open hand—generous! open!—struck my shoulder. I flew back and then up at him, slipping past his collar
rough as a dog's tongue. Mother screamed. I climbed him,
flailing; he was planted on the floor and he rocked under
my weight for a moment, both of us silently straining toward each other and apart, our sweat pouring together
while Mother screamed on and on—the malignant smell of
hate and fear becoming the myrrh of two men fighting, the
sweet cunning of love and death. I clung to his great neck
to strangle it. His beard scratched my arms. He hugged my
ribs, forcing them up—cracking!—pushing my hair out,
lengthening my bones, driving my voice deep. Savagely he
told me his life, wringing my childhood from me. I took
this after his long day and had nothing to give in return but
my unfleshed arms roped about his neck. We embraced like
this.

The broken blood fled for a window into my mouth.
I felt myself fainting.

Abruptly I lunged down, perhaps permitted to beg
free. His weighty old-country strength: my agile sporting
slyness: as he glanced for pity at my mother I threw myself

like a pole against his knees in a playground stunt performed without thinking. The trick uprooted his legs; he crashed; his forehead above the unsurprised Tartar eyes hit my mother's foot when he fell.

He sat up and started to his feet as she held him. I could not breathe, my chest frozen. I turned from his sprawling. I let him hear me choke and then ran to my room. Yes, I had wanted to win, but now, fatalistic, in an instant guessing ahead, I made the highest demand on a father: that he know he had beaten me too, only because he had let it happen.

"What's happening to us all?"—those first tears of old age. "What's happening to us?" Dad was crying in the bathroom with the door shut and the water running in the sink so that no one would hear an old man with an ingrate son. He had locked Mother out, who was dry-eyed now, figuring.

If I am bereaved of my sons, the first Jacob said, *then am I bereaved.* To fight back was all I needed; he had given too much. Economy in Pattie! my father a spendthrift!— such knowledge comes late to me now.

Susanna at the Beach

First came the girl. Then one fat man idly floated beside a friend in the water, lolling on his back, spitting, his great trunk rolling in the pleasure of himself. He liked to watch the girl while taking his pleasure.

Finally there were the people on shore. These September loiterers, with thin hocks and thick, with waddling rumps in dank wool or tendoned ones in Hawaiian shorts, with itching faces in devotion to sun or a suave glistening under the equivocation of lotion, all of them squinted and winked and finally moved toward her. They strolled, they turned on their heels, or they merely leaned. They came limping over the hot sand like the good wizards in a story.

The girl over whom the old men watched was diving from the end of a breakwater into the oily, brackish, waste-ridden substance of Lake Erie at Cleveland, Ohio. Her arms, deeply tanned, worked firmly; and heated from within, she scrambled up the rocks in haste after her discipline. She had fled all the billboard schemes of the life of a pretty girl. Lips soft and half-parted for a grand design rather than a Lucky Strike, hands taking the measure of ambition rather than the bottle of Coca-Cola, she had come to perfect her diving in a worn black cotton bathing suit which was already too small after her summer's growth. They were simple exercises, but she wanted them to be perfect. She had an idea of how they should be.

The old men, shaking off the sand flies which had multiplied among the refuse so late in the season, looked jealously to the thin cloth which held this girl and to the water which sheathed her. The girl measured the angle of her imagination against the remembered sting of an imperfect arc. Clean! she had prayed, but her worried brow was reporting, *No, another flop.* The black cloth gleamed in the wet. The droplets of water peeled down her body like broken beads as she climbed to try it again. The smile at the corners of her mouth was a promise to herself: Well! This time, then. Even in the brief instant of her stretching, a crescent-shaped slope at one shoulder flashed dry in the sunlight.

This time she went in straight and slender with the will of perfection.

It was a Tuesday afternoon, and a day of rare Indian summer heat. Still, only the most faithful had returned to the beach: the athletic grandfathers, white-haired and withered, with an eye for the weather; a student with his American history textbook and the glaze of sun in his face meeting the doze of exposure to knowledge; the kids pretending to fish and the dead shad belly-up at the washline of water on the sand; the occasional amorous ones, asking riddles, fondling each other slyly, their pockets a-jingle with desire and streetcar fare; women from the industrial flats nearby, sitting in housedress to recall, complain, worry, and take a sleepy hour's leisure together. Mostly, however, beneath the roar and thump of road construction on the slope above them, almost in the shadow of the Terminal Tower to the east, there were the old men: the salesman sunning himself with neck reaching out and pants rolled above the knee so that by evening he can look "just like Miami Beach, better even"; the flat-thighed wanderer in a straw hat and red woolen trunks with a white canvas belt, his sinewy breasts hanging—he sat in a patch of seaweed to observe the diver and stroke the sand from between his toes; another, the big-bellied swimmer, now paddling and spewing water, shaggily emerged onto the pier in order to get nearer to the girl. His friend accompanied him. Hairy-chested loungers, old-time beaux, their bodies both wasted and swollen, they joined the rest of the men along the breakwater. They watched the girl still diving, still climbing; her deep breathing pressed the erect buds of her adolescence against sleek black cloth, she rocked once on her toes, and then off she sprang.

This girl used herself hard, used her lightness hard; and each man there, turning to her from the beach or the pier, thought it a pity. A waste—her sufficiency unto herself silenced and saddened them and made their arms hang tensely forward. Challenged, they turned up the cards of their own sorts of sufficiencies.

The fat swimmer, swirls of hair on his belly and back, was now switching himself with a green branch as he talked business with his friend. They both studied the girl, and their discussion grew lyrical. They talked business and public affairs. He was saying: "You're John-cue Smith, let's put it, you want to get married—"

"I know! Got the taxes to pay, the down payments, the terms—"

"Yes, that's what I mean, to get ahead in life. The installments."

"I got the cost of living these days, Freddy."

"You got the government."

"Yes, Freddy, I got the taxes, yes—"

"The essentials of life."

"Yes, yes, all of that, yes"—and they both shook their heads mournfully and let their mouths fall open while the tips of the girl's feet, propelled by her dive, wriggled above water as she swam.

"Like to bite off a piece of that one, eh Freddy?"

"I saw it first, me, you want to say I didn't?"

A policeman on horseback on the beach looked for purse-snatching, nuisance-making, or drunkenness. Overhead, a pontooned airplane swooped low and up. The traffic rushed past the stillness of sun and beach and water, while, out on the lake, a single leaning sailboat, a visitor from the Clifton Club, kept its distance.

Two women, equipped for conversation with quart bottles of cherry pop, their dresses pulled over their knees and their stockings rolled down to their ankles, agreed on questions of mortality, bereavement, and the pleasures of a city beach. They sat on a log stripped by water and shaded their eyes first toward the industrial flats from which they had emerged, then over the lake and into the horizon and beyond. "My mama she die when she eighty-four," said the tanned younger one. "Just like baby, like new kid, she need milk to drink."

"Yah," sighed her friend, a fat and weary woman with concentric rings of flesh about her eyes. "Look that American girlie on the board, what she think? She hurt herself like that."

"She not able my mother care for herself or nothing."

"I know, dear."

"She die like so—sssst—after long life. She work hard."

"I *know,* dear."

"It ain't right, is it?" She nodded once, decisively, and said, "My father he still strong and smoke big cigar I buy

for him. He sleep with woman and give her money and
everything. Ain't nice old man like that. He make eye at
every young girl—"

"Bad young girlie," said the plump woman to the
sand, the water, and the figure now climbing back onto the
rocks.

The tanned one pulled at her dress and said, "That's
why, here in this country, many people go off on roof for
fall down. My children all go away to Detroit and *I* give
money to my papa."

"No justice on earth, darling," said the sad plump one.

2

The girl, the fine diver, went off the rocks again,
measuring only with a frown the interior demands of her
lonely stunt, absent from the beach on the parapets of
ambition. She had scraped the cotton suit on a rock. The
small split showed an edge of white breast, the first hard
growth of the departure from girlhood. Some of the idlers
had gathered in silence on the breakwater to watch her.
"You want to tell me no, Freddy? I'm telling *you* no," the
fat swimmer insisted. She did not see them; she had nothing
to say to them; her regard was absorbed by the patch of
black water and the rules of her skill.

Back on the beach, another immature and pretty girl
sat with her feet drawn under her on the sands. No one, not
even Freddy, the fat swimmer's friend, gave more than a
glance to this one, whose tanned plumpness in stylish knee-
length shorts promised an eventual stylish willingness while
her profile remained strict, suburban, and pure. Her
mother, shriveled to creamed skin rather than casual flesh,
squatted like the image of her age by her side, but this was
not the reason that the free-ranging eyes of the beach

passed over the daughter so lightly. The men sensed that she feared to lie on grass because of disease, dirt, and small animals, that she shuddered at the thought of diving into the tricky, steaming, polluted waters, that despite her prettiness she had put herself apart from the play of caprice, open-mouthed laughter, and the risks of pleasure. "Look at the girl on the pier, the one that's diving again," this cute creature said.

"She's headed for earache, that's for sure," her mother commented with satisfaction. "Maybe she doesn't read the paper and how the water's unsafe. Dangerous for bathing. Full of organisms."

"I'm getting hungry, Mother"—wrinkling her junior-miss nose and hugging herself as her favorite starlet did.

"I *said* we'd stop at the Howard Johnson's."

Meanwhile, the diver scrambled over the rocks, up onto the pier, took three or four mincing, dancing steps, and bent her knees for her renewed essay at a controlled style. Her wide temples glowed pinker and pinker with the blood under her skin and the impact of water. Her innocence—an innocence of lessons—was informed by the heat and by the pressure of her blood which brought her climbing, diving, repeating this gesture again and again past the heaped-up rock. Had she seen them and gone on, it would have spoken for an angry and stubborn pride; but her way was the way of habit, of grace, and of a passionate ignorance, a deep communion with belly-smash on the shore of Lake Erie at Cleveland.

The plump lady from the flats was disturbed. "My doctor say: Playsuit! no stockings! Like that you have no more colds for wintertime. You have upper repertory affection, Doctor Sczymanski say. Neighbor she look at playsuit, close mouth, she say: shame! What can I do, darling?"

"That American girl, *she* have no shame," remarked

the tanned woman whose father smoked big cigars. "Everybody is look at her legs"—and they both fell into a musing silence, and looked.

The beach was silent while a skin of complicity tightened like the dry sun about them all. Gradually these visitors to the September sands moved toward the breakwater, each one marvelously hushed because, if they said nothing, it could be presumed to be their habit and their devotion, an abandon to mutism in the heat, a pious thing superior to their daily selves: and thus, if the rip in the girl's suit grew longer, it was not their place to warn her of it. Let each creature hunger for itself alone—Freddy poked his pal to mean this—and thus send only appetite in the pursuit of others. The veiny old men moved fastest.

Within a few moments the beach was almost deserted except for the couple busily twisting and tickling in their well-worn place. The girl sat up with a jerk, spreading sand in an abrupt movement of her thighs, while her friend grinned, saying, "I'm not connerdicting you." He pulled her down again.

3

The tear in the diver's suit widened; the gash in this black second skin showed, to the fat man, the whiteness of belly, and then, to Freddy's bemusement, the flexing folds of flesh. Just once Freddy saw her fingers feel for the rip, but her body's intelligence calculated on nothing but the demands of perfection, and the thought of care for that clothing which was outside desire did not move further than the impatient, rummaging hand. She did not glance at herself. Turned to her idea, fixed on some inner certainty, she closed the split with her fingers, then forgot it, then let go.

She dived and climbed without liability to the give of

cloth or the alteration of her world which Freddy and the
big-bellied swimmer brought. She scrambled up dripping,
let her eyes roam absently over the tense strollers gathering
on the rocks, and dived once more. The pale wetness of her
flesh opened to them like a wound under the suit while the
girl, if she thought of her body at all, thought only of her
skill and of her rehearsals for its sake. She was secure
(small splash and ripple) in the exercise of method. She
was an expert.

"You trying to tell me no, Freddy?" Behind the fat
swimmer and his friend, past the city beach on this September afternoon, the machinery of road construction throbbed
and the insect hiss of an afternoon breeze occupied the trees
on the slope leading up to the highway past the tables, the
shelters, and the park restroom. Because his mouth was dry,
the fat man pointed to the girl and whispered, "Lookit."
He squeezed the muscles of his friend's arm, thumb and
forefinger twanging, and then they both moved forward
again. The heat and the effort brought shiny tears to his
eyes and a dampness to his forehead. The thickness of his
body in swimming trunks, sagging at the middle and the
rear, bulging beneath, looked enormous in the sunlight and
the intimacy of one leg's motion against the other.

Repetitious, formal, and oblivious, the girl's ambition
seemed madness or a mad joke to the watchers. It pleased
the fat man; it was a delight to him. He opened his mouth,
like a swimmer, and put his tongue sideways to breathe
more easily. Freddy—as to him—he could hardly believe it.
He wanted to float up an inner tube and go out someplace
to think about it.

When she climbed over the rocks once again, the rip
widened almost audibly, and still she did not see that her
suit was ready to hang in tatters. No one warned her—as
we do not warn a madman that he is talking nonsense—but

they sighed when she extended her arms for the dive. The fat man sighed. All of them leaned together now, men and women, sharing the girl and sharing each other, waiting for their world's confirmation against the challenge she brought it, an assurance of which they were in need before the return to autumn and the years rapid upon them. A whiteness of breast flashed out, its pink sprouting from the girl's body like a delicate thing nurtured in the dark. But the day was bright and the shadows short. Looking at this tender and abstracted girl, the old Polish woman shivered at her own memories of paleness, of resiliency, of pink colors. The fat man, too, partook of their communion, frowning darkly, the green branch switching at his flanks, his knees slightly bent. He pinched his friend instead of himself. Now, her hair flat on her head and the flush of pleasure high on her cheeks after the repeated slap of her forehead against water, the girl was diving in a diminished rhythm, worn out but blind to risk, finished but unable to stop. The moment when her breast and belly slipped by the surface was the fat man's favorite.

The diver, that object for the vindictive imaginations of old men and old women, seemed to pause to acknowledge their study of her, but saw nothing, saw nothing again, and went on. The fat man's eyelids had dropped. He was moved. As she climbed, dripping and critical, bewitched by mastery of her body, feeling, if the presence of the others had come through to her at all, only a reward of praise earned through the long summer, the fat man released his friend's arm to break the silence at last with a shrill whoop. Then the old Polish woman screamed, "You're nekked, girlie! *Nekked!*"

The fat man, his friend, the salesman, the student, many of them were now yelling their cheers at her. Poised for her dive, she must suddenly have seen them and seen

herself in their sight. Her look was one of incredulity. Her
eyes turned from herself to their shouting, gaping, heavy-
tongued mouths and back to the loose cloth dangling from
straps. She did not speak. She turned her face from them.
Its stern and peaceful determination hardly altered. Then
suddenly the extended arms flashed down: she ran, she did
not dive, she jumped and rolled into the oily water. Despite
this folding upon herself, their eyes searched out a glimpse
of sunlit flesh, white and pink and tender. While the crowd
applauded, the student shouted, "She wants to drown herself," and leaped into the water.

"I'll get her! Me too! *Me!*"

The young man reached for her hair and only touched
it before she wrenched free. She doubled under, holding
herself, and then she was swimming. The crowd was roaring. Four, five, six of the men had pushed to the edge of the
breakwater. The girl kicked forward and swam with short,
quick, sure strokes, straight out into the lake, while a cluster
of young men and old, their smiles strict in pursuit, tumbled
down the rocks to be first to catch her. The fat man, paddling furiously, was ahead of Freddy. The righteousness of
a mob's laughter urged them to be swift, but the girl was
very strong, very skillful, gifted, and encumbered by nothing but her single thought.

A Celebration for Joe

Cousin Joe said: "Stay young? Live more? But can you stop the wind from blowing?"

I wanted to wear the black for him. For this departure I needed a band of black rage, tucked into my collar like a bib to catch the gravy of tears. "Don't be in a hurry, Joe," I said.

"The wind from blowing?"

It was agreed that he had to die. The doctors and the nurses whispered and clucked and hurried to present their bills and went on to other consultations. The house was full of death; it moved in the corridors as if the windows had been opened to this subtle breeze. His room was flower-soft with it. His great head lay embedded in the wide bull neck and the mouth grinned its gold teeth at us. His wife cried, Elsie and the other daughters cried, I cried. Joe wept for us all, told us to be brave, but did not interfere with our pleasure in tears.

"It's not so bad, they're finding a cure for me," he said.

"Wh-what?"

"Next time it won't happen again. I'll go to the doc, he'll give me an examination and a pill like in the maga-

59

zines it says you should. They got a foundation working on
how to cure it."

"Joe!" everyone sobbed during those last days.

"I'm an old man anyway. It would have been something else," he said.

When the telegram came, I rushed to him without closing the door to my room, perhaps dreaming of revenge
against my father's flesh, death the one answer to love,
health, and power. But he was Elsie's father, not mine, and
I wanted to see him because it was Joe: Cousin Joe, the
good cousin in our family. Once he had peddled fruit, then
sold yardgoods, then opened and closed a shop without even
a fire sale; then suddenly he talked his way into the brick-
layers' union. A mason who could lay thirteen hundred
bricks a day, although the union said to him, "Please, Joe,
six hundred is enough. *Plenty.*"

"Okay, the vacation's over," he had answered. "Only
six hundred." And he got married. And he had four daughters—two married, two working for pay.

A second cousin, a skinny adolescent with a new col-
legiate flannel sportcoat and a mouth freshly astounded by
Contemporary Civilization (A and B), I came to visit him
because I was lonely at school and because "you can always count on the family for thicker blood than water."
(My mother's insight, of course.) Now, the blankets pulled
up high, I was aware of fixing the memory of his huge bald
head shiny and bulging like a honeydew, with phrenological
bumps and glints as he turned on the pillow. The weight was
more than a pillow can take. A tuft of feathers was working
itself out. "What you looking, Danny?" he asked me.
"Dropped a penny in the sheets?" His nonchalance at present was a sign more deadly than the lamb's blood. The
other nonchalance—the one mated to him which he had
put on his family and no human being but Elsie had over-

come it—was a thing which, under the watching of his daughters and his wife, might make him ugly or comic to himself in the sight of his finish. The cheeks cracked for his grin, but this was no longer the grin that he enjoyed for the way it did justice to his teeth.

"Pa, be careful," said Elsie, the art school girl, her father's favorite—the ballet-slippered and flush-cheeked and hanging-on-her-father's-neck girl. She had never grown too tall or too heavy to take him about and jump to redden her cheeks against his. The dark hair, captured behind, of course, in a rubber band, leaped when she shook with laughter; it leaped now, although she was not laughing. "Do you want something, Pa?" Elsie held her hand on his forehead.

"How did you ever learn construction?" I asked, because he liked to talk about it.

Doris was saying, "He's not going to die." (He can't do this to me.) Sandra was saying, "He's not going to die." (He never did before.) Sulky Marilyn was saying, "He's not going to pass away." (Knock on wood.)

Elsie's lips were moving. She turned her tears toward me in a complicity of bereavement which, when Joe discovered it, included and eased him. Elsie moved her lips to say nothing but their silence. Her father wanted to talk for her.

Sarah said, thwarted as always, first by her husband's health, then by his sickness, now by both: "Don't! Don't! O don't, Yussel!"

"That's all right, Saraleh."

"So don't wiggle around so much, you heard what the doctor said."

He had never kept the promise which America was for them: *You will be comfortable, my children.* They could not believe that he would leave them alone now after hav-

ing bothered them so long. (But Elsie believed it.) They
could not accept that he would depart without ever once
calling out in need of them, furious in their sense of his
flaw—he needed nothing except himself and his work. Stubborn? the nervous shake of Sarah's head asked. That man
is stubborn, the shake replied. (But he needed Elsie.)

"He's going to be all right," I said, patting the nearest
soft back without looking to see who it was. He had been to
the hospital twice already. Both times he had threatened to
walk out unless they carried him home. Once they found
him standing in the hall with his pants half pulled on.

The back jumped and said, "Don't!"—it was Marilyn.

"So how did you ever learn construction?" I repeated.

"Brick-laying," he said, grinning.

"The mason trade was all right, you have a good
union," I argued, "but you could have opened a fruit store,
be your own boss again, or a little ready-to-wear place.
There's money in dry goods. The war proves it."

The blankets rippled; he was laughing, which hurt him
but was still worth the crackling in his chest. "Whoever!"
he choked. "Whoever! Whoever! Whoever heard of a man
was his own boss? The Jews were in Egypt, they built the
pyramids, you think they'd take a chance like that crossing
the Red Sea if they were thinking about semi-annual inventories? At least bricks you do it and you're done, ready for
the next job, you get a habit to stand off with the Irishers
and look at it."

I looked.

"Yes, yessir, just like that, Danny. A pile of bricks is
nice." He thumped himself, wheezed, unbuttoned the pajama shirt and showed the gray-black hairs curling off his
chest.

Because the wheezing embarrassed me, I repeated a
childish joke—"A man's best friend is his mortar"—and
blushed.

Such generosity! He laughed in his biblical fatness, a fatness of oil, sleek and glossy. He laughed in his fatness and his sleekness while death chipped at his heart in this house which he had built, brick by brick, himself. He could afford laughter and patience even for a pimply boy in sport clothes and abashed by illness. "You stand off from the lot and say, Hum, with bricks. You say Hum to them. Listen to me, Danny. With bricks you carried that wall on your back, and that one. You carried that house, you set it down, you stuck it together."

"Okay, it's time to be quiet," Doris said.

"You go from job to job, and what you carry with you is how-to-do-it. Plus the union card, I didn't forget. You can build your own like that."

When it came to his own house, someone helped him with the plumbing and wiring. He had taken his wife to the country and given her a shack like a skeleton. A man of sixty with four grown girls left behind in the Bronx, he had fleshed out this skeleton. "They cry, they don't have to bother with us no more," he said. "Let them cry, it makes them feel good."

"*Sh!*"

"I was only saying what is true."

"Pa, you promised you'd be good if we let you come home."

There was a sad slanting fall of eyelid, and a hilarious fleshing at his mouth. "*Let* me," he said to Elsie. "*Let—*"

"I meant it another way, Pa."

"Be careful, girl," he said. "Don't stop it from blowing."

Upon the idea of a house which was this shack, he had begun to lay bricks. He learned support and insulation and joining; he had friends to give him a Sunday. And he learned carpentry, his voice ringing over the hoarse ravening of an electric saw. Mostly he lay bricks—that's how I

remember him. Rising from a shack on a weedy lot came a
house, while his bald dome glistened and he leaned against
the hod and shook his head *yes*.

"What for?" three of the daughters had demanded.

"What do you mean all by yourself to build a house?" I
asked, falling by respect into a parody of his speech. "With
your bare hands?"

Elsie said softly to me: "You know how he likes it."

"Sometimes my friends help me weekends and the
fourth of July. Sometimes I wear gloves. No bare hands—
you want to try?"

"Don't bother," the girls had counselled me.

I even learned to mix cement, that grainy spitting soup
with bubbles like saliva.

When it was closed in for the first winter, there occurred a moment of pensiveness in the family. "Well, a nice
little bungalow," murmured his wife, Sarah.

"I don't know," said Marilyn, "no modrun conveniences yet."

"A house!" he yelled. "A place to live, getting bigger
every year. Look! Taste it! Workrooms, storerooms for our
junk, places to sleep."

Elsie admonished the others. "Pa gets a kick out of it.
That's nice. Be quiet already."

"It's almost a ranch-style," Doris mused. "Stanley,"
(her husband) "he says you could sell it and get a nice
little apartment in the Bronnicks." She pronounced the second syllable of *Bronx* with the negligent culture of a girl
to whom museums come natural.

"What could you get for a home made house like
that?" And the answer was easy: "Beans."

He didn't blame his children for being American; it
was a waste of exasperation. Besides, Elsie was American
plus—plus something which felt like the pleasure of work,

which he could not say in any of his languages. But he announced: "I don't want no nice apartment. . . . Want to see how I mark off the ground?" he had asked me. "Every man his own surveyor,"—and he paced exactly one yard with each straining thick-thighed step.

On that October day his daughter Marilyn had gone to the kitchen, which still smelled of wet cement. He watched her rub the dirt from her shoes with a newspaper. "Clean children I raised," he said. "They lived in the city with smoke and garbage, no real dirt, no work-dirt. Well, everybody enjoys like he can."

"It's not their fault," I said.

"Who said anything was wrong?" he said. He had learned in middle age to wield tools, to lift, to carry, and to swing down with his legs apart and the fixed grin of labor running with sweat. He was barrel-staved with hair and tight high-colored skin, a house-builder with ambition for red bricks mixed with straw. "I ain't building me no pyramid, it's a house," he said. But it was a memorial all the same.

A sphinx—that monument of brick stolidly facing out over the deserts of Connecticut. Foundation and insulation by the builder, windows by the same. It had been brought on the back of a hard squat round old man from the Bronx. This, and not the bitter unleavened bread, was to be carried across the desert. And Elsie loved him! Is there anything more? He would sit in his kitchenette and eat buttered saltines and radishes and figure how to keep the fireplace from smoking.

The fireplace was smoking and he was dying.

I found him among the paraphernalia of death. Back from the hospital to finish himself out at home, he panted and gasped like a played out child, still wide-awake and challenging his family with the suspicion that they wanted

to put him away. Except only Elsie. The room was filled
with a melon-fragrance, the sweet ripeness of decay. Under
the sheet—it was now summer again—illness had tightened
his skin. His body had swollen, containing death, holding it,
embracing; he had swollen like a mother's breast groped by
famished death, the blind baby.

"Aie!" wailed his wife.

"Oh! Oh!" said his polite daughters. More than their
love for him, they felt and feared what remained of him in
his dying. Elsie said nothing.

"I know," he said, "I didn't make no wills. Split it up
someways, but don't sell the house."

"What should we do with it, Pa?" Marilyn demanded.
"You can't expect us to live out in the sticks."

"Hello to Danny," he said to me, "come to see an old
man off. The terrible thing, let me tell you, is all those doctors and relatives in the hospital. At least now the docs
went away. Glad to see you, boy, but don't bawl me out. I
had enough from them already."

I couldn't cry. He seemed pleased. A happy death?—
that is, sad with the sense of waste which increases the glad-
ness that such waste is still possible. Another way of saying
it: Bricks were piled in the yard, mortar was dying in a bin,
windows still wore the glazier's stickers, but the house was
finished enough. You could live in it already, which means
that you could die in it. He said to me at one time during
those hours while we waited, astounded by his wakefulness:
"It's tough on the women." And then: "Well, take this
house for a for-instance. It might be hard on her, but it's
something to remember with."

The doctor had anticipated a paralysis, but there was
none. "Stop talking so much. Don't be a dumb bell," Marilyn said.

"Eat your dinner, it's getting late," he said. "Make

them something good to eat, Sarah. It's getting dark already."

It was as if we were waiting. He waited, too, but did not insist. "I build a house, I make my own mortar. Bricks dried in the sun with red clay and straw—the straw sticks the clay together, the mortar sticks the bricks together." Naked under a sheet and pajamas, the chest rolled like a barrel and the tight high-colored skin shimmered like a ripe pear. Obscure disabilities and failures were occurring one after the next within his body, but Joe's eyes still recreated Joe at each instant, blazing from the great fat expanse of his head. The bald lids of his eyes fell in a moment's respite. If there was pain, we knew only by his withdrawal from it. Elsie, all youth and agelessness, waited by his side in complicity with this old man.

Someone's tears awakened him. In the air of his daughters' discontent his mouth gulped like that of a fish. "What's the matter?" he asked. "Should I hurry?"

We pulled closer as his face darkened with blood, smooth and strange with effort. His wife whispered, "What's the matter?"

"This time it's for me."

"What?"

He pulled himself half out of the sheets. "I got to go—"

"What?"—and she pushed his chest with her hands. "Lie down. Don't move."

"To the bathroom!" Part of his face went awry with laughter. "I got to go to the toilet."

"Stay in bed, Pa!"

"Yussel!" his wife cried. "We'll get you the pan."

"Get away from me," he said.

"I'll tell the doctor on you," Sarah said.

He pushed her away with a slow sweeping motion, unhesitating in will although, to his face, there came a look of

surprise at his own slowness. Still smiling, uncaring about
our watching, he grunted and ponderously rolled off the
bed onto his feet. He stood swaying naked before his daughters, his wife, and me, his pendant belly dark and rolls of fat
over the cord of his pajamas, his huge swollen old man's
backside bulging. "I can do it myself," he said.

No one moved.

His daughters stared as if they had never seen him
before. Elsie turned away, but the others went on looking.
There was a bluish bedsore like a beetle on his back, and
discolored marks where the pajama cord had cut him.

"Some baby, eh?" he said.

"Joe!" his wife cried again. She was too afraid of him
to touch him.

"All right, all right."

"Joe!"—I heard my own voice. He could not get to the
bathroom alone; he would take no help.

"I told you he'd try something like that," Marilyn
hissed. "In the hospital they got facilities—"

"Listen, everybody," his voice came. "Listen, don't cry,
anybody."

My tear-ducts and the apple of grief in my throat
turned with regret that his shoulders and chest and belly
could give none of their strength to the sapped limbs. His
glare was fixed on the door. He stretched, propped with his
thick legs straddling. He stretched again and scratched the
hairy flanks under cotton, but his face was pulled tight with
effort. "Don't say nothing," he muttered stiffly, and he
stumbled, and his arms beat at his side, and he scampered
against the bed which creaked and rolled, and he fell half-
naked to the floor while we all jumped to him. *Oh no,* Elsie
turned her head away into her arms. I think all of us yelled
at once, but he was silent now. There was even a slight
bleeding where he scratched his flank against the bed. The

heart was unequipped for his desire. It heaved, it turned over, it busted.

Afterwards, long past suppertime, I remembered that he would want me to eat, and with this thought in my throat the warm tears came loosened to wash me. At midnight I took the bus, then the subway back to my dormitory. I sat in a Bickford's and ate.

The bin of mortar in the yard hardened, whitened, flaked until his wife threw it out like spoiled soup. But even ten years later, the three times of Joe and all of us are joined in a single moment which still hovers over his bed in that house where his legs were a-straddle on their way—the past time of the idea of a house, the present time when he does work with bricks, and the time to come when, nothing yet finished, Elsie would sacrifice her bereavement in order to marry. Their presence in a moment supposes a law about the happy and unwilling death of the man who finds a work that he likes.

The Burglars and the Boy

Let me tell you a story about how the most necessary illusion of them all was invented, engraved and fixed with acid in the whorls of character—this time not the other story of lost illusions.

When a boy, "poor but dishonest," as the saying goes, I imagined myself Dick Whittington and delivered the morning paper in the suburb in which my family lived. Creeping chill and resentful among the predawn chatter of the birds of early springtime (although it is not always spring in these memories), I gathered up the papers from my porch and carried them in a bag, folding and then sailing them over front stoops. *Zip-zippo,* said the thrice-folded *Plain Dealer* onto a porch. Zip! zip! zip!—bearing Walter Lippmann swiftly across slivers to bring me money in the pocket, which means freedom and power, which meant a chance at cute and bestial Pattie Donahue. Zippo again for all our suburban tips toward immortality, which means a nice career!

In addition to two side streets, I distributed the *Plain Dealer* at the apartments above the row of stores at the shopping center. I had neither a dog nor freckles, and rarely whistled as I went, but otherwise I must have been all-American enough to be lithographed onto a calendar over the title: "BOY IN MARCH. . . . Easy Credit Terms At All Our Outlets." The discordant note in this patriotic fantasy is that, for sweet integrity's sake, my dream of Pattie Donahue, impossibly voluptuous in honor of my thirteenth birthday, should have been put like the conversation in a comic strip in a balloon above my head. I was obsessed with what I called *Love,* browned, tenderized, crisped, and capitalized in the toaster of my imagination. (This passion is not the illusion already mentioned.) My secret self also spelled both profanity and deep commitment as did the Katzenjammer Kids: "% #&*!!!"

The streets were coldly aglitter with street lamps, starved by shadow, frozen in the distraught sleep of inanimate things. Near the end of my route, an occasional early-riser's alarm clock would clatter, a light switch on, and the clop-clop business of bathroom and kitchen begin. Sometimes an abrupt chink of light opened onto a porch; a dog was set free. My libertarian thoughts roamed with it in a splendid solitude, without responsibility to this real world of ambitions and economies, from the aspiration toward Buck Rogers in his Twenty-fifth Century to the Pattie Donahue of my unleashed flesh, with license in this odd dead-asleep suburban hour to give myself up to doing that which would have brought a fierce blush to the cheek of Jack Armstrong or Dick Tracy. I cried out to the pneumatic specter of Love, "Life! O Everybody!" Translated from the fakery of my heart, this meant simply: "Pattie! You just forget about that Lewis Snyder, give me a look. He's got boils on the neck."

Pattie and the others stylized by unpracticed desire into either boils or immortal Beauty and Truth, I kicked the dew from the bushes and marvelled at my mystic identity:

"I'm really Errol Flynn, I'm the mad scientist from Buck Rogers, I'm King Carol of Rue-mania's long-lost son, if he had one, maybe." And went home for a bowl of Wheaties and the back-of-the-box literature. The dog, busy with its own work of imagination, would finish with the lawn and then doze on its master's porch.

The shopping district at Detroit Avenue (so convenient, so friendly, such free delivery) held its commercial counsel, the night lights as murky as pigs' eyes above the hams in the butcher shop; the barberpole rested its stripes from their daily screw toward infinity; the awning was folded within itself over Tintoretto Fruits & Veg. As I sneaked by the drugstore window, white-coated Dr. Spellitbackwards and his scientific finger admonished the empty air. Once a drunk lurched at me from the alley to say, "Whatcha doing, kid, yeah?"

"Working,"—this an exaggeration. I was a somnambulant whose dreams, to my surprise, brought a qualified pessimism (Lippmann) and a serial optimism (Orphan Annie) to this corner of the stupefied universe.

"Hey! C'mere, yoyo!"

"Got my root to cover. . . ."

Both the electrified alarm-ribbons and the NRA stickers on Jasper the Jeweler's window reminded me of the brigands said to be abroad, not in our Lakewood, of course, but in many publications. "Watch out for prowlers, roughnecks, bad company, nasty old men," our teachers told us. "Don't forget to beware of fiends." Sometimes, in the apartment house above the row of shops, I heard a groan from behind locked doors as I put the paper under a footmat. I knew it to be normal and natural, the way of adult sleeping. I expected it; I scowled with piety and anticipation. While passing the years before I too might rise to this mature misery, I consoled myself with fancies of doing good—

curing sick friends by an occult exploration plus pure will power, convincing Charles Laughton to be nice to the Bounty mutineers, catching Pattie Donahue in my bare hands as she leaped (languorously) from the bedroom of a flaming house. She then pinned a medal on my new covert suit, saying, "Just for you, my only darling. It was interpellation beyond the call of doody."

Folding the papers on my way past the darkened storefronts, I twisted my lips cunningly in the imagination of her kisses.

One March morning I was brought to life abruptly by a flicker and dim figures at the rear of the jewelry shop. There was a glimmer of flashlights, a shuffle of feet. Two men, irresolutely moving, were whispering together. I stepped to the door and found that they had removed the pane; they must have worked out some way to disconnect the alarm. I boggled while they scooped tag ends of jewelry into paper sacks, but it was only a few seconds before they saw me.

"Hey, kid! Lookit the kid!" It was the barrel-bodied drunk of the night before.

His friend, less astonished because seeing me for the first time, took three long steps to the empty door frame. The breath of command steamed over me: "Get in here, yoyo." A gangling narrow-skulled man in a plaid lumberjacket, he jigged and held his toe, which he had stubbed on the way. His flashlight swept me toward him. "Tarnation, goldarnit," he was saying.

I stepped over the door jamb.

The barrel-bodied burglar, jumping at me and growling, bustling, noisy-breathed, thrust-lipped and pouting, prodded me with two fingers and said: "Who the hell you think you are?"

I did not have the answer to his question.

"Shut up, yoyo," said the slower-to-anger tall one, leaning back into darkness and watching me with the dreamy brooding of a hibernating creature, driven out by hunger to forage in early March. He nursed his toe in his hand and clucked his tongue.

Short-burglar charged back and forth in the narrow space: "Get that flash out! We oughta make time now! Somebody's gonna notice the Pinkerton's off!"

"I said shut up, so shut up," the tall one said, looking cock-headed at his friend. "I banged my foot for real that time."

"*Jeez*-zuz, Fred, what we gonna do with the yoyo?"

I wheezed with fright because they did, but said nothing. There was a communion in asthma and, for the moment, no other sense between us. I was asking myself alternately, stupidly, three question: Would Pattie Donahue give a care if she knew my peril? Would she say only, *O dear me?* Is the tall one from West Virginia? ("Hill-billies very often cut your head off, they decapitate it," Dorothy Dillon had told me. "Most irresponsible people.") My awful privacy had been peopled with a rush. Radical Rosicrucianism and Spicy Detective were turning to smoke before the fact of these nervous men. *Do you want Money-Love-Power?* I quoted to myself soothingly, but could no longer remember the advice of the free booklets in plain wrappers. I harrumphed to clear my throat and my head, said, "Arrgh," decided not to risk the treble of my changing voice.

The tall one sighed. "Listen, yoyo, we got half a mind to—"

Get thee behind me, Dotty Dillon, I prayed.

His voice trailed off, but as it seemed a comfort to him to threaten me, I looked up attentively. "Yoyo," the short one grumbled. I waited, my unfurled heart spinning like a fine toy inside; and yet, even in my breathless funk, with my knees going flooey and an ache in my chest, it seems to me now that I was more devoted to the particularity of this event than I had ever been before. In that narrow aisle between two long glass cases of jewelry, I took the risk as necessary, and with pleasure.

These sparse-bearded and unhealthy young men could not be murderers, I promised myself. Not the type that Humphrey B. had to face on Saturday afternoon. They didn't look like monsters. Their hands jittered in and out of their pockets; the paper bags of knick-knacks rustled; they looked miserable. Were they scared enough to hurt me?

"What, Fred? What?"

Within all that world of suburban sleepers, I had never confronted such unease—not so much in the expression of faces as in the slump and jerk of discouraged limbs. The tall Fred had a high peaked forehead, straining with thought and vanishing back into pale hair. The dark barrel-bodied one kept looking at him, barking, "What? What? What?" They had not even tried the safe where the valuable pieces would be kept. They had scrabbled their hands for trinkets through the green felt of the display cases. "What? What?" They were all jumpiness, conferring lips, and bumping thighs. I had learned their word already, and they looked more like yoyos to me than I looked like a yoyo to myself: a clumsy sentence and an ungenerous thought. It would probably have done me no good to say that I was sorry, so I kept silent.

"What? What? What?"

"What you figure to do with the yoyo?" Fred asked.

"That's what *I* was just saying, Fred. Jeez, whyncha listen?"

If only Pattie could see me so brave now, I was thinking.

"What you aiming at, yoyo? Leggo your mouth."

I had felt my teeth to investigate their movements. I wondered if they were chattering. They were not, but the rattatat continued. Short-burglar, the one I had seen prowling in the alley, must have been poorly tuned. "Jeez, Fred, what we going to do now?" he moaned.

"Wait! Don't you move," the other commanded. I had not considered moving; I was worrying about short-burglar. What kind of a duel could this be if my adversary fainted?

"Okay," I said.

They were leaning to me with disgust and fear. My paper carrier's sack was slipping down my shoulders; I hitched it up again. At this movement short-burglar twitched visibly. "C'mere," Fred commanded, knees and elbows, plaid gangle and stoop and wounded toe.

"I'm here already," I pointed out.

"Listen to that backtalk, Fred," said the barrel-bodied burglar. "No backtalk from yoyos, yoyo." They led me into a small washroom at the rear of the store and again stood breathing heavily, as if in the prayer that this might dissolve me. They were wasting their breath. Short-one peeked at his flashlight, saw by the liverish yellow that the battery was wearing out, switched it off. They had closed the door and we three were jammed up against each other and I smelled something which I have come to remember as the smell of burglary, thick, sour, and heavy, a very different thing from the swift tang of larceny. The burden of my lust after Miss Pattie Donahue was nothing more than a string on my finger (with a yoyo atttached), very little compared with the awful weight of my existence on these two break-and-enter souls.

"Sit down!"

There was but one place to sit; I sat. My *Plain Dealer* bag kept slipping; I hitched; it slipped again while the two burglars wheezed and sighed hoarsely and shifted their feet in the stuffy washroom. "Go on, go on, so put the papers on the floor," the barrel-bodied one said, scowling as if to punish me. He was becoming uncomfortable at my discomfort. It was more than an inexperienced burglar should be asked to bear.

"Okay, let's get going," the tall burglar said, peering at his long hank of a wrist. He had no watch.

"Where?"

It was clear that they knew neither what-next, what-now nor what-how. They were apprentices with no calling but the Depression. What-then was also a mystery: they had troubles. They stood in front of me, bumping my knees in their confusion, occasionally shining the light in my face and then apologetically switching it off. I was a trouble-maker; they appreciated me at my value, alas. The bulky short one offered threats: "Tie him up! Fix him good!"

Fred was theoretical. "Maybe the yoyo already called the cops, maybe. Naw, but maybe the cops patrol this here street."

I strangled my voice down to a male bass and volunteered an answer: "I never saw one here, a copper, a bull, Fred. You could probably amscray and not even get bollixed by the John Darms,"—triumphant in my command of argot.

"Who told you my name? Shut up."

"The way I look at it, Fred, me personally, I think you fellows could probably take it on the lam, see, and then—"

"*Please,* kid," Fred appealed to me, "it's hard enough like it is. Please."

Short-burglar had ducked behind and returned with a sharp, blue, and cold-looking roll of wire. "Whyn't we roll him up in a nice little ball?" he asked Fred.

"Fix the yoyo up good for the night?" In short-burglar's

presence Fred poked his face at mine in order to restore our old relationship and measure the effect of his ruthlessness.

"Yeah, sure, great,"—and then, after fumbling in-effectually with the wire, they decided, "Naw, takes too much time. Slips." Fred's fist-like head was thrust forward on the stalk of his neck; he scowled his warning to accept this version of their failure to get me securely out of their way. "You just better look out," he said. I could have sug-gested some boy scout knots, but knew that adults resent interference from yoyos.

They ran the light from my face to my feet. More threats, more theories. They didn't look happy enough to be Robin Hood and Friar Tuck, nor sinister enough for Dill-inger and Pretty Boy Floyd. They looked seasick. I worried about daylight. At last, realizing that they were the ones who were obliged to act (it was not my place), they warned me to stay put while they finished, and then not to move for half an hour, or else:

"We'll plug you full of holes, kid," the short burglar said without conviction.

"They'll carry you out of here in a box," the tall one murmured unhappily.

"Like swiss cheese," said the short one.

"Not like swiss cheese in a box, like a stiff in a box," Fred explained.

"Yeah," they agreed irresolutely. There was an embar-rassed silence. They seemed to feel that they had committed a faux pas, while I did not have the true courtesy which would have consisted in cowering and taking them at their word.

"Okey-doke," I said, "I'll just sit. I don't mind, me per-sonally, but just my papers'll be late." I realized that Mr. C. R. Brown, 13577 Detroit Avenue, daily and Sundays, would this morning not have a *Plain Dealer* for the streetcar downtown. He was my most matinal client. "I just like sitting sometimes," I added, peeking up at Fred, worried about the silence on this social occasion. *With a good book,* I was ready to say, *with a good book just thinking.* "Only the customers don't like it. My root-man he gets excited—"

"Never you mind the papers," short-burglar said ominously.

"They won't mind, kid, just only one time," Fred promised me.

"Okay now, don't move, you got us?"—Fred limping slightly, skinny-necked and slope-shouldered from behind, short-burglar sweating and puffing and busy.

"I got you," I said.

They shut the door on me and I heard the leafy rustling of costume jewelry as they finished filling their bags. After their crowding, breathing over me, shining their lights in my eyes, I felt abandoned in the closet which had suddenly become, despite the plumbing, as huge and as empty as a palace. I wondered if a policeman might happen along, but reassured myself against interruption, having never seen one during my route hour at this block. (Further down I had once spied Officer Campbell curled up snoring on the seat of his squad car, the motor running for warmth.) Through the tiny alley-window, I heard the drifting of papers in the early morning breeze. Rustle-rustle, scratch-scratch, and the playful scrabble of breakfasting rats. Then there was silence, both outside and within the shop, except for Fred's hoarse breathing. I put my ear to the door and tried to guess what they were planning.

Bump me off? No, they weren't the types, too slow, too much thinking.

Tie me up? No, all thumbs and all tongues, they knew their clumsiness too well to try it again.

Lock me in? No key.

Then what?

The door fell open and I nearly toppled onto my leaning ear. "Listen, kiddo," short-burglar said.

"Listen, yoyo," said the tall one. They were both trembling. "Listen, you stay in this room for a half hour or we'll fix your string good, see? You know what that means?"

I nodded solemnly, thinking, O Pattie Donahue will be sorry if I come out dead dead dead. And: When I'm a hero after all, then she'll wish she didn't snoot me, that Pattie. My sense of fitness was baffled because Fred had failed to draw a finger across his throat and make a slitting noise.

"Okay, we need a half hour. Then you can peddle your papers, call the cops, we don't care. Thirty minutes. But if you tell the cops what we look like—"

I closed my eyes. His remark had wounded me. *Now* was the time for the slitting, strangling gesture. No, they were too embarrassed. Impressionable, having lived in their world so long already, I accepted their standards. I shared their sickly social unease because we had been brought together like this with no introduction and, at least at first, with very little in common. We had burgled in each other's distracted hearts. I blushed because they thought that I might describe them to the police.

"It's no use," Fred said, his roosterish eyes half-shut and his neck bent for the cropper's barrel-stave.

"Okay, we're getting," said short-burglar.

They remained one more moment. They gazed glumly upon me with pleas, with shame, with suspicion, with their paper bags of jewelry dangling in their hands. "What a yoyo, ain't he?" Fred croaked. There was a hopelessness and a resignation. They looked like Lakewood husbands doing the Saturday marketing.

"Bye, kid." Tenderly they closed the washroom door.

"Bye, yoyo,"—this appeal, muffled by wood, was in

Fred's hoarse whisper. He was waiting on the other side. I could imagine the gobble of his Adam's apple. "What say?"

"Bye," I said through the door, and hooked the latch. "Hey, Fred? You Fred? Don't worry."

I listened for their shuffle in flight together down the alley. Then I sat whistling on the toilet, folding the rest of my *Plain Dealers* for tossing at doors, until I decided that it was time to call the police. What else did I owe my two fellow-worriers? When I emerged, the dawn was full on the suburb, and I blinked thrice for the long night of incomprehension and selfishness which was over for me. Now I had a glimpse of how others felt about things. Of course, new nights were coming.

I had forgotten Jasper the Jeweler. He was a tired, trusting, owl-eyed man who had neglected to keep up his burglary insurance. He had a sick wife, too. Feeling for others is far from a moral quality, and very complicated.

Encounter in Haiti

I would like to tell you how, as a scholar in Haiti on a fellowship sponsored by the State Department, it became my duty to give fifty cents to a part-time peasant prostitute, half her fee for servicing an elderly and retired French fascist.

Climbing to the cool mountain village of Kenscoff, thousands of feet above the heavy-scented tropical hurly-burly of Port-au-Prince, I left my family for a few days and settled myself in a friend's summer house in order to finish a job of writing. I was completely alone except for the gardener who brought me coffee, bread, and fruit in the morning. The village itself is as peaceful as a Haitian settlement can be—the sounds of singing and calling in the fields, the tattoo of hands on water cans, insects and birds, occasionally the echo of drum, *asson*, and chanting from a co-operative plowing or house-raising back on the slope. Once the village coffee speculator chased a peasant woman down the road, morally outraged, screaming *"Voleuse!"* because she asked the unheard-of price of thirty-five cents a pound for her coffee. Apart from such rare interruptions, I was alone with my conscience, the smell of eucalyptus, and the long fresh days and the long chill nights.

For the two main meals I walked up the road to a small inn, the Hotel des Fleurs Froides. At this season there were only two other pensionnaires, one a Haitian of good family, a former professor of law who had dropped his marbles and now, while benevolently presiding over difficult sessions in his pith helmet, lived by a ritual so intense that he would knock down a chair which stood in the way of his pre-meal forced march across the dining room. Swinging his heavy aristocratic *cocomacaque,* he paced back and forth, for exactly one hour, murmuring the text of one of the defunct constitutions of the Republic of Haiti, smiling apologetically but treading straight upon you if you didn't scurry out of the way fast enough. "Monsieur Manot has organized his life," Anna, the waitress, told me. "He has an income. His family comes to see him sometimes, but he is happy without them. *Le climat de Kenscoff lui va si bien.*"

These words—"The climate of Kenscoff suits him so!" —were to be echoed later by the other pensionnaire, the former officer in the French army whom I will call Colonel Climate. He was permanently settled in the Hotel des Fleurs Froides, where in 1954 a room with three meals cost three dollars a day and less by the month. Old newspapers and fresh coffee are available at any time, and these conveniences, plus the mountain air and the companionship of Anna, constitute the chief pleasures of the hotel.

At lunch one afternoon the Colonel sent Anna across the dining room with a glass of wine from his own bottle. When I looked up from my book I saw him nodding his head briskly, grinning, lifting his own glass, removing the toothpick from his rapid mouth, signalling me to *drink! drink!* I drank and then, of course, came to thank him at his table. After introductions were made—he stood up and clicked the heels of his sandals—he explained why he had been so forward with a man whom he did not know. "You too resemble an artist, a person who, like me, admires wild orchids," he stated. "Join me at dinner, please. You speak French well for an American. I would not believe it! And French is the most difficult language in the world because—yes, it is so—there are sometimes two ways of saying the same thing. If one speaks French well one has no strength left for foreign languages. But you do, Sir!"

I bowed under this ravishment by praise. How disabling to be born into a language like English in which there is only one way of saying things!

"Another glass?" I would have accepted his wine, a fine ambiguous red, but he interrupted himself: "Try some water instead. The water of Kenscoff is preservative, is free from microbes and modern chemicals, and in addition has the prime virtue, Sir—it is diuretic." He gave a short, fine-toothed, military smile. "Sometimes I wake up from four to six times a night."

He poured me a glass of this risky water and I toasted the athletic old man's face before me, a bald, smooth, sleek head, the skin reddened and flaking off his scalp, a face of furious health, scorched from without and all burned up within. Apart from the heavy mole winking on one eyelid, giving his face a curiously unpleasant joviality, his expression was unmarked by anything but muscle along the jaw—the habit of command uncorrupted by thought, a wiry self-indulgence, a girlishness of caprice and malice in the pink mouth separated from the pale blue beard by a still pinker expanse of flesh. His head was as smooth as an egg.

But the soul of an artist also inhabited the Colonel, who was all tenderness for the climate of Kenscoff and the wild orchids of its woods. "It's against the law to pick them in French colonies, so I just look at them. *Ah que c'est belle l'orchidée!* Have you ever been in Dakar?"

Haiti, of course, has not been a French colony for a

hundred and fifty years, but for the Colonel French law was
still in force. He began to tell me about his family when,
masticating fiercely, touching the napkin to his mouth, he
cried out, "Wait!"

"What's the matter?"

"Wait, Sir!" He pushed back his chair and fled out
the front door.

"???" I went on eating.

He was back in a moment, puffing through his damp-
ened lips, nodding fervently, I-told-you-so-saying, sliding
back into his place at table. "Fourteen degrees Centigrade,"
he pronounced. "And in Port-au-Prince it must be a veri-
table inferno." He took up his fork again. "Modern urban
life! Barbarous!"

We had left the subject of orchids and proceeded to the
true passion of his long career on earth: the perfect climate. All his life he had sought the ideal, and now this
reduced Platonist had found it in Kenscoff. Martinique was
too hot, Sweden too cold. California, which he had tried
for a time with his wife, was too dry. Numerous other places
were too wet. "In sum, Sir," he stated, "only Kenscoff is
truly ideal. I will live here forever."

"Aren't you lonely for your wife?"

"I miss my wife," he said with a faint pout of sacrifice,
"but my days are full. I walk. I exercise. I do physical culture. There is too much reading in the world already—I
have no need to tire my eyes. I need them for looking at
flowers. But then, in the evening, when it is too dark to be
outdoors, well, I write to my wife. Every night but Saturday
—every man must have a little relaxation, Sir. I am a loyal
husband."

His wife, ill in the States, would like to see him. He
would like to visit her, too, but: *"Le climat de Kenscoff me*

va si bien." And besides he had such beautiful memories of her that it would be a shame to look upon her now, all wasted by illness. "In her youth she had a body!" he cried, raising one finger as testimony. May the Good Lord who sees all strike him dead if his wife had not been rich in flesh. "Now, alas, she is old and scrawny," he finished mournfully. "Her biceps lack firmness. No tone to her pectorals."

He stopped Anna and held her arm. The back of his hand was plump, pink, and freckled. She pulled away, smiling, saying, *"M'occupée, M'sieu le Colonel,"* but consented to bring him some more lettuce and parsley salad.

"Creole is just French babytalk," he commented, bending, nibbling. "I don't encourage it. I always speak the pure French of Racine and Tardieu with them. But anyway, I understand the colonial peoples just by looking at them, that's how they know what to do." Over his salad, ravenous for vitamins and empire, he informed me that losing Haiti was Napoleon's great mistake. "Russia was nothing, just snow, ice, and Russians. But St. Domingue—our pearl, Sir! A treasure of a climate."

Occasionally, in my walks about the countryside, I would meet this aged, brisk, red-faced athlete, his pants secured at his ankles by a bicyclist's clips, his feet in sandals without socks, his erect little body jaunty in sport clothes. To his proposals of walks in the woods to see the finest wild orchids in the French empire, I could always plead other occupations, but it was now impossible to avoid him at mealtimes. The gentle maniac pacing up and down in the dining room was no distraction. Taking food, like love, is a sociable procedure. The French empire and I spooned up our soup together.

2

"In a few days," he announced one Friday evening, "I too will begin a book."

"What book?"

"Not to read one, my friend—a waste of time—but to write one." And he smiled and nodded. *"Oui, ah oui,"* he said, "the time has come." No secrets from his dining companion! The eye with the mole on its lid was somewhat inflamed.

"The story of my life and why France fell. I did my duty, Sir! It wasn't my fault. I told them in 1935—" It seems that France fell to the invasion because of a lack of balance. No equilibrium.

"What balance was lacking, Colonel?"

"The balance between Intellectualism and Physical Culture—there is the theme of my book. I could not restore the balance all by myself,"—and his fine, high-toned, soldier's face darkened with memory of hopeless effort. "I told my brother-in-law in 1935. I told him again in 1937. I predicted it. I told him to tell the *Chef d'Etat* without using my name, for, as a military man, I could not, of course, mix myself in politics."

Monsieur Manot was pacing and murmuring, "And this court further holds that the property may not be transferred to an eldest son alone without, without, without . . ."

"But you were interested in politics, Colonel?"

"No, no, do not misunderstand me. Politics is not for a soldier, Sir. I only saw then, in the simplicity of my soldier's heart, that France needed a Man."

It seemed that there were other passions besides orchids and the climate of Kenscoff in the Colonel's heart, and these were of a sort which changed my first view of him as a whimsical old fellow. France fell because of the rabble of

Paris. France fell because of the unholy alliance of Bolshe-
viks and International Bankers. France fell because Polish
foreigners who pretended to be Frenchmen sabotaged the
Army and prevented deserving officers from being pro-
moted to general's rank. "I know. I saw them at work. My
eyes were open. And they are still alive."

"Who?"

He did not answer. He studied his plate, slicing all the
meat into tiny morsels, then lining them up in formation,
then popping them into his mouth. First the piece farthest
away, then the next, embracing them steadily toward his
small neat belly. When he had refuelled, he began to talk
again. There was one man, he remarked, a man in fine
physical condition, who had tried to save France. He offered
up even his body. Someday the world will know the truth
about him.

"Who was that?" It was pure malice to pretend to
ignorance.

He removed his toothpick before pronouncing the
word: *"Le Maréchal!"*

I persisted in my wickedness and went on chewing,
trying to drawl like a middle-westerner even in my careful
schoolboy French. "Which marshal, Colonel?"

"There is only one—*Pétain.*"

Anyone who noticed the last war, and particularly
those who have lived in France and seen what the spirit of
Pétain has done to a great people, can perhaps be forgiven
if a curious encounter in a mountain village of the Carib-
bean republic of Haiti arouses a complicated set of emotions. Like many Jews, I feel ashamed to mention, even to
anti-Semites, that most of my family was destroyed in gas
ovens. This is not simply tact. I might want to speak of
it. However, the chasm between the emotion which it is

possible to express about these people and that which their martyrdom deserves is too great to cross in social talk. The discontinuity between the ovens and Colonel Climate, despite his evident place as a stoker, was so great as to be, properly, comic.

I contented myself with saying that I found Pétain stupid, unpatriotic, and—

"What!"

"And in *bad physical condition.*"

His rage was deep, genuine, and immediate. He leaped up and out of his seat, crying aloud, almost weeping, sputtering, his arms jerking with his intense, highly willed, old man's vitality. The spittle formed at the corners of his mouth. "B-b-b-blasphemy!" he stammered, near to tears. And then, because he was a Frenchman and I therefore could understand nothing of his life, he put his face close to mine and hissed out a formula which made him happy: "He who has not eaten of chocolate does not know the taste of chocolate."

Equally wild, I shouted, "But I've eaten of that chocolate! The Pétain militia delivered my cousins to the Germans." We stood, mouths hanging, and gasped at each other. *Chocolate,* I remember thinking.

The educated Haitian maniac, called back to sanity for a moment by our madness, paused in his pacing and tugged the Colonel's sleeve, *"Calmez-vous, Monsieur, calmez-vous."*

Anna, setting a pot of eucalyptus tea on the table, touched my arm. *"Quittez'l tranquil,"* she said. *"Gros bagaie cé pas nécessaire."*

The Colonel turned, his short arms pumping, and marched out. I sat down to my root tea, hot inside, quenching my thirst with a green liquid-like bile, consumed by shame at being brought to put the weight of my resentment of Hitler on a half-senile athlete. If he could upset me like this, then it was time to take the *camionette* down into Port-au-Prince. I stayed up that night with a horrible loneliness for my wife and my two daughters. Family and community are a great comfort against stupidity, even against the murderous stupidity of my orchid-loving friend.

By changing my dinner hours the next day, I managed to avoid facing the Colonel across the dining room. Once, sucking his teeth after supper on his way out, he hailed me in friendly fashion and—why not?—I greeted him in the same way with a half-military salute and a rapid aspiration through the spaces between my upper bicuspids.

"*Bonsoir, Monsieur! Bon appétit.*"

"*Bonsoir, Colonel. Amusez-vous bien.*"

It was Saturday night. Veal cutlet. I began to know the habits of the kitchen. The Colonel's pants twitched and constantly reshaped a triangle from behind as he went out for his evening walk. I bent in solitude to my plate—string beans, rice, a slice of crusted meat—and a frayed copy of *Match* with a pro-and-con discussion of Ingrid Bergman's romance with Roberto Rosselini. It was later than usual and Anna, who had had her own plans for Saturday night, showed her displeasure with me by slapping the cupboards to and sweeping under my table before I had finished. I turned away the eucalyptus tea and asked for coffee.

The drums had begun already. From all the hills about Kenscoff they were summoning the faithful, and judging by the immaculate white dresses of the women and the pressed khaki or blues of the men, this was an important ceremony. I asked Anna which god was expected.

"Loko Atissou," she said.

"Will the *loa* come?"

She took away my coffee before I had finished, with a

quick, crisp, disapproving gesture. "If he comes, he'll come," she said.

I would make friends with her again tomorrow. Outside, the cool evening was crowded with peasants standing about on the road in holiday dress, blinking and talking, unaccustomed to being awake at this hour of the evening. Saturday night in Kenscoff, Haiti, with its big-footed peasants lounging in groups and the close-mouthed chatter of earned pleasure among them, made me lonely for Prospect Avenue in Cleveland, Ohio. Of course, the *vodoun* drums of the Rada cycle are no substitute for the jukebox cacophony down the canyon of Prospect. I decided against attending the ceremony, where I would probably find the Colonel, and in favor of the weekly peasant dance in the *choucounette*, a mud and straw hut ten minutes' walk up the mountain. There would also be a battery of three drums with perhaps an *asson,* a metal rhythm instrument, and I could have a glass of *clairin* in lively company.

Gros-Fils, the proprietor of the *choucounette,* discontented with selling only *clairin*, had lately grown more enterprising. He had constructed a little compound in his clearing. There were two smaller *choucounettes,* built this week, leaning like kennels against the smoke-darkened walls of the old one. These were for the girls that he had recently taken under his protection. A small, self-effacing man with a long sad Indian face, assuming the dignity of sunglasses even at night, he stood behind the crates where he sold *clairin* by the glass and bottle and said nothing to indicate his new commercial status as participant in the twist-and-twirl business. His smile was as modest as ever and his nose still had its self-effacing snuffle. A girl brought me my glass and then asked me to dance. I hung like any college boy at Nick's in the Village about Ti-Celestin, the chief drummer, and his two "secretaries." Their variety of tone, not just beat, is difficult to imagine—they scratch, knuckle, rap, and scrape the taut skin from which a faint animal odor still rises and to which a few clinging hairs still bring the luck of the beast. The skin of the drum made me think again of the Colonel.

Another *clairin* improved my mood. *Clairin,* a raw white rum, seems to reach the soles of the feet and the top of the brain with about the same speed and with the same urgency. The *choucounette* was lit by kerosene railway lamps. There was a fine orange steam in the air. The dancers hipped and clashed and jigged and fell apart again without a word. Haitian dancing is a lonely and impersonal thing.

The less lonely business in the two new kennels outside took place on straw mats with no light but the moonlight through the straw roof and banana-leaf screen. A discreet and modest man, Gros-Fils inaugurated the annex to his *choucounette* with no special fuss.

For the first hour.

Gros-Fils was the first to respond to the quarrel. He tucked the bottles carefully into the crate and went out to the clearing to see. I followed him. There was a shouting fight in a mixture of French and indignant female Creole. Colonel Climate, natty as usual, was saying, *"Ah non! ah non alors! ah, ca non!"*

The girl, disheveled and unhappy, plump and bulging her buttons, with a safety pin dangerously open in her blouse, explained to everyone—the domino-players in the yard, the dancers, the other girls, the drummers who had come out to see, and to Gros-Fils himself—that the old foreigner had come and bothered her and then given her only two gourdes and a half, which is fifty cents. She wanted one dollar.

"I won't be exploited," he stated. "I'm a soldier, I know what you're worth."

"Vicieux!" she screamed.

"Just because I'm a foreigner, I'm no American tourist—"

She appealed her cause to the group, first closing the pin, then arguing with the night, palms up and eyes rolling. "He's so ancient he can't do anything but bother me, the old pig. Go drink some *bois-cochon!* I should get paid double for such an immorality."

"I gave you fifty cents," the Colonel said, obviously regretful now but too stiff morally to retreat before the scorn of natives. "As a soldier I naturally inquired the price in advance. If you make a mistake, am I to blame?" He cocked his head to wait for her reply. I admired the aplomb and confidence which comes of long years of certainty in one's own way, supported by an institution.

"Vicieux! Cochon!" She moved shrilling upon him. The excitement was aging her, blotching her shiny skin, crooking her fine healthy mountain-child's grace. She could have been no more than sixteen. She turned suddenly as if she had just caught sight of me, stamped her bare feet in the dust, and invoked my sense of justice: *"Mes z'amis!* another foreigner! Tell me, Sir, what would he pay in Port-au-Prince, and especially for viciousness? Tell us all for him to be ashamed, please, Sir."

The Colonel was astonished to find me here. He peered, mouth open, into the smoky starlit darkness. Charcoal from the outdoor cooking of *griots,* a fried pork delicacy, put a light mist over the compound. Someone had carried out a lantern. Colonel Climate pointed his narrow trembling face to mine and said, *"Pas un mot! Pas un mot!"* It was spoken as a command, in a fury, but the sense was to beseech me to silence.

"Tell me! Tell us, foreigner," the girl said, taking my arm.

"Pas un mot!" His eyes were red with rage and he was half-crouched like an animal in his pants with the bicyclist's clips about his ankles.

"A lot of foolishness," the girl cried out contemptuously. "A *vicieux!* He can't do anything anymore, but he still wants to play."

The amusement in the crowd had changed to grumbling and unpleasant high reports of laughter at my silence. They were waiting. I remembered the words of my instructions: "Abroad you represent more than yourself as an individual . . ." This terse State Department version of John Donne's dictum that not even Ernest Hemingway is an island unto himself had pleased me. Anyway, whether or not it pleased me to have the responsibility for symbolic international relationships rather than a simple duty to a girl short-changed, these people were looking to me for a crucial decision of solidarity with them.

"Give the girl her money," I said to Colonel Climate.

"You stay out of this."

"Give it to her, Colonel."

"Get away from me!"

Gros-Fils interrupted unhappily: "No, if you please, Sir, let the young foreigner judge."

"What's the matter," the Colonel inquired of me, "does she work for you? Are you in business here?"

My exasperation made it difficult for me to take him seriously, but it was obvious that his last perverse pride was to be found in not giving the girl what she asked. It was all he had left. The red face, the pale eyebrows and the white fringe of hair, the crazy skinny old-man's athleticism were all ashake before me. But no Haitian peasant would interfere in our quarrel. None of them would dare to settle with him, and he knew it. He was potent on this ground.

"Don't be an imbecile, Colonel."

"Pas un mot!"

"Okay," I said.

Crouching in the lantern light, crazy with his forlorn-ness and his desperation to accomplish some feat of will, he cried out, "You think I'm an imbecile, you? But I found out about you." He moved his mouth open and shut for an instant without being able to speak. "Does the *putain* belong to you? Is she yours? I found out all about you, Jew."

The resolution to all my problems with the Colonel and the people of the *choucounette* was easy. I gave the girl her fifty cents. "For the old pig," I said. The words which I had shouted—and had their shouted laughter in return—are the same in French and Creole: "He's senile! He's not capable!"

The girl threw back her head with pleasure and kissed the coin at me. "A lot of ga-ga foolishness," she said, "is all *he* is good for, Sir."

I paid for him, and paid with joy, because we all live in the hope that the Colonel Climates of this world will someday not be able to do anything anymore. I paid because all foreigners in Haiti are judged together. And I paid with dread of the years still to come because, although he can make no pleasure in the world now, the Colonel is capable of many sorts of clinging, bitter, and destructive efforts toward the girl and me.

The Colonel had picked his way through the group and down the path without anyone's touching him. They drew fastidiously away.

"The pleasure is mine," I said. The next day I went down the mountain in a *camionette* to my family in Port-au-Prince. The name of the *camionette* was "Everywhere, and Kenscoff, Too."

Ti-Moune

Monique first came to me one morning when I lay upstairs, sweating with blackwater fever, in our house on a road just outside Port-au-Prince. She already knew my wife. I heard her downstairs asking, in French, "And Monsieur, how is he today?" She spoke with the sombreness and concern of a little girl grown used to illness, trouble, and sorrow. Because I was not really very sick, it seemed to me another of the incongruities of life in Haiti that Monique should have enough sympathy to be able to squander some on the visiting Americans in their splendid house, with its refrigerator and running water, next door to her family's clay-and-straw *caille*. "May I go upstairs, Madame?"

A moment later, she was at my open door, curtsying, smiling with many teeth but shyly all the same, and asking, "*Comment va Monsieur?*"

"Better, Monique. Tell me, how old are you?"

"Eleven. You will certainly be well soon, Monsieur. This is the fifth day already."

"Thank you, Monique."

I sat up, and she walked over and took my hand, then curtsied again and went out. That afternoon, I felt a click in my head, as if I had suddenly switched off the disease, and half an hour later I was strong enough to sit on the gallery. I felt grateful to Monique.

Skinny from rapid growth, although not tall for her age, knob-kneed, barefooted, and venturesome, with enormous, watchful black eyes and with her kinky hair tied up in little ribbons, Monique was the leader of the neighborhood children, who included her brother and two sisters and my two daughters—Ann, six, and Judy, four. She led them all by her imagination, which was both gay and grave, by her weight of years, and by the authority of gentleness and self-respect, which the children all sensed in her. Her dresses, faded to pastels by sun and soap, were always neat. Every button and every thread-made loop were in place. Once, I saw her with her mother in the ravine below our house, where the Rivière Froide sang past. She was standing knee-deep in the stream, soaping clothes, rinsing them, spreading them on rocks to dry, and then splashing them with water again and again to keep them from stiffening. Her mother, shaded by a tattered parasol, sat on a rock and directed her.

Monique's perfect skin was of a deep chocolate, but mixed blood declared itself in her straight nose and narrow lips. Sometimes a shiny black Oldsmobile would park briefly in front of her family's hut, and a lighter-skinned Negro man with bags of English mints would go inside. Monique was apparently the poor cousin of some family of money and station. She would share her bag of candy with the neighborhood children.

After I recovered, Monique, sometimes accompanied by her brother and sisters, came often to greet my wife and me and to ask permission to take our daughters out into the yard to play. She would teach them French and Creole songs, patiently making them repeat the words after her,

and then she would grasp their hands and whirl them in a
dance, as they all sang:

> *"Rond, rond, les écolières*
> *Sans rire et sans parler*
> *Celle qui rit la première*
> *Sortira du rang*
> *Un! deux! trois!"*

I remember particularly one dance she did with Ann. I
was watching from the gallery, and I tried not to let them
see me, as I was afraid I might disturb Monique's gravity,
which was deepest when she led a younger child in a dance.
This dance, like the others, was a modification of a French
children's dance, one of many introduced by the colonists
and passed down by their former slaves, who in freedom had
made the dances and the songs their own. Monique bowed;
our daughter bowed. Monique curtsied; our daughter curtsied. Then they joined hands, singing and dancing in a
circle:

> *"Ba-teau, ba-teau-teau*
> *Mon bateau s'est défoncé*
> *A la rue Saint-Honoré"*

Monique would also ask our children riddles and tell
them some of the Ti-Malice stories, which are folk stories,
something like Br'er Rabbit stories or fairy tales, and known
to all Haitian children.

When there was special cooking or baking being done
at our house, Monique would help peel the vegetables or
beat the cake batter. When she licked the spoon the first
time, it was for a taste she had never known before. And
when she bestowed her sedate approval on a cake, it seemed
almost an act of piety. *"Merci, Madame. Il est très bon, ce
gâteau."*

Frequently, she took lunch with us. Meals were so irregular at her home that it was never necessary for her to ask her mother's permission. (Her father, if there was one around, never appeared.) After lunch, she would insist on wiping the table and sweeping the floor. In a land where domestics receive as little as eight dollars a month, we had servants underfoot, but Monique *wanted* to do some of the housework. Once, while wielding a broom taller than she was, she sang in Creole probably the saddest child's song there is, the only one I know that tells of a boy about to commit suicide:

> "I need *corossol* tea with sugar,
> Biscuits and some fruit.
> My stomach hurts me.
> I am not a glutton, Maman,
> I am only hungry."

She never sang this song with our daughters.

Often she would stay all day, and in the evening, when she said good night to my wife and me, she at first shook our hands. Before long, however, she was reaching up and leaning forward to kiss our cheeks. She did this with such smiling grace that our embarrassment was only momentary. One evening as she left us, my wife called after her, *"Bonsoir, Ti-moune."* Monique smiled and ran across the way to her hut, where the oil wicks were already lit, and the charcoal smoke of her mother's stove sent up a screen between our evening and theirs.

"Ti-moune," derived from the French *"petit monde,"* is a Creole word that means "little one." It is also a word that has to do with a custom, now gradually passing in Haiti, under which a peasant family sells or gives its unwanted children—the children it cannot feed—to a more prosperous landed or town-dwelling family. The *ti-moune* works as a servant without wages, beginning at the age of five or sometimes even earlier. The word, partly because it is ambiguous, is not thought of as being uncomplimentary,

and anyway there was no doubt that my wife was using it affectionately. Monique understood.

Sometimes when Monique came to visit us, she would take our children into a nearby woods and teach them the Creole names of plants and trees. One afternoon, Judy received some painful ant bites while digging in a banana grove outside our house, and Monique ran into the woods and returned with an armful of leaves. She insisted on putting these into our bathtub and then putting Judy in with them. Trained to use drugs out of tubes and bottles, my wife and I felt foolish swishing a mess of oozing leaves about a bathtub, but when Judy emerged, the irritation had disappeared.

Monique, usually the most modest of children, said, "I know the leaves, myself," and wriggled with pride.

During the mango season, when the trees are so rich and heavy that even the poorest Haitian can fill his stomach, Monique showed Ann how to knock the mangoes down with rocks and then how to peel the luscious fruit neatly. One day about noon, having eaten a giant Madame Francis mango and a sweetsop, Ann came home to say to my wife and me, "I already had my lunch. I had lunch with Monique."

We later thanked Monique for her hospitality. Her pleasure betrayed itself in her shy smile and in the twisting of her handkerchief.

One afternoon, Monique made a rag doll from an old dress while Ann watched. When it was finished, she offered it to our daughter. Caught by surprise and delight, Ann took it and in return gave her a magnificent plastic doll with swivelling eyes of china blue—the gift of an aunt when we left the States. Monique brought this doll to my wife and asked if Ann would miss it. "Sometimes a child wants her own doll back," she commented solemnly. My wife assured her that Ann had made an excellent trade.

I had come to Haiti on a State Department fellowship for a year's study of Haitian culture, and now the time was almost up. We began getting ready to leave. Ann told the news to Monique, but without emotion, for she did not believe we could really leave this fine place. Monique came to my wife and me for confirmation. We said yes, but we hoped to be back someday. "*Ca me fait de la peine*," she said in her sedate, grown-up way. "It grieves me, Monsieur and Madame."

The next evening, as my wife and I were having our after-supper coffee on the gallery, Monique's mother walked over to the foot of the stairway. Strangely, it was the first time that we had seen her at close range. Her skin was quite light, and she had what Haitians call "*bons cheveux*" —straight hair. It was a reddish color. Her appearance surprised us. She could almost have passed for white. I had somehow never doubted that she would have Monique's chocolate color, and glimpsing her from a distance through a banana grove or down in the ravine, I had even seen her as dark. She had a thin face, tensed by poverty and anger against poverty, with none of the patient resignation of the peasants.

My wife asked her to have coffee with us, saying that we were pleased to meet her at last. She thanked us and said that she would come up to speak with us but that she wouldn't take coffee.

When she joined us on the gallery, we insisted that she sit down, and she reluctantly did, perching on the edge of her chair. We insisted also that she have some coffee, and at last she consented. She was an extraordinary Haitian, having to be urged to accept a cup of coffee.

We made talk with her. It was odd, of course, that Monique should have spent so much time in our house without our meeting her mother, but we had long ago accepted this aloofness. Perhaps the formal Haitian rules of politesse, under which she would have called on us long before, had been thrown awry by the presence of a grand house, full of foreigners, in a settlement where a roof of tin instead of straw is the great sign of coming up in the world.

Neighborly gossip came hard to her. Her stiff perch on the edge of the chair seemed to say that only important business could have brought her to us. She smiled the fixed smile of convention; she obviously was uneasy among us— "Americans! *Blancs!*"—although, tanned as we were then, we were hardly more *blanc* than she. When she had finished her coffee, she put down the cup and then sat up very stiffly again. By this time, we were as uncomfortable as she was.

"I see that you like my Monique," she said. "Thank you very much." The tone was chilling—a mixture of fierceness and unction.

"She is a fine child," my wife said. "You must be proud of her."

"Her French is excellent, is it not? I forbid Creole in the house."

"Yes. She's very sweet, Madame," my wife said.

"She is in perfect health. Strong. A willing worker." Monique's mother folded her arms as if challenging us to disagree.

My wife and I both understood. I gave a little start of surprise; my wife began to pour more coffee, stalling for time while we figured out how to respond. The woman did not touch her coffee.

"Monique will never again have such an opportunity to go to America," she said, her voice softening. "I have considered and I think you will not mistreat her—yes? Therefore, I do not even ask a *cadeau,* a gift, for my other children."

I tried to explain how impossible the suggestion was.

There were no *ti-mounes* in the United States, I said. She was not our child; she had her own mother and her brother and sisters; we could not accept the responsibility of taking her from her family and country, even if the laws permitted it. It was out of the question.

She smiled faintly, as if she had already foreseen these difficulties, and then she shrugged them off. "No, no, that is nothing," she assured us. "Monique is very happy."

"What? You have said something to her?" I asked.

"I have already told her, Monsieur. She has heard that there is ice on the earth in your country, but she knows you will give her warm clothes. I am confident also."

"You have really told her already?" my wife asked.

"Yes, Madame."

We were astonished and miserable. Could the child's sweetness have been motivated all this time by the hope of a voyage and the sight of snow, and adoption by us? No, it was unthinkable; she could not have been pretending all these months. I remembered her worried frown—two creases between the eyes, and the corners of her mouth pulled down—when Judy whimpered over the ant bites.

"How could you say a thing like that without first asking us?" my wife demanded. "How could you do it to Monique? How could you, Madame?"

"I thought you liked her."

"We do, we do—but we can't take her with us," my wife said. "We can't adopt her, either. She wouldn't be happy. Anyway, we're not rich—"

The woman looked scornfully at us, and then around at the furniture of the gallery, the entire house. How, an American not rich? Such foolishness. She smiled again, stiffly.

Her obvious conviction—that only our selfishness kept her from getting what she wanted for Monique—angered me. "It is completely impossible!" I said. "It is not done, Madame."

"But she can wash, clean, cook, run errands. She can sew a little already. She is very strong. She has good character—"

"I know that, Madame. She's a lovely child. It's not the point," I said.

"She will not complain, no matter what you tell her to do. She is good. I will miss her. You cannot refuse now." She paused, fixing me righteously with her eyes, and then went on, "You will never have to beat her for laxness, Monsieur. She has even learned some English from your children. If you have a telephone, she will answer it for you."

"America is not Haiti," I said.

"This is not permitted in the United States," my wife said.

"Ah!" Monique's mother abruptly stood up, as if really hearing us for the first time, and stared down at my wife and me. I got to my feet. She put her hands caressingly, almost coquettishly, to her straight, reddish hair. "Ah!" she said again, smiling and bowing, and the resemblance to our lovely, shy little Monique made my heart turn. "Ah," she said. "I see. You Americans are all like that. Because she is black."

And she went swiftly down the stairs, and was gone.

Monique, of course, said nothing. During the few days that remained, she came to play with our children, as always. She helped with the packing, quickly learning how to fold clothes neatly.

On the last day, when the house was cluttered with trunks and crates and we were waiting for the moving truck, she came inside to wait with us. The only difference in her appearance was that she had new ribbons in her hair and wore shoes. Our children, excited about leaving, hardly had time for her. She stood quietly at one side of the room.

She accepted the little gifts we had for her and her brother and sisters but did not look at them. She put them outside the front door and returned to stand beside us. She watched the truck come and go, then walked outside with us and watched us climb into a friend's automobile. At the last moment, Ann remembered her, and called out, "Bye-bye, Monique."

Leaning out of the car, I lifted Monique to embrace her. My wife held her for a moment. Ann said, "Come on, Mommy."

Monique's shy smile and brilliant eyes were as for any other day, but instead of saying "*Bonsoir, Monsieur, bonsoir, Madame*," she said only "*Adieu*," and stood smiling and waving to us until we were far down the road on our way back to America.

Paris and Cleveland
Are Voyages

"—for all those who step the legend
of their youth into the noon."

Even before he noticed the
girl, he had already taken to the easy habit of strolling into
this panelled, chandeliered, and interior-decorated suburban library of a late afternoon in Cleveland. He liked to
pry on the travel writers gasping over the places where he
had spent his wanderyears with Helen: Paris, Florence,
other pleasant towns. Nothing is so mysterious as the de-
scription by a stranger of a well-loved old friend. Such dimwitted joy in these arty photographs! What smiles for him
in the mislabeled halftint of the very street on which he had
lived in Montparnasse! "A meal can be obtained on the
Left Bank of Paris for three to five dollars. Wine not included." (When did Helen and Gran pay so much except
under the obligation of a holiday or a visitor?) "The greedy
life pulses on Saturday night in Naples. A good nylon dress
is recommended." (Apparently the lady expected to be
eaten by some greedy pulser, gobble-gobble, buttons, and
all.)

Who was this girl approaching his table near the travel
section? He recognized Elliot Paul in her pretty little hands.

The poor child probably wanted to dream that the rue de la Huchette would be the last time she saw Paris, too.

Today he would try the Blue Guide to Italy and maybe Paul Morand, a native wanderer, on Paris. With a luxurious sigh, he sat down near the girl. Dr. Granley Hattan allowed himself this smugness of nostalgia in his afternoon pleasures, the pleasures of loneliness at thirty when Bohemian days are past and the kid makes too much noise to let him work at home and the thesis is published ("Francois Mauriac: A Double Regard") and his tenure and rank as Assistant Professor at Western Reserve University are assured and maybe he doesn't have anything better to do anyway.

"Excuse me," he said to the girl, just touching her purse to move it. Otherwise it would look as if they were together.

She did not answer. Could Elliot Paul's prose be so loud as to deafen her? Gran was suddenly aware of his crew-cut hair and the touch of useful premature gray in it and his whole lounging length of critical body. She moved the purse and moved so that the long red scarf still hanging from her shoulders—as if she had been so eager to get to the rue de la Huchette that she could not undo her clothes— touched his knee as it fell.

That was a kind of answer to him, Granley Hattan decided. A nice rise and fall of breathing at her small intent leaning body. Without a word he picked up her scarf and put it on the table.

2

College girl in velvet slacks, red canvas shoes with white crepe soles, fine tweed coat thrown over these items, that red scarf undone but never taken off, carelessly cropped hair, crisp little ears, strong small pretty animal mug of a face, a bright girl with her own ideas (the studied sloppiness) and a moneyed father (the coat)—these were Gran's notes on her into the pages of the book he thought he was reading. She was flushed with Elliot Paul, actually copying out phrases! The leather notebook and the chewed pencil were a studious touch, and the brightness and pallor perhaps stood for impatience with that rich father of hers.

Gran congratulated himself for knowing her well. This was not the kind that sat in the front row to try for an A by showing its knees; this was the kind that learned all the forms of "être" and "avoir" and read *Le Livre de Mon Ami* as if Anatole France meant something. Maybe this one even wrote poetry.

But it was odd how the fact of seeing her for the first time in the suburb, off-campus, made her different. Her body had the alert charm of youth, the trust in that charm, and the baby-fat gone. Looking about at the vaulted church-like fakery of this suburban branch library, he thought of his graduate course, French 410. Didn't the lovers meet in churches for Stendhal? Of course, travel folders and anno-tated memoirs could never replace the door to the con-fessional.

"Oh damn."

"Pardon?"

"Oh damn," she whispered to him, insisting on it. "Can you lend me a pencil?"

He grinned and touched the scarf. You broke it on purpose, he wanted to say, but said instead: "Surely, but if you take notes on Paris, at least don't read Elliot Paul. That's for schoolteacher tourists."

"How do you know?" And she answered the question herself: "You've been there?"

He knew by the way she said *there* that the sea was steady and the winds favorable. "How about some coffee and I'll tell you all about it."

"Yes," she said simply, packing up.

They strolled out together. She was an inch or so shorter than Helen, not her willowy type at all, but nicely turned. Helen, his wife, had worn her hair long at this girl's age, clipped in a ponytail behind. He had taken Helen's prettiness as the normal thing, his right at the time; perhaps it was; yet now in this strange girl at the same age ten years later, he was astonished at so much unmarked beauty, unquarreled, unsuffered, pouting and dusky only with resentment of parents. Yes, the freshness of her skin went nicely with the dark disputing rings under her eyes. Helen had not had them; she was another sort, married young for other reasons—pure gaiety perhaps, so romantic, blind, easy, and fixed in her own family that she could not suspect how hard it is to live in family.

The librarian's hairy librarian-face turned on them, but it meant nothing. They could be fellow students, neighbors—they probably were near neighbors, anyway. He still looked young enough to be a graduate student. Down the steps, he watched this girl again, thinking of his wife and of himself. He had hickies on his nose then—the word was still *hickies?*—and his pictures showed him too-smooth, untried. Surely he was better-looking now at thirty, the youthful spring of his step chiming well with the fret of thought in his face; experienced laughter is best, less braying.

"What's your name?"

"Carol."

"I'm Gran Hattan."

"Carol Dent," she said. He liked the way she gave her first name alone, as if they were playmates. Apparently she did not know that he was Dr. Hattan, the new man in Romance Languages. As if to answer this thought, she added, "I've seen you on campus. I saw you here yesterday, but you didn't see me. I knew you spent two years in Paris, wasn't it?" She looked at him with her bright red lips damp and slightly parted: "It's my *dream.*"

Gran laughed softly because it was such a childish thing to say and because it nevertheless told the truth about a bright and adventurous suburban coed. Her saying it like that, *dream,* sent an odd little shiver up his back; perhaps she meant it to. Helen and he must have said it the same way.

"Funny thing," he answered, "this beer place at the corner serves the best coffee in the neighborhood. You usually don't find that at bars. I had a Fulbright in '49—first year it was. We were the forty-niners with our meat cards and travel allowances and our leftover khakis to sell to the Arabs. We were some smart babies!"

"But that wasn't really so long ago, Gran."

3

This was only the first time that she read his thoughts with such flashing amusement. I'm older than you, he had meant to say. Six years ago was another age: we all still had boots and field jackets.

O not that much older, dear, her smile with buds of teeth replied. Clothes are only clothes, something to sell to the Arabs for a silkscreen print or an album of Gregorian. Bop existed already; so did Van Gogh and the uplift bra—even if we called bop "bebop" at Shaker High.

But then the baby fat would suddenly reappear, softly enveloping her understanding of him in the book-struck, dream-struck, mirror-struck adolescent's pout: "I'm perishing for St.-Germain-des-Prés, Gran. Is it true they've remodeled the Dôme? It's one tricky job convincing Dad how Paris won't ruin me for life. Really, he's a pain sometimes. Used to read books, but you'd never know it now with the television." And she tossed her head, which made the scarf-ends twirl. He had been touching them with his hand again.

"Don't try to reform your father, it never works," he

said. "Just get your way out of him if you can, it's the most
you can expect."

"You've escaped the father image, huh? Luck plus
hard work at independence, I'll bet. How old were you? I
will, too, I escaped Mom's domination in junior high already, and without turning dike, either."

"Congratulations. Lucky men of this world."

"Don't tease me, Gran, this is serious to a girl." She
smiled—where had she learned that nose, that quirk of
grin?—and sat very still for an instant. Untroubled by her
bold words, she now blushed a new thought and leaned forward with her smile renewed and whispered near his ear—
she didn't have to, but she did—"I'd take a beer, but
wouldn't it be embarrassing if they asked for identification?
I'd die—"

"Of mortification?"

She gave him the turning-away three-quarter view.
"Of embarrassment. I wouldn't *ever* say mortified, Gran.
You're not sardonic at all today, you're only sarcastic."

He understood that she expected him to do better than
coffee for himself. Wine in a neighborhood bar would pre-
cipitate a bad case of sarcasm at the eyes; he wanted to
take himself seriously. Beer the same at the mouth-corners
—too obedient to Carol. Oh Lord, someone had told her
she looked like a dark Audrey Hepburn. He ordered and
reverently nursed a bourbon on the rocks. She tapped her
ashes into her saucer and watched him meditatively. Now
not A. Hepburn, she was Vivien Leigh with phi bete her
junior year and Olivier and anxiety yet to come. This silence, fine-eyed and brooding, was succeeded by the information that she had memorized more than half of "Le
Cimetière Marin" and read Valéry's letters about it in the
original.

They talked. They measured each other coolly but with

a satisfaction which they were proud to admit. It's not so often you can be honest about liking a person, as Carol pointed out. You've got to have an agreement about basic personality. The bar, carved, panelled, and stain-glassed like the library, seemed to both of them the right sort of Elizabethan pub to be designed by a Cornell architect.

Late one afternoon, the third time that, without spoken arrangement, they had met at the library, she put out her cigarette decisively just as he said, "Carol, whatever made you start about the Dôme? That's Montparnasse, by the way—"

"Tell me about your wife," she demanded. "What's she like? What time do you have to be home for dinner?"

"Such curiosity! Which are you interested in, what she's like or when I have to be home?"

"Oh!" Boldness is fine, rather exciting, her piping *oh* seemed to say; indiscretion, however, is too much, and sometimes sordid. She pouted and withdrew her hand. He had been touching her fingertips over the table. This time she had removed the scarf and the short tweed coat, and his heart was sharp and busy within him at the sight of her untried ripeness, her sharp, flesh-and-muscled, held-in, held-out body, the rich expanse of well-tended woman rising and falling beneath sweater and fitted skirt.

"Carol, you're an extraordinary girl," he said.

She was not answering. He needed punishment.

Could he tell her about Helen? That she was too thin to be worried about getting fat but she worried all the same. That she took care of their boy as if he were precious silver that had to be polished and wrapped and stored or it would tarnish to death. (Gran Hattan was dissatisfied already with his mama-calling six-year-old—a softness in him, a female dependency of spirit. Bud wasn't his vision of a son, who should be shrill, tough, and bruised by hard play.) And that Helen and he quarreled over buying better furniture than they could afford—dare he tell Carol that? No, it was more penance than he needed to pay in the exact economy of the first contest between married man and suburban girl.

"My wife's taller than you, blonde," he said. "Wears her hair up behind. Our kid was born in Paris."

"Isn't that marvelous! Doesn't it mean he can never be President?"

"Yes, but we cross that bridge when we come to it. I'm thinking about a constitutional amendment—"

"Was she pretty?"

That *was!* Such elegance! The sly creature had struck hard. That *was* spoke for her acquiescence in the erotic sense which their meetings had for him. Girl of innocence and craft! he thought. Wasn't it true, as one of his friends argued, that any woman is always at least ten years older than every man?

"Yes, Helen is pretty," Gran said.

Having made her point, she did not need to listen. He found her back in Paris. "Born there—the American Hospital, I suppose?"

"No, the Hôpital Foch."

"Ah,"—so pleased. She busied herself sleekly with other words after her triumphal *was*. "Paris, this best garden of the world . . ."

"Shakespeare, only he said it about France. But Gérard de Nerval—I think it was—said about Paris that she's the paradise of misery and the capital of hope." Combining and misquoting two writers in thirty seconds, impressing her with his epigram and his memory and his pronunciation of Nerval's name, Gran was impressed himself by his eagerness to delight her, that is, to make himself pleasing. It takes a light and sure foot to gain ground in this slippery contest. Outside the leaded windows with their rich tinting

—drinks ran a good twenty cents more in a bar of such chic—the autumn weather was heavy and one Heights bus after another roared home with late shoppers up the hill to the suburb.

"What's Cleveland the capital and the paradise of?" Carol demanded. "White Motors and Glidden paints, that's what. I used to think I couldn't bear it another week."

"And you had to bear it all by yourself, Carol?"

"Sh! Stop teasing. Of course, Gran, now I'm growing up, I'm patient to get what I want."

Paying and signalling without saying it that his wife really would expect him now, Granley Hattan asked himself if Carol meant to tell him that he was her patience and what she now wanted. You could never know for sure about this girl. She always refused to meet him on campus; she only once refused their late afternoon meetings at the library. He never said anything except, "See you here tomorrow?"—too proud to come off his age and tell her about his desire, just the desire to see her, to watch her toss the scarf about her throat while he took his pleasure in her high brightness, that subtle and gaudy play of first youth against the elemental needs of love and knowledge and power over others. Was it really any better to come to desire power over things, over self?

Finally it was she who admitted, "Meeting you saved my life, Gran. I don't even fight with Dad anymore. I even forgive him for making me dorm at home and take my B.A. at Reserve."

"I like you, too, Carol."

"You mean something to me, Gran. I really mean it."

He took to carrying his wedding band in his pocket when he met her. Once she caught him slipping it off before touching her hand, and her freshet of laughter poured over him in a fine light shower.

He smiled.

She understood and did not judge him. Growing up to his needs as she felt sure of her own, she even liked him for it. He asked if she had ever seen the old Slavic settlement down in the Flats near the Cuyahoga River—onion-domed churches and clapboard houses with vines for their age and good places for the usual coffee together.

No, she did not know it. Was it nice? Picturesque? Could it interest even a travelled man like him?

Yes, they would walk there someday, soon, late this week, maybe. Even if he could not walk Paris with her, he could show her the first place where Cleveland was settled, those cobbled and winding streets where every other shop is a shoe-repair and each drugstore an "apteka."

In the meantime, in no hurry for anything, all patience, Gran would talk with her about literature, the world, himself. He had long ago formed the habit of walking at night; past the image of himself as a poet (or so many poets), his long walks now enabled him to plan his classes in peace and get the regular exercise which preserved his leanness of belly and agility of step. Often Helen was asleep by the time he returned.

Carol Dent met him under a streetlamp three nights later. That it really happened made it almost as good as a novel. Of course, he had spoken of his custom. She laughed and caught his hand. "I've been looking for you over five blocks," she said. "Which way do you usually go?"

"Varies." He took her arm across the street—the long scarf draped over his guiding hand—and did not let her go, because she had added:

"I wanted to talk some more. Forgive me! Am I disturbing you? You know so many things I want to know. Dad doesn't know what to make of me lately, says I'm getting so *cooperative*,"—and a little wry face.

Her frank pleasure flattered him, yet made him uneasy. If she worried about how he felt about her—if she saw him at all—wouldn't she need to be more cautious, reserved? Wasn't that the economy of the suburban girls? The investment of stay-away-closer, the capital gain of come-to-get-me-for-I-do-not-care? She dared to care; she dared to admit it. So sure of herself, she saw no risks at all. Dangerous, dangerous. How did she manage?

What if he were to show impatience with her? He knew she was a child: she knew he knew. Very dangerous.

Gran Hattan was confused by so much irregular honesty in a lovely and pretentious child. She had no investment, it seemed; she liked being with him; that was all. What was the status of his own increasing investment in her? Where then was his protection?

But these doubts were not scruples and scruples would be a poor shield against the pure delight of her presence. He could not turn away from this sweet brashness. It was a lucky prize; luck is part of the well-planned life. Even her bracelets made a soft jingling in the warm after-rain autumn evening. He would give her a little silver bracelet. Why not give freely? It was time to let down the guards.

This time, admitting nothing but easy companionship through wet autumn leaves, under wet autumn branches, while they touched and jumped away in the hazards of walking at night down a dark suburban street, the skittish brush of arm and arm, shoulder and shoulder, leg and sometimes leg under raincoat, served their long silences most garrulously. In full flood of desire, Gran labored against the tormented tenderness of his overwise blood. Electric it was! Her scheming innocence a blessing! They pulled away. They both liked scenery.

4

The day they walked in the Flats, far from the University and far from the suburb, he took the role of guide ("St. Aloysius it's for. Quite Byzantine, isn't it? Those towers like tumors, aren't they?") and shut up finally when she did not answer and then abruptly, without pretending anything at all, he put his arm hard around her waist and let his fingers spread and luxuriate. They did not break step. It was a harsh dry day of early winter, the sun flashing over slate roofs and hot icy blue through the blue air over the industrial valley just below them. Thin streams of crystalline smoke arose straight into the sky. For answer to him, she let her body's rhythm speak, hard-soft and soft-hard, her hip moving against his, her cropped head leaning for a moment against his shoulder. No, no, at the moment he seized her like that, her hand fluttered against the small of his back, then fell.

They walked in silence, looking for a place.

The thought of his wife came to Gran Hattan only with relish. Helen would not wonder why he was late. He had managed well. She was off with their one docile child to pay a visit to the wife of the Chairman of the department (three pampered children and a fourth on the way). Nevertheless, something about the sunny winter day and the abrasive midcity air put him out of time again as they walked and looked, and his breathing, frozen and excited, was almost a retrospective pleasure—a pain of desire, a dry pang of memory. The frank taking of Carol's hand had been a similar shock. How could a married man of thirty go so silly over the knuckles of a college senior? Did his boredom with Helen and his job require exactly this revenge—a warm small submitting hand that squeezed and then lay at rest? Yes, it was a pleasure to admit it, his grand discontents of Cleveland could be assuaged by a child who wanted to know all about Paris. He had talked to her, then, about how Hart Crane was influenced by the Symbolists and when he first came to Cleveland he had looked up Crane's friends, an old man in a bookstore, a retired high school teacher, a fairy cook—

She did not blink of course.

"A fairy cook who went to Akron with him. They even wrote a poem together. Now this guy is a fat bald old codger in a businessman's restaurant on Prospect Avenue— wears perfume even in the kitchen . . ."

"Will you read Hart Crane to me?" she had asked. "I know it's not done anymore, but I bet you read beautifully."

Permit me voyage, love, into your hands . . . He had let go of her hand because he was confused. Even then he had rehearsed his vengeful fantasies. Helen had it coming! No right to worry, fret, take it out on spoiling the kid! He was still a young man. Exactly ten years older than Carol. At her twenty-five he would be the same man—thirty-five. At thirty, forty—caught up and identical. Every woman always ten years ahead of any man? They know what they want.

He would take her back to Paris (back, Rodin's belly-ing Balzac at the Carrefour Vavin!), get a fellowship, settle the couple of thousand he had on his wife and the boy. He had a novel in him, too, why not? What about all the great men who deserted their wives, and sometimes with the kids in double bunks? (But what about their one son? And what if the novel were no good? And with her parents or some-where in a too-small-flat—that Helen who had taken the *prix fixe* with him on the rue Hautefeuille when she wore her hair long and clipped behind until the sixth month of pregnancy and then had it cut for three hundred francs. What about it? Well, Helen was a great one for neatness.)

All the time he had been thinking these thoughts, just from taking and relinquishing Carol's hand, they had been walking; and now a few days past his memory they were walking again, this time his arm tight around her and the same thoughts; and now he had made a small progress, a triumph of the neatness required, a jolliness of relief just because Helen was safe and busy with Mrs. Professor Chairman Durand until the kid's bedtime.

The sun was white, descending. Then, at the horizon above the factories, it performed for them: suddenly a winter rose and the dry clouds set afire! Away with Helen, a citation for Carol: *Let us walk through time with equal pride* . . . Harold Hart Crane of Crane Chocolates was a local boy, too, although it's more complicated when a poet likes girls.

"Gran?" They had found their way around the steel-gray Russian Orthodox church, back behind the winter-closed pikes of the garden, in the wind-shuttered shadow of the turrets and domes, here just above the industrial valley and the rubbled river and just below the ramps of commercial Cleveland's great bridges, the sun lacking warmth in December but lovely, lovely—"Gran? Gran?"

Now he kissed her; now they met and made vain walking steps against each other; hot and busy-fleshed, they moved under their coats. They played out of time deep within the body's deep hungers.

Jeez, we were necking each other standing up like kids, he remembered later.

5

Driving primly back to the proper Heights, they watched the road. A signal turned green, but a stalled car blocked them. Carol looked out the window, remarking,

"Last days for Christmas shopping already. It wasn't even Thanksgiving when you met me."

"You met me, too. Does it seem so long that you have to remark about it? A month almost."

"What are you so chilly about all of a sudden?"

"Nothing, Carol, I'm sorry. I'm crowded. This kind of driving makes me irritable."

She waited while he honked and they were moving in the thick passage again, then said: "Gran, would you like to see me some evening?"

"Yes."

"When?"

"I don't know how I can."

This small creature, hot and crafty and surely untouched, had it all figured out. "Tell your wife you have a meeting, papers to grade, late work in the library." She wrinkled her nose and shrugged. "You're doing an essay on Hart Crane and the Symbolists for the Romance Languages Quarterly. Figure it out. Do I really have to tell you how, Gran?"

Could there be another girl like her?—this cool brashness, this hot certainty, this virginal purity of intention in a girl who had bit his lower lip unnecessarily, a too-hard, over-ambitious, biting first kiss for him, just because she had studied up by reading Van der Velde or other deep thinkers on how to win lovers to be crazy about a person and influence their passion. Although she probably planned all day to give him a broken lower lip as a souvenir, he liked and licked it and took the salty taste with pleasure. A coldsore or bumped it, he would tell Helen.

"Where?" she asked, still counting the Christmas shoppers.

It was flattering and yet disquieting to be so obviously nominated and so quickly used. How young she was! Their

evening walks and their bar and their visit to the Flats had
no resonance of the past for her—how could they? They
were pure potentiality, a thrust into the future; the first time
for new love may be eager and happy, but it is dominated
by the desire to move on. Innocent buds of teeth experienced in biting! What for Carol Dent was the first deep
waking—as much as she could yet awaken—was for Granley Hattan an aching reminder of the long early play of love
in many towns. Satisfactions recalled, dissatisfactions recalled complacently, what difference? Carol, however, admitted no memory at all.

"Where?" she insisted.

He thought he knew a place, yes.

"When?"

He told her that he could figure that one out, too.

"Is your wife the suspicious type?"

A role-player himself, Gran felt tolerant of this quick
bright red-scarved creature's playing her wickedness with
such sweet, keen, and joyous directness. He suggested that
she need not bother herself with worries about his wife, who
used to be an artist herself, sort of, and did some very good
painting for a student and did not ever nag or bother him
like many wives.

"Helen was that?" Carol asked, using the first name de-
liberately, her bright gaze winking toward him, fingerpads
touching at the eyes with their new fawn-lines in black pencil at the corners.

6

Jitters, itchings, headaches, dizziness, faintness, all
those boyish pimples and twitters had reawakened in
Gran Hattan. Dark jealousies, lightheadedness, angers and
switchings of his voice mid-sentence, midword—Hattan's
unexpected yea-saying to another for what he had set in

motion himself, for pure self-love, brought a pitching fleck of terror to his eye when he looked at her. Carol turned up her lips for smiling and lowered her eyes.

Had he really begun this himself? Was will and self-willing ever enough? Would not the will to love overthrow even irony? He woke once strangling with excitement at the thought, *Today, today* . . . And it only meant that they had set an hour to stroll in the garden behind the old monkey-house in Rockefeller Park. If the adventure could no longer end with ennui or any other French word, how could it ever be ended?

Was it possible at last that *this* was love?

All his dreading body asked a no, no, no, and the hurt of it did not grant him retreat. Pleasure is awful. Sweetness is dangerous, the bittersweet most threatening. He had forgotten what a girl is! Complication, trouble, divided gaze, and washing with strong soap to be sure his wife did not sniff out Carol's scent on his shoulders and hands—poor Helen.

It would help to arrange a sharp quarrel with Helen and lump all his discontentments in one ripe justificatory gesture. Funny, although he had planned for it, that the quarrel was unexpected when it came. As always, their neat little, clean little, precious little suburban flat exasperated him. Leaving the murmurous early evening of winter for the cold gleam of all those modern lamps—cones on pulleys, aluminum reflectors, three-way bulbs in many cute disguises —he felt like another bleached modern gimcrack among the foam-rubber furniture, the driftwood pinned against a fire-place blocked with red plywood, the Lautrec *affiche* (not Dufy at least!) and the *original* Matisse etching, drawn by the Hand itself (one of twenty-four in the series, then the zinc destroyed)—extravagant anniversary gifts from his loving wife, yrs., Helen.

She had moved her own paintings into the hall, first,

and finally into the attic. He had not noticed until weeks later, but who looks at the frames in a hall? She had given him that large mouth of pain for days until he noticed, refusing to tell him the matter, and then refusing even to let him move the paintings back down (she had studied with Hans Hofmann and at the Leger school in Paris).

On the dark afternoons of late classes, Bud customarily stayed up to have dinner with him. Arriving home tired, Gran found Helen frowning and hot, the house overheated, the boy in bed with a mound of toys heaped about him.

"What's up?"

"There's a measles epidemic going around. I think he's getting it."

"Any spots?"

"No."

"Does he have a fever?"

"Not yet."

"Then what's the matter?"

"I don't know, he's been so irritable. I wanted to get him off his feet. Spock says the complications—"

"Daddy! Daddy!" the excited voice piped thinly. "Mommy says I'm sick! I had softboiled eggs! Come and play with me!"

Without saying anything more to Helen, Gran put the thermostat back at 70 degrees, peeled off his clothes to the T-shirt, splashed cold water on his face and neck—the windows were all in steam, the house was a hotbox—and went to sit like a doctor on the edge of Bud's bed. The kid babbled away at him about all the recent exciting events, thermometer inserted so queerly, intensified attentions, consultations by home medical guide and telephone. Gran felt his wrist and forehead. The eyes had a hot sparkle, but they were clear and the pleasure and the grin (my own mouth,

Gran thought) were nothing abnormal in an excited child. "I'm sick, Daddy, I'm gonna have quarantine!"

The kid was not sick, no matter how many goddamn measles freckled out in the neighborhood. Gran felt deeply convinced of his diagnosis: too much mothering, overdose of fret and fuss. It would give any child spots of red in the cheek and a suspicion of fever. "Member how I had a cold and drank ginger ale, Daddy? That was when it rained all day."

Yes, and July is when Mother is convinced that you have polio, darling.

And fall is the time of burning leaves and an acrid beauty to the industrial skies and Buddy has possible vitamin deficiency, Mother thinks.

And winter is the time of struggling over the thermostat and penicillin for headcolds and one fidget after another.

They waited until the kid finally fell asleep. Helen would deserve what she would get. She could pull her mouth down and let it spread with reluctance to answer him, but this would not stop him. He knew her well! "You're going to make him a hypochondriac! We're raising a goddamn sissy! Wait till he's sick before you jump!"

"*You* don't have to take care of him. You don't care. Measles can affect the eyes—"

"But I tell you he doesn't have it yet."

"You wouldn't care if he did."

"You *want* him to be sick, you want to make him need you more—"

She looked at him full, her tired, pretty, thirty-year-old face flaming: "Maybe you're right! I read those books, too, before I became a housewife. Dust, clean, cook, but don't touch your papers! What an existence! Maybe I need a husband in addition to a son—"

"*You* need? What about me?"

"Oh, what's the use, Gran? You'll never learn."

Of course, when there's learning to be done, it has to begin on both sides, and maybe it was time to admit the fact of Too-Late. You have to exchange needs; you have to have a will for it. Gran admitted (yes, why not?) that he had withdrawn the will. They defined their rancor to each other hopelessly, helplessly, rehearsing the old lines, with Helen strangely cold and adamant and Gran finally the one to break into tears of rage although, yes, he had predicted, planned, and even desired this quarrel. He was a moral man: the quarrel gave him rights while his rage kept its purity. It was best to hate Helen's tall grace. Young matron! Handsomest wife in the Department! Tea, somebody?

"All right, Gran, I'm sorry, you're sorry, let's go to bed or something. I made your supper . . . I suppose you don't want it now . . ."

It was silly of him to show tears; it was not required, although it added to his rights to himself. He gave himself no added credit, however, because he was thinking of the way Helen used to be (a great walker with him in the market of the rue Mouffetard) and that was fine but probably not so fine (who can remember for sure?) as Carol would be even at her age. And Carol's gaucheries meant nothing because Carol would learn to be smart and better than Helen and smartness isn't everything—look at Helen! It didn't help her to have a Master's and to have thought seriously of a career in art history or advertising or maybe doing books for children. No, he granted that he deserved very little extra credit for those tears before Helen. Many times he felt worse but did not cry. Nevertheless, the tears produced their pain even in him, and he said what seemed to stand most for that pain: "You're ruining my son."

She turned away, large-mouthed and sick, shoulders drooping, the housedress damp under the arms. "My son, your son, *our* son. Oh, never mind, Gran. Stop it now. You'll wake the kid. I'm sorry you feel bad. Please, I'm sorry we're not good to each other anymore. Would you like something to eat?"

No matter, no matter. He had put down his deposit; she would pay. He went about switching off the lamps because the light hurt his smarting eyes, and then submitted to supper while Helen, her hands folded in her lap, sat silently watching him try to eat.

7

The obliging hotel near University Circle had a chic dark bar for first and an opulent stillness for later, mirrors with black hangings in festive mourning, music discreetly from nowhere. Gran assured Carol, only because she asked, that he had arranged things. Things had been arranged by him in the most fantastically simple way: he told Helen that he was going out and would be out late. They were numb to each other. Maybe she simply took it as an extension of his walking habit. No matter for Helen now.

Carol met him in the bar, dressed-up in dancing clothes and her subdued excitement signalling to him in every rich movement—older, yes, womanly, walking toward him now, possessed and possessing by the slip of hips, that great eternal female clamor! She seemed to have revised even her inner self-portrait: from sweet gamine with scarf to sleek lady with pumps and hat. Courtly, calm, Gran rose to greet her, biding his pang of regret for the red sneakers and the scarf and the velvet slacks of their first meeting, and the volume of Verlaine with every line pencilled into English, plus critical notes in the margin:

Et on donne a Lui
And one gives to Him (Capitalized, must be God???)

But of course, like any vital creature, she could not spend her brightest flashing in the reading of French poetry. And she could not display in a hotel bar the pert, small-wristed, small-footed, dancing-after-life gaiety which was uniquely hers and could perhaps be his. She looked at his finger with a turned-up smile. The ring was in his pocket. Please don't do your Vivien Leigh cheek at me, he wished to her. I want you just to be Carol tonight, the girl I met.

"Please," he said aloud.

"Please what?"

"Please stop smiling and say something."

"Isn't that up to you, Gran?" And in a low voice for her new clothes, hat, and heels: "I'm happy, that's all. I'm glad to be here."

Better.

"You know, Carol, I was afraid maybe you couldn't come."

"I said I would, didn't I?" She pouted and pulled her hand away. "Never *couldn't*—I just decided, that's all. Never a question of couldn't with me."

"You're beautiful. You're prettier than Vivien Leigh."

Or was it Audrey Hepburn that she was supposed to be prettier than? No, stop that.

"Smell me, I wore the Lanvin you gave me—"

"Later, Carol." And he was thinking, not of her perfume, but of the tricks and straps of a dressed-up woman, so much loveliness in so much machinery, the flesh breathing, slippery, scented warmly deep within the frills and the lace and the elastic.

"Mind wandering? Penny? You like me in a hat?" She glanced at the card on the table: TRY OUR MANHATTANS. THEY'RE MADE BY THEODORE. "I want one," she said. "I got all dressed up so they'll serve me and not—"

She blushed. They had the drink. Then they strolled to the elevator together and rose to the top floor.

Sometimes things are as they should be! Carol was very happy, showered, fragrant, pleased. Therefore Gran was happy. She learned with athletic ease and delight. Therefore Gran was content. She frisked and played and was loving in a way which seemed almost abstract in its lack of complication—perhaps only because new, perhaps only because mystified at the miracle of flesh within her rigorous embracing of novelty. Blessed by the hot immediacy of her small, pointy, unused, and eager body, Gran nevertheless wondered at this abstraction.

Well, therefore something left to explore, he decided later, drowsy and pleased and thinking: Painless? So simple? Well, surely some deeper reticence. Therefore lovely, therefore fine in health, therefore—*O Carol!* He put his lips near her cheek on the pillow.

"Gran?"

She would not let him dream of her even now stretched cooling at his side. She propped herself on one elbow. "Gran, I have to tell you something."

"What?"

"Listen, there's big news in my life, Gran."

He was shocked full awake at once, and with a watchful irony. "There is?"

"I'm going to Europe! That's it. I saved it to tell you now. I knew you'd be so happy for me. Paris! It's my graduation present."

"If you want to talk," he replied dryly, "then let's get up."

The moment of silent modesty while she bent and unfolded her things (he had not noticed how carefully she had thought to fold) and then dressed, this odd shy empty moment was over before she had finished straightening the

seam in her stockings. "Gran, I'm so excited," she said. "I've
been wanting to tell you for days, but I thought I'd save
it for—" And incredibly, at *this* moment she flushed.
"—Saved it for now," she said. Was it a blush because she
had kept a secret from him? "Oh I'll miss you so," she
added, wriggling her toes into the shoes and turning her
foot to look at the heel.

"That's all right, Carol, I can give you some addresses."

"Would you? Darling! Some good cheap restaurants?
Some friends?"

He sat at the desk and took a sheet of hotel stationery
and could not write. His hand was shaking. She watched
him with a fixed, self-regarding smile, the eager compla-
cency of the dedicated art and artist collector. He was part
of the preparation for the voyage. Typhoid injections, small-
pox, triple tetanus, and this. A hotel room for practice.

"Of course, the left bank has probably—the rive
gauche—changed since your day."

"Practically nothing but a memory," he said. "That
happened in history when Gide was still alive. 1950. You
were at Shaker High."

Her desire to talk was unquenchable. She had guarded
her secret for him, well, this was a tribute of a sort. She applied her lipstick before the closet mirror. "You're teasing,
I know! I was a senior then. And you of all people *know*
I'm not a baby anymore,"—and then came to slip beside
him on the short bench before the desk. They faced each
other in the glass over a hotel print, "Hunters in the Snow
near Erie," and spoke into their doubled, dusty images—this
bright slim creature, this rumpled and tired young man:

"I wanted to tell you all now, Gran. Surprised? Daddy's
giving me the trip for my marks in French, thanks to you,
kind sir!"

He had drilled her privately on her irregular verbs, was that it?

"You're such an *incentive,* an *example,* Gran darling. Don't be sad. I'll write to you. If I were a man I would want to be just like you, so tall and lean and sensitive. I'll never forget you for ages and ages."

Is this the note of admiration to strike as one rises from bed beside that incentive?

"Of course, I do have advantages as a girl. I suppose I'll meet somebody and get married in Paris—a young poet maybe, who knows? Do you think I'm pretty enough? Do you think it's silly to think so far in the future? Did you meet Helen in Paris?"

"Yes."

"Do you think I'm pretty enough?"

"Ravishing," he said. "No, I guess everyone thinks ahead. You're ravishing, plus cute as a button."

Pouting, she mittened at his hand and peered into his face in the glass. "That started out like such a compliment, Gran, that ravishing. But I don't *want* to be cute as a button. Isn't that a cliché? Mom was cute as a button, and cute as a button only married a lawyer."

"Don't worry, you'll be a success in Paris." Gran was beginning to be pleased with himself. He was amused now, in another way from the way he had thought to be amused, that was true; but pleased and amused all the same by this busy Carol. He felt wide-awake and somewhat drunk, as if it were the last quick walk home in the snow after a late party. She's not a monster, he thought, she's only the new bright suburban girl thrilled by her adventure. She'll come back from Paris and marry an editor, or maybe be one, and pluck out the clichés for pay. She loves life and art, that's all. It only seems monstrous. "Carol, I'll tell you what I'm

going to do. I'll give you some people to look up. Some
great friends."

She was really ready with pencil and notebook from
her purse, the same notebook which she had used in the
library to copy from *The Last Time I Saw Paris*. This was
too good! She had brought the notebook with her! With
deliberate hesitation in response to her impatience (afraid
he'd change his mind? an attack of prudence about gossip
somehow finding its way from the Fourteenth Arrondisse-
ment to Cleveland Heights, Postal Zone 6?), he wrote from
memory, *Philippe . . . Michel . . . Stanley . . .*

She watched, her lips spelling with him. Then: "Who's
he? Who's he?" She listened, and at last she let go the words
which put his despair upon him, gave him what he knew
he deserved (but afterwards aren't all animals sad?) and
must finally have brought the weather change to his face in
a way which communicated itself even to her:

"Philippe who? Stanley who? What does he do? They
were all your friends back in 1950? You don't think they're
too old now, do you?" She clapped her small hand to her
mouth. She turned from the glass and twisted to him on the
bench. "Oh! Gran, how can you *look* like that? Don't *take*
an innocent question like that. I didn't mean that about you,
old. I just meant they're probably busy, attached, married
and settled already, *you* know. Don't take it like that, Gran.
Don't you *stare*. They will probably all be just *marvellous*
contacts."

He remembered his responsibility and stopped staring.
When he finished the little list of contacts, he had satisfied
her. The bar was closed already, so they could not have another drink. She linked her arm in his and told him not to
be like ice. He drove her home carefully over the January
slick. He had been generous with all he could give.

Then he went back to see if his son's irritability meant

that he finally was coming down with something. There were infections in the neighborhood, but the resistance had to be low first for a fever to take hold.

No, he decided at his own door, there was another precious gift which Carol had taken from him. His responsibility to her and to this gift for her had gotten him over the moment near tears when he had so stared and stared. There is that matter of nostalgia for the past which, more and more, the hard and arty person will come to need.

Aristotle and the Hired Thugs

Antione and the Hired Thing

In 1933 my father had two mighty enemies. Against one of them he struggled all the long fruit-and-vegetable day, hoisting the crates and loading a top-heavy truck in early morning, at dawn, in his sheepskin jacket, then meeting the customers until evening in a store built narrow and dark in the alleyway between a bakery and a Peerless showroom. Against the other enemy he fought all night, tossing and groaning in his sleep, fierce with that strange nightmare which allows an angry man to be pursued without ever retreating.

His daytime adversary was one shared by most other Americans—the Great Depression. The one of his nights was that beast clanking and roaring in the streets of fantastic Deutschland. "Hitler!" he said at breakfast, shaking the sleep from his head. "I'm almost ashamed to be human. The other strawberries don't like the rotten strawberry, they blush rotten red if you don't pluck him out—"

"Have another cup of Wheatena for the strength in it," chanted my mother, grieving with him like a good wife because of the need for strength on a troubled planet.

"Sorry, no time—look at the clock!" He hadn't meant to complain; it was the only earth he knew. "The lettuce is

145

in already, and the pascal comes with it." And standing up, jacketed in sheepskin, shod in Army-Navy boots, he drained his coffee, dropped the cup in the sink, and was off to the market downtown near the flats of Cleveland. Before light on a May morning, he fought the battered reconditioned motor of his thirdhand truck, cursed, lifted the hood, wiped the wires and plugs. Mother opened the kitchen window to watch. Then fits and coughs, then action. Mother watched him go, and waved. *Action*—his pockets filled with knives, hammers, dollars, a deck of cards, and funny pictures to show his friends in the chill damp of a spring morning. Down the suburban streets, up the suburban highway he rattled; and through the sleeping city where the street lights abruptly died in the dawn; and only rare bedroom lamps and kitchen noises greeted him on his way.

But the Central Farmers' Market was a city in full life. Carloads of vegetables steamed with the haggle and babble of selling under corrugated zinc roofs and no roofs at all. Hot fat soup was sold from great tureens by farmers' wives —nickel soup for before the sale, coffee and steaming pies for later, ten cents, to be wolfed down whole by desperate eaters who could not remember whether this was their second or their third breakfast. My father paced the aisles of lettuce and tender peas, the green corridors of spinach, deep into silent back parlors of early fruit off the railway cars. Private, at one with food, he sniffed gratefully, at his ease, homely, taking the pleasures of business on his tongue and in his deep-breathing lungs. He went to the produce market as to worship—putting Hitler and bank holidays behind him in the glory of America's bounty. He squeezed a plum until the wine spurted. He wiped his eyes.

Joe Rini surprised him in his shadowy lair. "What you doing here, Sam?"

"Same as you! Good, eh?"

"But can we sell it? I still got last week's plums left over."

My father shrugged, the sheepskin ruffling against a crate. "They get soggy in the cooler. What else can we do?"

"Nothing—and these look like prime. Here, let me taste."

"Taste, go on. Me, I'd like to buy."

The fruitmen rivalled, of course, for the favor of the farmers, who were of another breed, not washing in those days as a protest against the cost of living. Their best produce many times rotted in the fields, and the farmers often suffered terrible bellyaches from the hopeless eating of an unbought crop. Even striated beefsteak tomatoes, warmed by sun and dusted with salt, can be too many! The farmers suffered from mortgages, skin diseases, unrepaired fences, chronically pregnant wives. Regularly removed from their lonely land to confront a crazy urban cackle, and perhaps returning without the profit of seed and fertilizer, they too passed cards among themselves.

The immigrant Italian and Jewish fruitmen, with their occasional Greek and Negro colleagues, exchanged printed jokes and dirty pictures. They first competed and argued, then huddled for eat and gossip, sharing each other's hard times in the pleasure and intimacy of these early mornings. They left at dawn with regret, jamming their trucks into gritty day.

The farmers' wives, bundled and red and unfragrant as men, dipped up the last coffee and watched without a word. Drops of fat cream whirled round like crazy fishlets in the tin cups. The farmers too had their whispered consultations, but these never ended in a burst of laughter as they got the point. Their little cards were other dreams, dreams of riding and hunting, gothic fantasies of ritual, celebration, and chastisement. The Black Legion haunted

the countryside around Cleveland. It made contact with the
Klan in Parma and the Bund in Lakewood, and there were
histories of drilling in open fields, the youngsters standing
guard with broomsticks. Their cards made them members
together for sacred order and vengeance. Cousins who rarely
saw each other came out on Sunday after church to listen
to screaming harangues from the platforms of pickups. During the dark winter of 1933, some farmers discovered that
they had the call—or at least as much a one as the man in
blue serge sent down from Jackson, Michigan.

Al Flavin was a farmer with whom my father had dealt
for almost ten years. They had never been friends, but my
father gave as good a price as anyone and Flavin took good
care of his lettuce; they met in commerce. An angry man
who had sometimes wrestled at country fairs, a giant with
magnificent hairy paws, he began to know glory for the first
time since abandoning his boyish victories on sweaty canvas. Men listened to him. He became a Commander or a
Knight or a Dragon, whatever the Black Legion name for it
was. He could not pay off the loan on his greenhouse, but
he could gather the Legionnaires in before-dawn consultations at the edge of town.

It must have made Al feel distant from himself to
break up the meeting, give the mystic handshake, crushing
the wrists of men less mighty than he, climb into a truck
with a load strapped on, and then go meekly off to do business with Sam Stein.

"All right, make it eleven crates for ten," my father
said.

"Ten crates," Al repeated stubbornly.

"Eleven. Or ten and my last price."

"No. Ten crates. My price."

"Al, listen to me," my father said. "You *know* I can't

buy it your way. Joe Rini will undersell me, he'll throw circulars on all the porches, and then where will I be? You got to make sense in business."

"You heard me."

"What's the matter, you don't feel good today, Al? Something hurting?"

"Joe Rini don't buy from me. I bring in first quality stuff."

"I know, I *know,* that's why I stand here and argue with you. I *want* your stuff, Al. I like it."

My father rocked, smiling. Al Flavin stood behind his barricade of lettuce. Patience, patience—the soul is tried on earth. At last they were agreed, some place between demand and offer, and then joining in the traditional aftermath of successful negotiation, the two of them completed their deal by hoisting the produce into my father's truck. Hot and sighing when this was done, the cash changing hands, usually they came to a moment of benevolent treaty, and the plump fruitman would light up with the burly, brooding farmer. Al Flavin was busy behind his squeezed-shut eyes trying to remember who he is, who other people are.

"Okay, Al," my father said, "have a cigar."

Now he remembered. He felt his card and sorted my father out: *"Kike!"*

"Wh-wh-wh," said my father.

Flavin's shoulder caught my father and halfspun him around as the man stamped off in the flapping galoshes which he wore almost into summer. My father stammered, wh-wh-wh, meaning *What?* and *Why?* First amazed, then stooped and solemn, pouting with thought. It was well past dawn now, but suddenly the nightmare toppled onto his daytime dream, and he was standing in the sad, crooked streets of old Nuremberg.

My father stopped dealing with Al Flavin. This did
not put an end to it. He heard Flavin's word every market-
day morning, first whispered, then called after him, twice a
week. The single note grated on his nerves. The market is
supposed to be a pleasure. My mother made him promise
not to fight. Flavin, huge, profligate with his wrestler's flesh,
yearning to brawl, would crush him in his paws. It was
policy. Flavin was a Commander. He hoped to convert the
waverers by rolling with Sam Stein in the running wash of
the market gutters.

"I'd get him with the peen of my hammer first!" my
father yelled.

"Sam, Sam, we don't want trouble."

"I'll break his head with the claw!"

Mother petted him, stroked him. "Think of your business. You got a family, Sam, you got to count them."

"I'LL KILL HIM, BELLA!"

"Shush, you're making noise, the neighbors. You got
to count me, too. No trouble, please, for your kids' sake."

"No, no, no." His eyes were red with sleepless thinking.
There was an angry scratch in the tender eye-flesh. He
breathed as if he were struggling for air. "No, you're right,
Bella. But if he touches me one more time—"

That time came, however, on a morning during the
dog days of July, when even at early market hours the
men panted and sweated under the bloody-eyed sun before
it reared up onto the exhausted city. Ice trickled through
the crates of lettuce, rustling, and evaporated on cement
still hot from the day before. The overfed market rats loped
along on seared paws. Flavin sprang from behind a heap of
crates, pretending to be in a hurry, and struck my father
with his knee at the belly, so that he lost his balance and
stumbled like a drunk. He grunted. He tried but could not
quite sob out his breath. It was caught, trapped, extermi-

nated some place within, and he lay sprawled on the soft market refuse while the little world of pain in his belly spun faster than the earth's turning, and only a moment later, when the hurtling agony at the center of his being slowed down to weakness, and the weakness to a sour sickness that drained into his mouth, did he remember again who he was. It's an assault against life that brings this gnawing, liver-eating agony upon a man gasping for his breath with his head against a crate of lettuce. The blood shrieked like eagles in his ears. It's a wish of murder—extermination. It's a terrible pain that makes a man forget he is Sam Stein.

Flavin roared, pushed the laughter forward with all his weight, and stood with his huge arms welcoming. Once taciturn, he had learned the tricks of oratory: "Looks drunk, don't he? Ain't he a rummy? Never did run into a rummy kike before, did you ever, boys?"

An offering of laughter. The rest would gather when the rich noise of brawling crashed out. Flavin was in boots, kicking free of a broken crate, ready.

Sam Stein pained badly in the gut. He climbed up dizzily and shook his head clear. He felt for the silver-pronged crating hammer in his back pocket. Flavin crouched, his long jaw twitching with desire. The buttons of his pants were stretched and a tab of shirt came out his fly. Flavin could wait another moment to find and make himself real. The usual hubbub of commercial dispute hid them now; the life of the market swirled unknowing about the two men, food rising in great towers and vaults above them, around them, and only a couple of farmers watched. Joe Rini, terrified, blowing saliva, also watched.

My father had promised my mother.

He loved life and the right and *to win*.

Flavin might kill him.

My father walked away rapidly, hunched, turning red

for shame and white for planning, and grabbed Joe Rini by the sleeve and took him with him. "Joe, Joe," he said, "I got to talk to you. I know you got friends. I got to talk to them, too."

"What you got to say, Sam?"

"Oh maybe I could kill him, but then again maybe not. It wouldn't be so good if he gave me a beating. Those other cossacks would feel too nice about it. Or worse. A bad precedent. No justice in that. So. . . ."

Eagerly Rini talked into the void. "So you know how they drink. They're drunkards. So don't raise your blood pressure." My father's eye made him stop. Rini agreed. My father decided slowly:

"The way things are going on the market now, Joe, it won't be safe for any of us soon."

"What you thinking, Sam?" Rini asked.

He was thinking, but in his own words: precedent, morale, example. This was a political question to be answered in the impure, compromising way of politics. A passionate answer—Sam Stein's face bloodied, a crowd secretly smiling over Sam Stein's fallen body, an inflamed Al finding his dream of power fulfilled—this was the worst possibility which my father's furious body had almost given him. The philosophical thing to do was to master that hot inner twitch, and then, only then, to think out how to discourage the cossack mob.

Job and Noah had patience; yet Job was permitted his anger. Not an educated man, my father knew that the patriarchs had even spoken for passion on earth, properly used. And he knew no other place for justice except here below, on earth, where he hoped to have more children.

He breathed deeply once, twice, again, that's better, and then thanked God for giving him a sense of responsibility. He thanked the Lord of Creation that his healthy, willing, complaining wife had come to mind. Wistfully he thanked the Almighty for prudence—and also for his friend Joe Rini. He said to Joe Rini: "You're going to help me now."

That very night Joe found the three young friends whom he had in mind and brought them to the house. My father wanted to meet them . . . "make your acquaintance." How formal we become under embarrassment. For fifty dollars he could buy a beating with any refinements he named. Except nothing vicious, of course—what do you think, they were queers? They were mere administrators.

"No, *no!*" my mother cried. "So then he'll kill you next, and what's the good? We can't afford it."

"We can't afford not to," my father said stonily. "We're going to do what the Frenchies won't do. When he makes his noise, we march into the Rhineland and stop it good. You don't have to listen to that noise. You stop it the best way you can. You stop it. You *stop* it."

"Sam, O Sam, it's dangerous, it's fifty dollars."

"It's the cost of living, Bella."

Joe Rini's friends, three young chaps with slicked-down hair, nervous hands, and old jokes, were very sociable. They jiggled and dandled and played beanbag with me, as if I were a baby, although I was eight years old already. They took time over the business because my father likes business. Also he wanted to be certain. Mother served liver *with,* the rich slabs covered by curly, glistening onions. How can businessmen discuss serious matters without keeping up their strength? Mugs of strong black coffee, too.

"For fifty dollars, Mr. Stein," said the leader of the group, "we can maybe kill him for you. It's no extra. We'll be working anyway. His truck has got to stop for a light on the edge of town, and there we are."

"No, no," my father said. "Put him in the hospital, that's all."

"Mr. Rini says he used to work in the commission house with you. He says you're buddies from way back. It's no trouble at all."

"No!" my father said. "The man has a wife and kids, just like me. His big boy is too dumb to run a farm by himself—"

"We got smart kids," my mother interrupted, smiling, politely patting with a napkin, pleased by their appetites. "My big boy, he gets such marks from his teacher—"

"Bella, shush. Go call up somebody on the telephone if you got to talk. Listen."

The businessmen shrugged apologetically, being brought up in a tradition which favors mothers, and turned regretfully back to hear out my father and his scrupling. They were unaccustomed to fine distinctions, but they came of devoted families; they enjoyed a mother's pride. "So don't do that what you said there," my father repeated. "I just want him to learn a little, have time to think a little. The hospital."

"Okay," the leader of the trio said reluctantly, "you're the boss. You get a hold of us if you change your mind, will you? To you the price remains the same."

"The hospital," my father repeated, making them promise.

"Let us worry about the details, Mr. Stein. Fifty goes a long way these days."

My father arose angrily, sending his cup ringing against a platter. *I said the hospital!*

"The hospital, hospital," they intoned mournfully, and filed out.

The next morning Flavin did not show up at the market. It was so easy to follow him from the country in a flivver, stop with him at a red light, get rid of the cigarettes, and pile quickly onto his truck. So instead of Flavin, a weary, hardworking young thug appeared and nodded to Dad, saying that they had been careful, just as he said. But it would have been no extra trouble, in fact, the reverse.

My father was undelighted. By his veiled eyes he signalled regret at the weight of the world: he was obliged to send Flavin down to defeat without earning the kiss of victory. Life had provided him—as it does everyone—with one more little blemish on the ideal of brave perfection. He found it a necessary business, nothing more, a merely rational victory, and he foresaw the possibility of being ambushed in his turn by a man who might not bother to think of his wife and children. Nevertheless, reason consoled him.

"What if he does it to you now, Sam? Where will I and the kids be? Where will *you* be if you're dead?"

"Well, it's a risk. But in this life you have to take chances and defend yourself like you can. And now let me answer your question: If I'm dead, I'm no place."

He sent Flavin a five-dollar bouquet of flowers, followed the next morning by a two-dollar plant with thick wet leaves and a decorative sprinkle of spangles. Joe Rini approved. A friend who went to see Flavin in the hospital reported that they were the only flowers he received.

The moral which my father drew was one which he wanted to teach England and France in 1933 and after. Still strong and capable, Flavin came quietly to work in his bandages about ten days later. He sold tomatoes to my father, and they haggled like gentlemen over the price. They mistered each other warily. There was further talk of the Black Legion, but not a gesture from Flavin. In a few years even the talk passed.

Sometimes my father thought that he might be beat up,

but it never happened, although once he was robbed. That was not Flavin's work.

Flavin had taken instruction well, administered according to Aristotelean principles, with moderation, by a man whose fundamental passionate mildness led him to a reasonable strictness: the hospital for Flavin, nothing worse. Nightmares go on, but they have answers—albeit risky, rational, incomplete, and not ideally valorous. Poor Flavin, unused to surprises—he was discouraged.

And my mother was consoled. Dad made another fifty dollars to replace the ones spent in good works.

The Panic Button

Numbed and icy, his wife's voice through the telephone enveloped him in its dangerous calm. "Don't worry," she was saying, but too often for best efficiency. "Don't worry, don't worry, don't worry, I'm all right."

"What's the matter, Barbara?"

"I'm all right. They just flew up in my face like pigeons."

"What's the *matter?*" he almost shouted.

"But they're not hurt. Three children. One boy, two girls." Precision always gave her a sense of mastery over herself, over things. She was winning when she was exact. "The boy was the youngest," she said. "They ran across straight in front of me. I had the right of way, I was making a right-hand turn, really quite slowly. I scraped one—skin cuts, nothing more. I don't think I even touched the boy, but he fell. I hit a little girl—just touched her was all—I think she's only scared. Emotions. I don't think it's anything. They took her to the hospital to make sure."

"Which hospital? I'll go right there."

"No. That's so like you, Dan." The voice was one of disdain. The chemical crystals of her calm proliferated

wildly, like the spray of a fire extinguisher in a shaky hand.
"No, come here instead. The police are questioning me and
I can't move the car. Now listen, I'm at the corner of—"
She gave him the location.

"Don't worry, I'll be right with you."

He heard her saying as he put down the receiver, "But
I already told you I'm perfectly all right. Perfectly." He
stood a moment at the telephone. He could not possibly
have heard her say that. It was just that he felt what she
would think.

Although this event had never happened in this way
before, he found it very familiar and watched like a dream-
watcher barely awake as the cab took him through the
scattered Saturday afternoon traffic. A kid with a rod and no
muffler whooped by; loiterers at the corner glanced up from
their weekend editions; he did not bother asking the cabby
to hurry. No haircut today, he decided. No something else;
he forgot his other plan for the Saturday afternoon. The
children just flew up in her face like pigeons. Barbara's
words for it excited him, troubled him. The children flying
up like pigeons to disaster recalled something—she was
calm, he was less calm—and all at once, in front of a billboard selling insurance (ARE YOU READY? ARE YOUR LOVED
ONES SAFE?), he sat forward and remembered what it was.
Calling for a doctor. She had been normally pregnant, and
wild with fright and a consequent petulance, and wanting
with tears and fury—wanting him to be other than he was,
wanting some fantastic ideal husband and no husband at
all—and then she had taken ill. Calling for a doctor, calling
for an ambulance. Flying up in his face like pigeons.

While in terrible pain, coolly, calmly, with fine control,
she had lost their child. The white inwardness of her suffering had drawn them closer than they had ever been, and
then, with the receding pain, they had fallen away once

more. Another time, when he was ill, she had nursed him with marvellous tenderness. And then his return to health. And the falling away.

With all her mastery of herself under the shadows of danger, crisis, illness, and death, she had never learned to drive their car in his presence. He rattled her, she said, and she would fly off at him. He judged her, he lacked trust, he . . . thank God I wasn't in the car with her, Dan Shaper thought, and guiltily stared at the cab driver's neck, remembering the children.

He thought: When the panic button is pressed and everyone is in full confusion, there she is, fully competent. Beautiful, beautiful. The crisis mentality. If I would oblige her by being an invalid or an alcoholic, if she could find herself at the edge of hell itself, then she would charge into the Furies to defend us both. She could fight for me, she could murder for herself. She would be a hero and we could love each other. But all I need for her is to stand with me in love and confidence without the panic button, the way things are, just living together.

His cab pulled up before the little huddle on a sun-speckled November street corner. Their Pontiac was where it had stopped, with a few feet of black skid marks on the pavement. Two policemen, one with unfolded measuring tape, had their bored, busy policeman masks slipped loosely over their bored, lazy policeman faces. There were the curious, the loitering, and, as it turned out, three witnesses. "Your missus wasn't going five miles an hour. She made a stop. I told the officer," an angry little knot of a man reported to him at once. He smiled at this friend, moved his lips "thank you," and reached for his wife. He made her lean a moment against his shoulder. He could feel the mobilized little body, hot as a bird, even through her coat. He felt a flood of tenderness for this slight, firm girl who now needed him very much. He wanted her to feel protected and, for himself, he wanted to touch her cheek.

"Don't worry about a thing," he said.

"Everything is all right," she answered, pulling away. "Why, are you upset?"

There was also a grim mother standing with a weeping boy, his face smudged with tears, the tears still furrowing down his face, and a rip at his corduroy knees where he had fallen. The two girls had both been taken to the hospital. Of course he was upset! Shouldn't he be? Why should Barbara even ask and why should the question be sent flying at him like a judgment? He wanted to say something to the mother, something like "I'm sorry, I'm so sorry," but of course it wasn't his fault, it was his wife who was involved, and apparently it wasn't her fault either, and it was hard to say anything. Still, the mother and the boy were unhappy. The mother was angry. Still, how was it really his business? (I'm sorry, but it isn't *our* fault? my wife's fault?) He said nothing and avoided looking at the woman. He stood near Barbara and let their bodies touch as they moved. He wanted this unvoiced physical comfort to be the best love she now needed. Once her flower of a face with its huge dark eyes stopped its restless turning for an instant and gazed curiously into his face. It would be fine to give her what she wanted.

"Looks like your lady was in perfect control," the cop said. "Crazy kids don't look where they're going, don't cross where there's a guard. She couldn't stop them if she was the mayor. Of course the lady'll have to appear in court anyhow and I shouldn't say, but it's my opinion." He grinned and shook his head and used the quizzical word "lady," Shaper knew, because Barbara was such a lady, so cool about it.

"Your wife is such a lovely person," a woman came up to inform him. She paused to let him assimilate this information. Cans of cat food clanked in her mesh shopping bag. "I watched the whole thing. You should have seen how controlled she was, how she cuddled that little girl who was so scared, and she didn't think of herself and her own trouble—"

"Thank you," he said, touching Barbara to pull her away, but the woman followed them.

"The girl was all right, but she was so sweet to her anyhow. That girl just ran right in front of the car. She should have given her a piece of her mind—the brats, they're supposed to study safety first in school—if it had been me, I'd have been furious, me, but no, she cuddled and cuddled her—"

"Thank you," he said. "Where did they take the child?"

The woman rushed on, a bored lonely vacant creature in a cloth coat with a destroyed fur collar: "She had a right to be scared herself, she did, she did, but she only—"

"Let's go now," he said. He led his wife away, very much aware of his tall figure leaning solicitously over her. He felt the throbbing, shaking, inward heat of Barbara's effort at control—that hot motor which keeps the freezer cool. The policeman said that there was nothing more required. Barbara broke free of his arm and went to speak with the mother of the boy. She left him standing there, unprotected from the woman with the cloth coat. He followed Barbara.

"We can go *now*," she said when he took her arm again. "Now let's go to the hospital and see how little Jeanie is."

The woman with the cat food hung near them, shaking her head in violent wonder and approval. He held the door open for his wife. She liked public courtesies. He got in at his side. She sat there very still and white. He noticed that she had remembered to turn off the ignition, although the car must have stalled, and she had both put on the brakes and left it in gear. She said nothing until they turned the corner away from the crowd. Then he began to hear her breathing, and he felt her huge, dark, smudged eyes on him as he paid elaborate attention to his driving. "It's all your fault," she said softly.

They did not need another accident. He pulled over to the curb, stopped, and locked the brake before answering. "For what? How?" he asked. He put out his arms toward her in the hope of catching something. "How is it possible, Barbara?"

She whispered to him under great pressure, like a bursting vessel, "It's all your fault. Your fault." The tears were shaken from her eyes, propelled by anger, hatred, anguish. A droplet splashed on his hand and he felt its hot spreading. "Your fault for everything!"

"Let's go to the hospital first," he said, "then we'll talk. First we want to make sure the child is all right, don't we?" He felt a marvel of a smile gathering within and spreading its warmth through his veins. It was a wondrous calm humour that came to dwell with him. At last the connection was made between trouble and ordinary times and he could figure out what to do next. For him now to control, to manipulate; and beyond those items of approximation and accommodation, perhaps even to break loose from manipulating and controlling, which are the resort of weakness. The panic button had no more power over him. He would not betray it, no, but the smile nourished him.

"Your your *your* fault!"

"Poor Barbara," he said, "you're upset." He held her struggling head; it pressed furiously against his shoulder; he stroked her hair. He blinked his hot dry eyes and, to relieve them, focused as far down the street, as far away as he could without moving. "You're upset, but never you mind, Barbara honey. Who wouldn't be?"

Now free, free!

Sello

Among the several items offered Fred Stern during his first week as a Fulbright student in Paris were, of course, the usual wine, women, and instructions from the State Department, and also the opportunity to be associate producer of a monumental film on the subject of the French resistance against the Nazi occupation. The initiator of this project was a certain Monsieur Sello, a tall, skinny, yellow, unhealthy person who limped painfully in high black laced boots. He had lost part of one foot and most of the other in a mine explosion early in the war; he managed to hobble about on creaking shoes built up to approximate normal feet. The leather screeched as he walked. He lived in a furnished room on the rue du Bac, nourishing himself by his pension as a *mutilé de guerre* and his future triumph as producer of a masterpiece. His previous training as a moviemaker had come before the war when he had served as boy valet and coffee consultant to Eric von Stroheim, and in other obscure tasks which varied in the telling, according to his mood. From better days Monsieur Sello retained a brilliant set of teeth which he used with skill in smiling either pitifully or bravely (with graduations between) at crucial junctures in his negotiations.

Fred Stern, fresh from the State University of Iowa, was impressed by the prospects of glory through participation in the memorial. Sello's highest recommendations as to competence were his wounds and his connection with the great events of the war. With Sello creaking about on his stumps, leaning on café tables, blowing his old dog's breath into Stern's face, the student felt that at last he had made contact with real European life, the Realest of awesome Real Life. "For ten thousand francs," Sello told him, "you can join me as an associate producer. I have need of very little more to begin with. Then I have Pierre Fresnay and Jean Gabin, I have the banks, I have the director, the music, the studio, all. All!"

Dizzied by the unlimited energy of his few francs—they amounted, in fact, to less than thirty dollars in real money—Fred restrained himself by a midwestern commercial caution. He steadied his breathing by an act of pure will. He sucked in his belly. He asked further credentials, not because he lacked faith in the project—he had already secretly committed himself—but because he wanted to feel himself legitimately a part of the larger world. Otherwise it would be just like playing Monopoly on the back porch in Des Moines with these flimsy bits of paper which happened to have a drawing of Marianne on the back. Also his wife, Gretta, would demand explanations. "How all?" he asked with Iowa cunning in his best French. "Comment tout?"

"I have letters, commitments," Sello announced. "Monsieur Jean-Paul Sartre's enthousiasme pour le projet." (We will try to continue in English.) "Francois Mauriac is with us. Prevert, Paulhan, Queneau . . ." He pronounced some of the most formidable syllables on the left bank of the Seine. "Once the ball begins to roll, it will roll."

With such arguments were Fred's doubts calmed. He could become a catalyst, a ball-roller. Now all that remained for satisfaction was his esthetic taste. Could he see the working script?

"Of course! Without fail! Necessarily!"

There was a brief but significant pause between them. Sello made no movement but the brilliant one of his smile.

"Okay, when?" Fred asked.

For answer Sello ordered another café crême. They were sitting outdoors at Le Rouquet, a café on the corner of the Boulevard St.-Germain and the rue des Saints-Peres, just across from the shaded court of a Russian Orthodox Church and about a block from the intellectual bums of St.-Germain-des-Près. Even here, a good two minute walk from the Deux Magots, an occasional lovely turtlenecked philosopher strolled wiggling by; Fred Stern was in touch. The plane trees were in full, luxurious, green, and dusty flower. It was late spring. It was a time for commitment. Fred permitted himself to admire in particular one rump which made heroic but unavailing efforts to catch up with the rest of the girl's tragic, shapely, corduroyed entity. He sighed, and with an effort concentrated on a rapidly fading memory of his wife, whom he had last seen at breakfast. She did not twitch when she walked; she had played a dandy game of sand-lot baseball with the boys in Des Moines.

Sello was showing his remarkable teeth. And so back to business. Fred would pay for the several coffees and the croissant for which Sello was now summoning the waiter.

"You want to see my credentials?" Sello asked, breathing damp crumbs at him.

"No, no," Fred hastened to assure him. *Credo;* he believed. He believed in Paris, the Left Bank, the Liberation, the languid, eye-smudged actresses whom he rapidly imagined, and therefore he believed in Monsieur Sello. He could not demand a license or a diploma for becoming the producer of great films. But still, if only for his sensible

Gretta, he wanted an accurate idea, some written prospectus of that Sello superproduction, *La Résistance*.

Fortunately, it just happened that Sello travelled armed at all times with the preliminary script. He pulled a worn little wad of paper from the breast pocket of his jacket (English tweed acted as a mild tranquillizer for Stern), unfolded the three sheets, and handed them to Fred with a triumphant glance, the sharp tips of his teeth gleaming, but not a further word. His aching, crippled body shaped itself into a posture of negligent pride while Stern read. Very brief even for the prospectus of a film script, a few characteristic moments from it can be translated and condensed still further:

THE RESISTANCE

The entire world and Lady Justice herself were astounded by the magnificent phenomenon of the spectacle of the strongest, most virile segment of the French nation which rose up in its pain to smite the invader. Darting hither and thither, dynamiting bridges, freeing prisoners, printing leaflets, the gallant young workers, peasants, and intellectuals who remembered the glorious tradition of Freedom which. . . . (Comme Peguy l'Immortel l'a si bien dit. . . .)

And so on in that hortatory vein. Near the end of the third and final page, Sello seemed suddenly to have recalled himself to business, and an immense capitalized sentence, decorated with asterisks, spread itself across coffee stains and rusty creases:

***WE**MUST**CREATE**A**FILM**TO
IMMORTALIZETHE**LOVERS
OFFREEDOM! ! !**

The document moved Fred deeply. He was imbued with a guilty suspicion that both Des Moines and Iowa City had failed to become focal points of world history; he was steeped in a literary devotion to the idea of heroism, and Paris is still piled high with fuel for this piety—monuments, newspapers, renamed squares and streets, the corners with their neat little plaques and faded flowers. "Ici est tombé dans la Liberation de Paris . . ." The age of the dead hero was very often his own at a time when he had been merely a high school boy in Des Moines. His Civics class ("Sieve," they called it) consisted mainly of memorizing the names of Iowa senators; Hickenlooper had not yet been invented. Now in Paris the memorial flowers in the little vase affixed to the building at the corner of the rue de Verneuil and the rue du Bac were mysteriously renewed at intervals; in Iowa, Bourke Hickenlooper reigned. Surely Fred was dazzled more by sentiment than by hope of commercial gain, but Sello also pointed the way to great fortune through the enormous worldwide profits inevitable upon such an enterprise. Suavely Fred handed over the ten thousand francs without consulting Gretta.

"And now I must go," he said.

"Where? We must drink to luck first!"

"My wife is waiting—"

"Please! One moment! The receipt!" Sello made it official by covering a piece of paper and signing it with special grace, including his full name and title, "Organisateur-gerant-Producteur-en-chef." There would be, he intimated, a great deal of social jollity among all those participating in the film. Some of the most charming actresses and script-girls (pronunciation: *screept-gerrl*) would hasten to join the project. Words like "frou-frou" and "chic" and "le tout-Paris" passed his gleaming teeth after those other magic words, "Maquis," "F.F.I.," and "la France Eternelle." Fred left Sello waving byebye, languid as a lord, breaking the first of the thousand franc notes by ordering a Cinzano. An organisateur-gerant-producteur-en-chef must keep up his strength.

Gretta Stern that evening had several humid items of logic to bank against her husband's overheated imagination. "The Resistance," she pointed out, "is one thing. A film is another. Sello as poor cripple is one person. Sello as film producer is another. You have all these things mixed up, Fred—a stew." She took pity on him. "But never mind, you're probably right. It only looks, smells, and tastes like a stew."

The thought had barely occurred to him, but with a very few words his wife had abruptly made the thought palpable. "You think I've been conned? If he—!" And the muscles rippled throughout Fred Stern's honest midwestern jaw.

"Well, ten thousand francs is only ten thousand francs," Gretta commented cheerfully. "Let's go out for dinner, a cheap dinner, nescafé?"

"A lot of money," Stern admitted.

"Oh just forget it now, Fred."

"I'll have to borrow on next month's check to get us through."

"Well, I suppose it's worth it to imagine yourself brooding on the set in a canvas director's chair with your name stenciled and—Lord only knows what else you imagine."

Clever girl. Fred was conscious of his suspense without an immediate plausible reply to his pretty little, clever little wife. During dinner, which began with buttered radishes, and the evening, which ended indecisively, Fred urged her to have faith, to believe, to think positive thoughts. He wanted her to share his exhilaration, the challenge of their project. "Is ten thousand francs such a disaster?" she asked. "It's just a longshot bet, that's all." She did not exactly ridicule the adventure, but she described it; she made him judge it himself, and now he knew what it felt like to have tired blood. He had expected to defend his impulse, but what defense could he offer against her failure to attack? None. An aftertaste of radish.

"Well, it's done," he decided at last. "Let's not worry. We'll see."

"Ne fret pas, darling—"

"I said not to worry," he replied.

"That's exactly what I started to point out. *I* am not the one who is doing the worrying."

If Fred could then simply have lost the money and let the matter go forgotten, it would have been relatively easy. But now Sello felt a responsibility to him as partner. He came more and more frequently to their little quarters in order to report on the progress of the film. He had seen a writer, talked with a musician, passed word along to an actor, heard a rumor from a waiter. He limped painfully in; bravely, gravely he smiled; he came closely, breathing. Usually it was at mealtime. He settled sighing into a chair and went away after being fed. Fred gave him money for a cab to that distant corner of Auteuil where a banker awaited him—the expense of raising money in Paris is continual. Once it was raining, and Fred offered him an umbrella, in addition to money for the cab, so that M. Rothschild could not fail to sense that here is a man of means. Men whose corsets are stayed with bullion feel saddened and stiffened at the purse when their sensitive bodies pick up emanations of poverty. Gratefully Sello accepted the furled umbrella and waved a jaunty tata with it.

Having more than enough practice, Gretta and Fred came to recognize the squeak and complaint of Sello's boots

in the hall outside their door. Their nerves were sharpened
so that they even heard it when he was not there. Sometimes they had moments of crazy optimism—grand Monsieur le Baron de Rothschild had dashed off a check; the
bank had given its blessing and its loan; the picture was
about to start. Sello, sweating hard, straining on his worst
foot, entered smiling. He leaned on the door, poked his nose
through, recovered his breath, cried, "Bonjour! Bonjour!"
He sniffed, he sighed, he smelled something in the pan. It
was for this his optimism—news of mealtime. There was no
final word about the film, not quite, not yet, but there were
always good auguries. "The well known critic of the Figaro
smiled as I passed him chez Lipp, his father was a great
man. I have discovered the triumph of love without vulgar-
ization—symbolic love! I now know exactly the studio
where the interiors must be shot."

"The interiors of symbolic love?" Fred asked.

"Will you have a bit of supper with us, Monsieur
Sello?" said Gretta.

"Hm, hum. I hate to trouble you. Do not trouble yourself, please do not! But I might."

And painfully he lowered himself into Fred's chair.
"You are so kind. I must now tell you . . ." Fred pulled up a
stool for himself and listened to the tale of Sello's wander-
ings during the day. It was near the end of the month, which
is always a difficult time. "You understand? Life in France,
Monsieur Freddy—" His check would surely arrive on the
first of next week, or if not Monday at least Thursday, and
if not Thursday, then the following Tuesday. It makes one's
head spin! The postal system is infested with men of poor
initiative. In the meantime, the expenses of a movie producer mount; some cafés will no longer serve him—he cannot pass down certain streets; and yet it is necessary for an
organisateur-gerant-producteur-en-chef to offer an impor-

tant personage something to drink. Could his dear friend
Fred, for the good of the film and friendship besides, until
the first of the month . . . He would write down the exact
amount on a piece of paper, in ink, and put it away with the
pictures of his mother of blessed memory.

Impossible to hurry him out afterward. Each loan
deepened their intimacy. Sello sat, yellow, pensive, and per-
spiring happily at being at home with two such nice young
Americans. He felt that he owed them something. Therefore
he paid his debt. He uttered courtly praise of Gretta's cooking, which, he said, seemed almost French in quality. He
said this in several different ways. The flanges of his nose
expanded with the labor of gratitude. He smiled to show his
fine teeth. Then he remarked that French is an exceptional
language: one can make beautiful logic in beautiful ways.
Any effort to pry him from his seat would give them the
responsibility for his painful, tottering, balancing, half-
clawing struggle against the empty air. They preferred to
wait until he decided to leave. He brought his own tooth-
picks and sat until Fred served a bit of alcohol, as an aid to
the digestion only, of course, recommended by all wise students of the matter. Then he pressed himself out of the chair.
He grimaced as he took his first painful steps in the reluctant leather. "Ah," he announced at the door, "I have an
important, a vital rendezvous."

"Accept my congratulations," said Fred.

"But, but, but you kept me so long with your many
kindnesses that I am nearly late."

"Accept my apologies," said Fred.

"About the project. I dislike to be late." And pierc-
ingly he threw a glance at Fred as if the American might be
an agent provocateur, plying him with food and even drink
not for pure, disinterested, and estimable reasons of serious
digestive processes, but rather in order to make him miss

his appointments. "Perhaps, perhaps, but surely you will put me in a taxi so that . . ." Fred gave him the money for a cab and, in full jitters, returned to find his wife finishing the dishes without waiting for him to help. He was shaking with fury. He felt used, manipulated—the worst way to feel for a young American, not yet sure of his own powers. Gretta was humming, bustling, doing wifely work.

"What are you so happy about?" he demanded.

"Oh, I could tell you didn't want him here, I know you," Gretta said. "But the poor man really does look hungry, and it's a pleasure to watch him eat. Such gusto. Such appreciation. And it gives us practice with our French, too. He speaks so beautifully, he's better than a private tutor, did you notice his teeth? I've grown rather fond of Sello."

"So I see," Fred said sourly.

"I didn't think I would. Sometimes it's nice to be surprised. Well, if we're in business with him, we may as well like him."

At this point Fred broke out with a long speech, including a series of passionate rhetorical questions, influenced both by the style of French polemics and the style of ordinary Iowa inter-spouse nagging. Did Gretta really think that they were in business with him? Did she really believe that this film would come to anything? What on earth or in hell did his teeth have to do with it? Fred had only a few fillings himself. Did she really think that they were being treated fairly or were they being conned by an unholy left bank bum? Did . . . ?

"Well, it's only ten thousand francs," she said. "And what's so wrong if he does have nice teeth, poor man? And it's an *experience*. And don't keep saying Do-I-really at me. Really, Fred!"

He preferred to pass over these last irritable remarks. Irrelevance in Gretta was always a danger signal. The way she leaned against the word *experience* convinced him that she had mislaid her judgment for reasons which he disliked to consider. She was capable of malicious fun at the expense of the schoolteachers who came to Paris for "experience," and now she seemed to be using the same dodge herself. There needed to be an end to this experience, he decided, and so he told Gretta. It had something to do with mealtimes, Sello's breath, and her eagerness to feed the man— this he did not tell Gretta. He gave her joy of his conclusions in the matter, not his reasoning.

She listened to him with her head cocked to one side. "Well, I don't see any harm in what you say," she remarked. "If you don't believe in the miracle anymore, then of course try to get our money back. But don't worry about it, don't let it interfere with your digestion or your thesis. It isn't worth that much. And another thing, don't insult the poor man—"

"He isn't even a con man! A sponge!"

"I mean the poor unholy bum," she said.

In his dream that night Fred Stern found a dim, stooped, sallow creature climbing toward him, grinning, shoes screeching like devils. The man had become a haunt with teeth bright as threats in the dark of the strange city. Fred awoke huddled against his wife. He wanted to arouse her to talk with him, but he could not admit it. He tried to put his arms around her. She mumbled reproach at his proddings, turned heavily, slept on. When he fell asleep again, Sello stood patiently waiting in his dream. So sorry, mon vieux, the grinning cripple's face said, and the body climbed toward him.

These were the first words he spoke to his wife when he slipped, aching, out of their bed in the morning: "He thinks I'm just a dumb American."

"Who? Oh, the poor soul," she said. "That again. Him

again. Should I make eggs, a real American breakfast for you, Fred?"

"But he didn't say charity! He said investment! Sartre, Mauriac, Eric von Stroheim, who knows who else? I don't need to be sold like a stupid tourist!"

Fred went to Sello's room. It was eleven o'clock by the time he got there, but Sello was just finishing his dressing. There was now in operation a combine against sweet-smelling Sello. Because of the increasing summer heat, the heavy English tweed suit, the labor of lacing up his high leather boots, and the distance of the shower from the room, Sello had begun to smell strongly unlike a successful movie producer. He smelled like failure itself, angry, spiteful, and secretive.

Angry and spiteful he was, and secretively he smiled, when Fred explained his mission. Of course Monsieur Stern could withdraw his paltry investment. It meant nothing to Sello. He did not need a partner who lacked faith. Pah, he did not desire such a partner. Sello would merely have to find another man to take his share. (Fred omitted mention of the dozens of social expenses, drinks, meals, taxis.) Or perhaps, Sello mused aloud, he would simply buy out Monsieur Stern himself. It would mean making economies on his pension, but he would do it. Yes. Yes. Yes, that was it. In the meantime, could Fred help him down the stairs and into a cab? Business appointment. He knew someone who was a personal friend of Monsieur Rothschild's secretary. Excuse it, he was in a hurry; till soon, dear friend.

It became the steady ambition of Fred's life to get back the ten thousand francs. He took to resting poorly, rising early, cruelly bolting down his breakfast, leaving Gretta vague with sleep, and rushing over to find Sello still abed in his little furnished room. Fred sought the moral advantage of being dressed, but Sello did not seem to feel judged; he groaned, clopped his lips, and painfully arose. He complained of his artistic habit of sleeping late. Then he showed his teeth and asked, "But isn't it still very early?" Always affable, confident, fresh from a new encouragement from Eric von Stroheim, he always had an urgent reason for not returning the money at once. He also had immediate need of some small, infinitesimally small sum which no one could deny a friend. Suddenly caught again, bemused, yawning in midmorning, Fred gave him a few hundred francs, agreed to the delay, and went back wondering what to tell Gretta this time. Gretta herself was barely interested. She was learning to sew from an excellent seamstress. She no longer considered the money part of her plans. Her lack of concern and his too intense interest were, in different ways, accomplices to Sello.

The moviemaker, on the other hand, was cooling toward Fred. He still asked for small loans as before, but he seldom went into detail about his triumphs of planning, and the strangely white and healthy teeth were shown in smiles that had no legitimate cause. These meaningless smiles were gall to Fred—did they mean something? Without explanation, Sello gave him the sick yellow face, the glittering feverish eyes, the wet, badly-shaved cheeks, and the slightly panting breath. It was painful work to drag his two mutilated feet about the summer pavements of Paris. It turned out, however, that he sometimes visited Gretta when he knew that Fred would not be home. When Gretta mentioned this to Fred, he flew into a fury. There was no occasion for jealousy, of course. Gretta felt for Sello that peculiarly satisfying, peculiarly feminine emotion which is located someplace between sympathy and boredom. But Fred had reached the point of dreaming physical violence on the cripple; he hated him. When he recalled Sello's voice pronouncing the words "le film," speaking of "notre film" or "notre projet," he felt himself tottering as if he had run up a long flight of stairs, as if his feet were numbed and useless. *Feelm!* It was an obscene word.

And yet, when he met Sello, he fell into rituals of politeness. In the man's presence he believed that he had no right to anger. The man's effrontery was a close ersatz of dignity. True, Sello had tricked him, but he had also tricked himself, and all Europe was filled with stumbling scavengers like Sello. This was not logic. He simply could not yet prevent himself from giving Sello live credit for his injuries while in the presence of the wound.

On one unhappy visit, he had again come early enough to find the man still in bed. Sello lay under a tumbled heap of blankets. The room smelled of dust, old bread, close air, and Sello. The high twisted boots were standing empty by the bed, and on a chair nearby lay an alarm clock with a cracked lens, an uncorked bottle of medicine, and the three frazzled sheets of paper which Sello had apparently been studying once again before he fell asleep. "I think I have the summer grippe," Sello said. "I feel hot, then cold, then hot again. Would you happen to carry a cachet of aspirin in your pocket? Please look."

"No," said Fred Stern.

"Perhaps, so kind of you, the pharmacy down the street. . . ."

Fred did not move. He had rehearsed all his possibilities and planned the one to choose this time. "Today," he said, "is the day you promised to pay me. You said you would have the money today. *Today.*"

"If I can," Sello said, throwing aside the blankets. "I told you, I have a cold. A cold plus fever, not just a cold. A mere cold would not stop me, but the grippe, the summer grippe. . . ." He lay there watching Fred. Tentatively he tried his champion smile. "This week I have not been able to do all I planned." He rested a moment more on the bed, naked in his weakness, and then sat up and began to reach for his clothes. His dirty, unhealthy skin, his ugliness, his weakness itself seemed a threat to Fred. How could he have been manipulated by such a creature? There were long unshaved wet hairs flat against the underside of his jaw. Enough, enough, it was enough to make a man strike out murderously.

With an effort controlling his breathing, he decided to ask Sello a question about which he had been brooding during the long insomniac nights. It was just curiosity, he explained. (Gretta had slept undisturbed by his side.) Mere curiosity. To see their handwriting. Would Sello mind showing him the letters from Sartre, Mauriac, von Stroheim, the others who had promised their support of his project?

Not at all. With pleasure. Sello was delighted. His delight had an edge to it, however; he understood Monsieur Stern's motives. Shame, shame for vulgar suspiciousness, his freshening smile seemed to say. He sat on the edge of the bed in shorts and undershirt and reached under the mattress. He handed Fred the little sheaf of letters along with one of his old luminous smiles. He was delighted that the question had come up. He would never have thrust these so personal testimonials on an unwilling reader. He was happy; he rocked slightly on the edge of the bed; he contemplated his absent feet with cheerful disapproval.

Fred read the letters first with puzzlement, then frustration, and finally with a dizzying fury. The sense of the one from Francois Mauriac was: I will not oppose your project, Monsieur Sello. Rather, I approve of the principle and wish you good chance. Similarly, Jean-Paul Sartre wrote: I wouldn't say no, M. Sello. I find it an excellent notion. And Eric von Stroheim declared: Best wishes for success. You have set a mighty task before you.

These were his intellectual backers, and this politeness the extent of their backing! Fred finished reading and looked up to find Sello smiling and nodding, I-told-you-so saying. By now he was completely dressed in his tweed suit, only his mutilated feet hanging below the cuffs. He reached for the boots. He still wore a stocking cap to protect his head from drafts. "See? See?" he asked.

"*See?*" Fred echoed ferociously. "Of course I see. They favor your project the way I favor springtime! They don't say they'll do anything to help you, man. It's fraud! Fraud!"

"Fraudeur? Moi?" Sello asked in a very low voice, still smiling, as if asking information of some inner traffic control. The smile passed very quickly. He looked rapidly about the room and then at the naked purplish remnants of feet hanging below the brown tweed cuffs. His ankles seemed peculiarly slender, almost girlish. He bent, struggling to get his feet into socks, into boots, murmuring to himself, listening to his own voice and to Fred. In one dark moment he was moving from elation with the success of his enterprise into recognition that someone believed that nothing could come of it, that therefore nothing would come of it—and hatred of the agent of revelation. As he bent, moaning, to his boots, a tear trickled down the long yellow nose. He was having trouble getting the scraps of feet into place. Abruptly Fred Stern wanted to retreat, but did not know how or what else he could do.

"May I help you with that?" he asked.

Sello straightened up and dropped the boot. "No," he said. "No. No." He gave up trying to put on his shoes. He pushed himself to his feet, shouting, "No!" Toppling, trying horribly to balance himself on his purple stumps, he shrieked, "No, get out, get out!" and fell, flailing wildly, toward Fred Stern. Fred jumped into the hall. Sello fell heavily against the door and it went shut.

Fred stood listening in the hall until he heard Sello crawl back toward the bed.

A year later, back in Iowa, Fred received an envelope containing a thousand franc note. He wrote saying not to bother about the rest, but received no reply. About a month later another thousand franc bill arrived. Irregularly over the next two years the entire ten thousand francs were returned. With the last bill came a note, stating officially, "The debt is paid. Sello." He must have saved it from his pension, for of course the film was never made.

When the incident came up between Fred and his wife, he reminded her that there had never been an accounting of the small subsidiary loans. Sello had never returned their umbrella. Gretta answered little and suggested that he forget about it. As far as he was concerned, they could forget about all Europe now. He ended by deciding that the mistake had originated where bad trouble often begins. He had let Sello only partway into his heart.

What's Become of Your Creature?

A girl. A gay, pretty, and sullen girl, with full marks for both sweetness and cruelty. When he looked in her desk for cigarettes, there was a silken pile of panties folded like flowers in the drawer, perfumed like flowers, dizzying him with the joy of springtime. When she put on a pair of them, suddenly filling out the tiny petals of cloth in two paired buds, it was as if the sun had forced a flower into delicate Easter bloom. Oh he needed her, loved her, and so for honor to them both, let us tell the truth, as straight as the truth comes.

He taught one class at Western Reserve University just at the geological beginnings of the Allegheny Mountains in the city of Cleveland, Ohio—an abrupt slope after industrial plains. He told poetry students where Keats got his ideas (out of his head) and where Hart Crane got his (straight from his noodle). And why. And what therefore happened in the abstract line, "That is all we know on earth, and all we need to know." He, Frank Curtiss, about thirty, making a living one way and another, was very inspiring on the subject of eternal beauty and truth, urns, Popocatepetl, Sunday Morning Apples, etcetera; also very unhappily married.

Until Lenka, having registered late, entered both his class and his life with all those aforementioned desperately particular flowertime devotions. She seemed to have been bleached by centuries of the fierce cold Finnish sun—transparent skin showing blue veins on her forehead and pink capillaries on her cheeks, thick wisps of hair so blonde it was almost white, the bluest eyes with a brush of darkened lash above them and a savant use of crayon at the outer corners. She had a pouting mouth, she lazily and insolently strolled to her seat, putting on black shell glasses to examine *him,* she opened a frayed, thickly used spiral notebook. She turned out to be twenty-two years old and addicted to occasional efforts at gathering a bachelor's degree by evening classes.

During the first few meetings of the class, nothing much happened to Frank besides an exaggerated exaltation of commentary on:

> *But with the inundation of the eyes*
> *What rocky heart to water will not wear?*

Shakespeare was right: his heart dashed like water under her eyes. But he still had rocks in his head. Lenka stared at him, at a transparent, fidgety, too brilliantly nervous Mr. Curtiss, looked right through him with those enormous pale eyes, with that lipsticked mouth doing a lot of thinking about Frank Curtiss as he dissolved into foam and spray, with her vaguely pedantic heavy horn glasses being put on three or four times an hour. She bent her head to touch pencil to notebook, and smiled.

This did Frank Curtiss both harm and good at home. Good because it quickened his pulse, challenged his habitual faith that spring really must follow the dismal Cleveland winter under smoky, purple-gray, fouled industrial skies (at last the salted slush rustles into sewers, March scours the blue of heaven, sun tempts the folded leaves and forces open the bulbs in the gardens of the monkey house near University Circle); giving strength, it did him good in his private winter at home; and harm because it diminished his ability for loyal compromise in the hopeless bickerings, failures, discontents, silent starings over breakfast with his wife. Perhaps that was really harm and perhaps not.

Once Lenka smiled at him, for him, it seemed, for the first time. He had hurried through a late March snowfall and, swinging briefcase, wearing his old paratroop boots, dressed for the weather, there was a crust of white like a monk's cowl on his head. He brushed it off; light crash of snow to floor; meltings on his neck; wet hair flung back with impatient hand; Lenka smiled. He saw small white front teeth, very close, one of them just slightly wedged forward. *"What's become of your creature,"* Frank asked, *"in the transparent swirls/Where her heart plunged her?"*

"I left the book at home," complained a serious lady getting extra credit for her teaching certificate.

"Look on with Miss Kuwaila, please. *Jostled by the hurrying current* . . . This is about a trout. Now why does the trout, a mere fish—?" But he was confused, inspired, dizzied by the beauty of Lenka's wedged-forward tooth, and so said, "Let me give you the sound of the original. Que devient votre creature dans les orages transparents ou son coeur la precipita?"

The schoolteacher who had forgotten her book raised her hand as if she knew the answer. Turned out that she only wanted to declare that the lines lost a great deal in translation, so why bother? Jostled by the hurrying current, gravier ou balbutie la barque, her heart had plunged her to a compelling chauvinism about English language stuff, Americano-type sublimities.

Again Miss Kuwaila smiled! Lenka could be delighted! By regulation, of course, such a class included con-

ference time. Lenka wrote poetry and also what she called
—until he taught her better—"poetic prose." He forgave
her:

> *Love's wild beast, truth in the sword,*
> *Self-stabbing couple whom we isolate . . .*

And so on; ouch. Enough of that much-tamed beast, the
stainless steel sword which needs frequent sharpening, that
repetitious, myopic couple. Better she should dance, and
in fact, she danced. She made her living by teaching modern
dance to the children of Shaker Heights; training accounted
partly for the angle of her chin which meant pride to Frank
Curtiss (his wife was abysmally discouraged, querulous);
dancing and endowment accounted for the fine curve of calf
into knee, then tuck and dip, then high and healthy sweep
of behind. Don't forget ankle—slim it was. Don't forget
high-arched foot. Now take mind off leg. She wore honest
blouses, top button undone, second about to be, but she
was really reluctant at this moment to show him her poetry,
though Frank asked most sincerely (secretly relieved: he
was spoiled by much art, and even Lascivia, the midnight
angel of sweet lust herself, would have suffered if she wrote
verse-to-comb-the-libido-by or breathless doggerel or ran-
dom-focused Eliotic pretension). Lenka liked dancing,
however, she liked jazz, she liked jazz people in Cleveland
and hung around. "When I was sixteen I had long hair, I
pulled it back and they thought I was older. I sat in on my
first afterhours session when I was—no, fifteen, I think—
hair in a bun, dimestore earrings, very cool."

In music she liked Lennie Tristano, Thelonious Monk,
Miles Davis, and of course The Bird. Since Frank was igno-
rant in the matter, he only blinked to indicate piety. She
went as far out toward the commercial as admitting that
she could listen to Kai Winding, pass the time anyway, also
Bartók, Dessau, Carl Orff. No, she would never be caught

writing Eliot's last-gasp-of-Western-culture harangue or boyish Auden's plaint for Demo-Christian politics. Dylan Thomas was the great menace to a post-war adolescent who had gone to afterhours sessions with her copy of James Truslow Adams under her arm, revised 1948, new Questions for Study.

After the class, about 10 o'clock in the evening, Frank hurried straight home in the hope that some miracle had been worked in his absence, his wife had come to love him. Not this time. Another time? Hope had been his habit (flute music, dawn-rising, confidence that orange juice would always taste good); now duplicity also became his habit—he took coffee with Lenka before class in the early evening. They parted; they came to class separately and he called her Miss Kuwaila, though it was Lenka as they huddled warming over their coffee. She did not use his name.

After the first accidental meeting and invitation, they avoided meeting by design. They just went to the same little shop up the hill in Little Italy by accident at the same time, muttered greetings, sat down—soon stopped muttering. Slightly past the university zone, the privacy of this place cost them a brisk walk. Frank began gradually to feel that he was not a stick, a pruned twig, a failed romantic adolescent: he could be a successful romantic adolescent, meaning something to someone besides himself. He bounced on the balls of his feet as he swung back down the hill. Once an oddly exciting, disturbing event took place: she met him for coffee, they separated as usual, but she did not come to class. That was on a Tuesday. On Thursday he demanded, "What happened?"

"Oh, you know . . . Something came up."

She cocked her head, quizzical. *Say more, claim rights,* she seemed to be challenging him.

Jealousy meant private, most secret reassurance: he

felt a quick and unhabitual liveliness despite his wife. A roller-coaster thrill of dread and rising release: prickly sweat breaking out along his newly shaved jaw. *Felt!* He was jealous of the something which came up, but first she had met him anyway in Little Italy—invaded he was by rapid hurt and stubborn hope, by these things yearning toward a prideful chin, an awkward-graceful dancer's walk, her small, fresh-lipped mouth. He asked her to meet him for lunch the next day.

"Why not?" she asked. She opened her eyes very wide, stared briefly at the hat on the rack at the next booth, saw no reason why not. "Yes," she said.

Since they had always met at night, her daytime fragrance and colors astonished him, delighted—the rich blue within her pale skin, the lemon shadings of her hair, she smelled different—cologne rather than the lightly astringent perfume to which she had accustomed him. Lord knows he did not need novelty: it merely pitched him higher. With an effort he stopped fiddling, put his pen back in his pocket.

She told him first about her friends, local musicians, dancers, oddball types, and then cautiously, without the habit of confiding—subtle tribute to him—about her own life. She had made her way from a farm near Elyria, leaving her parents firmly behind; she had made her own life, her own living, since she was seventeen; she was, she supposed, "a permanent student—very treacherous—interested in too many things."

He smiled tolerantly. The jitters let up. "You're rather young to worry about it. Why should you feel out of place in school? You're just at the age when the mob graduates."

"I feel older, Frank," she said.

It was the first time she had used his name. Like a spill of warm honey on his tongue—*Lenka,* he wanted to say. It was the first certainty that her little stirrings under the table as they drank coffee, her brusque, bumping, bumping motions against him when they walked, were absolutely not accident. Gravity brought them colliding together, brushing, touching away. After class he told her he was keeping that book for her—please come along. He had an office and a key to the building, which was dark, almost empty at this hour. They entered, they went down the hall without lighting, he shut the door to his office, he still did not need light. April. Night birds sleepily twittering in the tree at the window. He turned, she turned, they kissed.

His heart thumped like a fish on a drum. Even through the coats they both were wearing she could feel his heart. She laughed, low and thrilled; she was perfectly at ease, his teacher now; she put her hand over his heart on the coat as if to catch the fish and squeeze it in her fingers. "You're *frightened!*" she said, and more gently, "Don't be."

"I never kissed," he said, "anyone else . . . I mean since I was married."

She put her face up to his, pressing her hand against his heart through the coat. Again her mouth asked his to search it while she held up his heart, calmed it.

"But you know," she said.

It is not as if they let their clothes fall and made love then and there, with muffled cries, on the dusty floor of an overheated college office at night, hastily plucking at each other, anguished, grappling, tender, thrusting, greedy. No. She was not that sort of girl. She insisted that first they go for a walk outside in the spring evening. The thumping fish of his heart was eased.

From fresh air, from deep breathing of budded April trees and crisp thickly tended grass, out of silent strolling by Lenka's side at night, he felt eased and content. Now they did not need to speak. They returned to his office. She was *that* kind of girl, intelligent and purposeful. The building was deserted, and anyway, the watchman, who liked to sit on his stool and contemplate his arthritis, never bothered faculty members working late. But after locking the door, Lenka also leaned a chair against the knob in case some joker came along with a pass key. She wanted no interrupting fantasies for that first time. Playful, delighted, breathless, but thinking hard.

*   *   *

Frank Curtiss found his late return home that night surprisingly uncomplicated. His wife assumed that he had merely taken a couple of drinks. No marks showed, no teeth, bruise, or joy interrupted his wife's dulled recognition of him. In fact, his controlled elation, his satisfaction and triumph, brought the unpredicted bonus of an immediate easing of his trouble at home. Thanks to Lenka, his wife did not grate his own edginess; she too climbed off the razor blade on which they had been sitting in slashed togetherness. His own rebirth seemed to provide a fresh resource for both of them. Since he was able to put up with her, his wife let up on him for a time. Success to the successful, he thought, ease to the easeful! How beautiful to the mind is the Christian ethic, and how helpless before the fact of a struggling soul! Far from inheriting the earth, the meek get only muck. Stunned by time, the lamb trots where it's pushed, sheepishly.

Inconsistent as the mind of a lover, however, it turned out that unsheepish Lenka, that creature of brave yielding beauty, also had her troubles. Frank was not accustomed to the calm and cool varieties of wildness. At twenty she had been sent to Europe to have her baby—"a public man" was all she would say about the father; Frank found the remark cryptic, unyielding. She had refused an abortion, but in Europe she had sickened, the baby had been taken from her dead—"I saw it, he looked alive, I didn't believe the doctor, I screamed and screamed and they put me to sleep again"; and now she could never have a child. This, she understood herself, had something to do with the intensity of dance study, poetry study, art chasing of several sorts.

Cunning and pity filled Frank's heart. Once more he suffered that wild thumping, as if the heart might crunch his ribs. This time Lenka did not notice; she was telling the truth about how it was before she knew him, and so his heart's labor could not now concern her. "I'll miss it more later," she remarked. "I always wanted a child. I try not to think about it. At least I won't let myself take dogs, cats, parakeets, you know. I'll make it work for me. I do dance calisthenics when I feel bad." Then she folded her hands, fell silent, fluttered her thick pale lashes, was a girl again.

In Frank's heart cunning and pity. Pity for this troubled lovely creature who looked so pure and innocent, who surely was. Cunning because he need never worry about pregnancy. (This had bothered him. He suffered the usual fears of retribution.) "Lenka dearest," he said.

"That's all right. No need to feel anything. Want to see how I can stand with my foot higher than my head?"

They were in her room. Confused by confession he too had talked about trouble in love. He got up to cross the lamplit space for a cigarette; then it was that he opened her drawer as she watched, in unconscious confirmation of intimacy, and saw the sheaves of tiny folded panties; no cigarettes in that drawer; naked, he started across the room again, and caught her eyes on him, and the pity and the cunning and the pride at his ease and at her watching his recently slimmed middle (surprise! he was just strolling naked here) and her own curled loving body part under the sheets, all these matters were brought together; her eyes shut, her teeth showed as he rapidly returned to her; per-

haps she smiled because she remembered his timid and boyish heart's pounding of a few weeks before; now he
brazenly strolled, sprang flopping, laughing across the bed.
They cleaved together.

* * *

Their meetings became more purposeful, deeper in
pleasure and trouble. Once he waited fifteen minutes in the
corner of the park which, by May, was their property forever. He was worried; time problems of married men. Then
he heard her sandals slapping the pavement, she was running, he saw her, *running;* she stopped abashed before him,
blushing, murmuring, "I was afraid you wouldn't wait." He
took her in his arms in the fading afternoon light, he kissed
away the little beads of perspiration on her upper lip. They
stood kissing, leaning, making passionate walking steps
against each other, that vain effort to disappear into each
other's bodies. He smelled her sweetness and heat and
wanted to sink his arm into her back, stroking the curve,
the yearning and folding into him.

But he saw his watch as he kissed her. "Later," he said.
"Stay home. I'll come by your place."

"Oh promise, Frank."

"Of course. Don't worry. I'll manage."

It was not so easy. When he got home he found his
wife worn and jittery, their child had an upset stomach:
"Four times this afternoon," his wife said. But it was the
heat, four wasn't too terribly many, she had given him par-
egoric and Kaopectate already. No, what was on her mind
was a telephone call, an anonymous warning: "Do you
want to know where to find your husband at this minute?"
Nothing more; just that and click.

"Students," Frank said, his heart sinking. "You deal
with crackpots at a city institution, especially evening

classes. Happens to everybody. Remember when Mel Bargin had that siege of letters?"

She was convinced, or worn out, or didn't care. Anyway, he was home in time for supper. They ate the silent meal of too many quarrels and the abandonment of hope. Frank knew that he would have to wait until she fell asleep before he took his habitual long walk.

She slept; he walked. Lenka lived on the bottom floor of a converted mansion. He peeked through the window. She had set up an easel and had been working in charcoal, a lamp was on, but she lay breathing gently across the bed, fully dressed, even shoes, the garter belt showed under the sprawled, slipped skirt. He tapped at the window. It was after midnight and the street deserted. She got up blinking, pouting, peered out to him: and oh then her beautiful smile on her beautiful pout and she opened the window.

Later he warned her of spies, his enemies or hers, most likely hers. She frowned, turned tense and worried—that was why he had waited to tell her. She admitted that she was the sort of girl who might have vengeful suitors lurking about. Covertly thrilled, forbidding this excitement, Frank rolled over and faced the window: Could someone have peeked at them under the drawn shade? She sighed. "Maybe it's my fault," she suggested, "breaking all the rules."

"Oh no!" And he thought: it's I who break the rules, crawling through a window for love like a burglar, and I hold on to my son and hope for my wife when it's hopeless.

"I guess both of us," she admitted softly, fairly.

But now they would have to be very careful. Frank could not be seen with her; they met in the park, in far corners of the city, or, most of the time, simply in her room. They sketched each other; they smoked, read, told each other stories; they made love. Frank found himself wanting to talk about his son, but bit his tongue. Self-conscious, self-judging. "Don't be frightened," she said more than once. Although almost ten years older than Lenka, he came to think of her as wise and anciently mysterious within the desperate yearning gift of herself, the will to be his of her open and lovely body. She had the patience of confident love.

Despite the secret isolation of their life together, the close confinement to odd places, then to her room, then, toward the end of the spring, in a rising pitch of indulgence and claim, to her bed, he had never considered his rivals. She had no right to be jealous of his wife; he had no right to think of Lenka away from him with others. The telephone call to his wife brought the others to mind. He asked questions; she was reticent, unspecific. A few words about her mother and father, the farm, a brother who worked it; vagueness about her friends—he knew none of them— though sometimes a knock would come at the door and they would lie still, listening to the repeated knock, the slow steps away, the outer door slamming. He was marvelously flattered by her refusal to answer the telephone. Their time together was simply theirs. Though girlishly hurt that he would go no place with her, she understood. She proposed a backroom jazz session on the West Side where he could not possibly meet anyone who knew him. He was too cautious. He tried to complete his knowledge of her by looking up her records under camouflage of his faculty credentials. Greedily he studied her previous addresses, the maiden name of her mother, full of K's, the solemn statement she had made on her first application. Her I.Q. score was extraordinarily high; this reassured him because he wondered if she had simply cast a spell over him—to some questions she merely answered with a stare. No, she was a human girl creature, not a witch. She had lazy grades, brilliant sometimes, sometimes mediocre. She was careful about picking up graduation credits. He felt silly when he handed her folder back to the secretary. "Hm, hm, yes indeed. Very interesting. Thank you."

There is a time in every man's life when he can do anything. It was this time in the life of Frank Curtiss. Despair with his wife had given up to deep gratification with a beautiful girl; he even did better at home; matters cooled and calmed; his work went well; he hardly needed sleep and did not suffer his usual rose fever during the spring he knew Lenka. No sniffles, no pink eyes. Expanded breathing, sharp sight. Of the occasional headache of fatigue and excess he was cured by the touch of her hand, her welcome when he came smiling, showing teeth, through her window. Slipping through, welcomed, he made love to her with the heavily settled industrial window grit still on his hands until it mingled with the secretions of love and summer—paste, caresses, perfume. Later he wrung his hands in soap, hot water, soap again, then cold water, in a gesture like expiation, rinsing away her smells, but soon became aware that this was not guilt—he found the scrubbing and splashing very fine to his summery blood. He did not think of the future; he merely lived and believed himself in love, in a kind of love, surprised by love's surprises, acquiescing.

Since he adored his son, whom we leave absent from this history, he could not imagine dissolving his home; but he thought: *I'll wait, I'll see. In the meantime, I'll ride.* Things were going too well to be interrupted by dreams of perfection. There is no perfection, anyway, in an imperfect world (philosophy of adultery); the unhappy husband has the right to save himself (more philosophy for adulterers); life on earth means a quest for the absolute, compromise, violation, tribute, delight in apples, worms, indigestion, purest love, gossip, peeking apes, donkeys, creeps, squares (still more philosophy, poetry, grand hysteria); *enough!*

thought Frank Curtiss. He had a son, Lenka could give him no child, and anyway he *had* a son. One last time, curled against him, Lenka murmured their password, "Don't be frightened, darling."

He began to laugh in the easy sprawl of his body, remembering the foolish creature he had recently been. "Frightened?" he asked, remembering mightily. Once weak and strict, now he floated down the river, agile, hale and strong. Or so Frank Curtiss seemed to Frank Curtiss. And he laughed, prospering, holding her away and cupping her gratified breasts which had changed, just as his body had, during the past months. "But I'm not frightened any more," he said.

He stopped laughing and very seriously, solemnly, thanked her for saving his life.

"I make you happy, don't I?" she asked. She had the sort of pale and delicate skin which flames at the first touch of a man's beard. With her downcast eyes, it gave her a perpetually astonished blush as they said goodbye. "Don't I make you happy, Frank? Oh I do!"

She did; the god of judgment had become an angel of mercy—had sent unmerited joy. No, he decided, everyone deserves to be able to carry a tune, find that wanton flush on a girl's cheeks, recall sweet love for a moment in the morning before going about the work of the day. "Oh I do love making you happy,"—she couldn't say it enough. He promised that it was the final truth and she should know it. Flowers, rebirth, ripening gourds, purity of delight.

It was therefore a considerable surprise to go home later and find a new lock on the door, a note from his wife warning him not to try to enter, and his clothes thrown into hampers on the porch. It shocked him that she had not even bothered to put out a suitcase for his use. In this numbed state he telephoned her from the gas station at the corner.

It turned out that she had prepared rather carefully. She had both keys to their car in her possession and advised him to take a taxi someplace, away. She suggested that he use the opportunity to spend a whole night with Lenka Kuwaila and see how he liked it. She remarked that she did not care to speak with him at all and that further discussions could be held through the intermediary of her lawyer. She gave him the lawyer's name and told him to look up the number himself. She paused before saying goodbye and added, "I waited until you finished final exams and you won't have to face so many people over the summer. I thought that was pretty considerate of me." She had also left about five dollars in their joint checking account.

He spent the night in confusion at a friend's house. For the first time he felt exhausted by his secret lovemaking with Lenka; he had left her with her smell still on his hands and come back to this news; there was an ache in his loins and a triangle of lead in his belly. It turned out that his wife had exact information about his connection with Lenka, dates and times and other, terribly intimate details. When her lawyer confronted him, he dully submitted, denied nothing, agreed to everything. Greater than the shock of his wife's action was his shock about the letters she had received. Lenka had simply recounted everything in tormenting detail, with obscene precision. He felt a lingering tenderness for his wife because of the jealousy she must have suffered, but whatever this secret suffering, it had now congealed to a buzzing, busy hatred and cold vengefulness which deprived him even of his sympathy for her. He was stripped bare.

Lenka left for New York without seeing him after his anguished telephone call to her: "Why? Why? Why did you have to do it that way, Lenka? Can't you see how it destroys everything between us, even the past?"

"I don't care about memories. What's over means nothing. Over. You didn't want to do more than crawl through my window a couple times a week—"

"But to write to her like that—what meant—how—"

"You cared more about a cold bitch than you cared for me. Just because you had a child."

"Why, why?"

She hung up on him.

He stood shrugging at the telephone. Women were hanging up on him all over the world. He was disconnected. Maybe it was really he, Frank Curtiss, they were hanging up on. He went on shrugging; it was a nervous twitch, a shaking-off-the-burdens tic.

Here we need not detail the prolonged anguish of a divorce when there is a child, when there has been a habit of suffering and also some distant memory of joy (this only increases bitterness and determination to hurt). He survived in a rapture of numbness, like a mouse in a paw. His wife tried to set rules about visiting their child; he raged and cursed her. But finally he saw her coolly from a distance, he saw her as impossible, for years she had been a stepwife to him. He was grateful to Lenka for the brutal surgery she had performed; the operation was bloody, but the patient survived. Things were arranged about his boy; he found a new job; he went to New York; a year passed. Where it went, he did not know, but now he considered himself a brilliantly wise twenty-two years old. He had been twenty-one when he married; the next years were poisoned by enough misery so that he wanted to leave them out; his year of liberation made him now twenty-two. This was mainly a joke, and he had a fresh sprout of gray hair in his thick cropped black thatch, but the world seemed to be on his side once more.

He was hungry, he ate, he had enough money to invite girls for dinner, he ate voraciously, explaining everything, enticing them on long walks through New York, exciting them with his tourist's freshness of joy in the great city. He found a girl to join him in biting into an apple, sucking the sweet juice of it at dawn, finally kissing in good friendship and turning on their sides to sleep. Life went on with the freshness of the busy mornings and the hesitating nightfalls of Manhattan. He found a good job writing coy letters for a chain of magazines, the sort that are printed to look as if they are typed: "You may have neglected to open our first bill. We know that you are a busy and successful man, but remember! The workman is worthy of his hire! And we here at *Daytime Magazine* consider our publication . . ." He had no automobile because of the responsibilities of parking, but could afford taxis (the workman was worthy of his hire). He felt free. He didn't even have a cold for two years after he separated from his wife: every change seemed to cure him of something. He threw away his bottle of aspirins. His married vision of himself as a heavy, shaggy, weary buffalo, head low and muzzle hurt, gave way to another image—he was lean, his posture was good, he was an agile bucko. When his former wife remarried, his last vestige of guilt disappeared. Free, free. He played badminton twice a week with a French girl who pronounced it "badd-ming-tonn." Free and agile. "I'd never have matured otherwise," he solemnly told his friend.

"You theenk too motch," she answered.

So finally he decided to telephone Lenka, though his little French friend advised him that this was as bad as thinking. Just curiosity about how she was making out, he promised himself. ("Don't be frightened, darling . . ." And how she had buttered toast for him, making coffee on a hot-plate. And the smell of her perfume when she had run toward him in the park, breathless at being late. "I make you happy, don't I?")

But after he told her how long he had been in New
York, she said that she was not interested in seeing him.

"I held a grudge, you can understand that," he said.
"I still think you were very wrong, but I'm grateful anyway.
It worked out for the best."

"And it's over," she said. She told him that she had an
official friend, a drummer with a well-known advanced
jazz combo. She named him with pride. Frank asked later
and discovered that her friend was known as "the Unholy
Wazuli"—a gifted wildman with two breakdowns and a
conviction for possession of heroin in his curriculum vitae.
He claimed to blow finer drum under the hooves of horse,
but others disputed the argument.

Disturbed by her refusal to see him, faintly jealous of
the Unholy Wazuli, Frank bothered the friend who knew
her. "Why do you want to mess with her more? She must
be crazy."

"Yes, but I just want to talk with her—"

"To do what she did to you is plain nutty, pal."

"Yes, nutty, sure. But she cared for me." This is very
important to all men, that a lovely girl cares, and especially
an unhappily married man will forgive anything for love,
even a good dose of nuttiness. The man unhappy in marriage may seem merely somber, but he is also crazy. Frank
had believed that Lenka cared for him.

Now, however, Frank was enjoying non-conjugal bliss
in New York, and although a certain sideways questioning
look while buttering toast meant girl to him, and a certain
springtime slap of sandals on the pavement made his breath
catch hard, his life went on without much thought of Lenka.
One spring day, now two years after he had first met her,
he was strolling through Washington Square when he saw a
girl walking ahead and he thought first of toast, and then,
recognizing the tilt of her walk, yes, this time it really was

Lenka. He had an hour before dinner. Without considering it further, he ran up to her, first closely studying her because he did not trust himself to see anything but her eyes when her eyes met his. She was still very pretty, but she showed early aging, a new fleshiness at her upper arms and a slight thickening of the legs, and when he said, "Hello, Lenka," and she turned, he saw the fine lines about her pale eyes.

"Well hello, Frank."

She waited coolly to see if he were merely greeting her. Before he lost himself in her, the thought came that she was paying the price for her ancient fragility, which had given her an almost adolescent grace: now she bore some unhealthy weight; she looked ten years older already. "You want to have some coffee?"

"Well, you know. No man, no."

"What then?"

She smiled, showing her fine teeth, and consciously imitated someone else: "If I could have my druthers, I'd druther have a drink."

"Sure, let's go." And he hurried her by the arm. He was shocked because one of her front teeth was missing, and it gave the smile a wild blackness, again breaking the seamless dancer's grace which he remembered.

They talked; she recited as if he were an elocution teacher and she were doing her lesson. She was still with her Unholy Wazuli. He had cut a great record, more than one, but you know, people put him down. Hard to get the gig when people put you down. The nut on his habit was fifteen dollars a day now. He couldn't make it by himself *no* way. It's no ball, a habit—people on the outside don't dig one bit—it's something to do—*you* know.

He did not know. Very squarely he asked. "Tell me what's bothering you, Lenka."

"A nut of fifteen a day."

"Explain."

"Well, you know . . ." Her man wanted her to work to support his habit.

"What kind of work?"

She shrugged. "Well, you know, man."

He was deeply shocked. "Don't! Please don't!" he gasped, shouted. He drew back from his own excitement, ashamed at how it might look, and tried to be smart, a man of the world, her way, and at the same time trying to make her feel his way about it. He said, "Lenka, promise. You probably think I'm still mad at you—"

"You want to put me down, man."

"I don't any more, Lenka. It's over now, past."

She smiled, showing the black place in her teeth. It was what she had said. What's over is over. What happens last night is dead.

"OK. But I still care about you, Lenka. Promise you won't do that? God! To buy heroin!"

"It's usually why girls do it," she said. "I know lots of girls, that's how they join up—"

"Promise!"

"That's how they get in The Life."

"Promise you won't!"

She only shrugged and thanked him for the drink. He asked if she would like to meet him again soon. She smiled thinly and said, well, her friend was jealous. He remarked that this jealousy did not seem to go with the work he had in mind for her. "Well," she said, "you know."

Manhattan is very large, but sometimes far galaxies engage, interlock. Frank was not certain how it happened: he found himself with friends in the jazz world. The hipster bit, as they said, was very big that year. He knew his way around. The Wazuli was a famous character, "a crazy big talent, impossible," Larry Arnold, an editor of *Down Beat*, told him. They also knew about Lenka, though all they said was, "Cute. Unholy's chick." Was she with him, Frank wondered, confiding, under his conditions? Larry explained, "It ain't the old days, mon. America has really changed in this here regard—you dig like Riesman, Kinsey, Fromm, those cats? A girl can't just patrol, just sell the basic product. Sex and air are but I mean *free,* mon. It's the specialties pays off now. When you're tired of air, you want to be gassed."

Frank was thinking: she called it The Life.

"She's just an unusually stacked chick is all I meant," Larry said out of pity for his friend's troubled frown. He took the black line between the eyes for jealousy, when everyone but a hipster knows that jealousy is a butt in the stomach and bile in the cheeks. "Besides, I got no news of her—just the Wazuli's chick is all I hear, and he's banned from Manhattan clubs. Tried to play the Embers stoned out of his head. Park Department, Hon. Robert Moses-san, Commissioner-san, picked him up for stepping on the grass. Joke. Yok yok. Whyncha laugh with me, Mister Shelley?"

Frank fought down his imagination of her cool pale dancer's beauty being used in that way, the Finnish farm girl from Ohio with the I.Q. of 155 . . . He wondered if she had taken to horse herself. Someone who seemed to notice better than most said that there was no space in her teeth. She must have had money to get it fixed. She had seemed to lack vanity about it (and he recalled the confident disorder of her closet in Cleveland, the smell of her perfume and the bending body, dressing with her back to the mirror on the door).

Another year passed. Frank rarely thought of Lenka, though she was a part of his blood, his suspicions, and his tenderness with girls, and when he found himself liking a girl, he found himself reminded of Lenka's ways—tilted

chin, curve of back, lazy easy dancer's walk. He now found
one whom he liked very much and he was about to try
marriage again, with hope. Settled in New York, his telephone number was in the book. And Lenka looked it up
and called.

She asked if he would meet her. It was important. He
agreed and named places, but to each she said, "No, not
there. I don't make that scene." Finally she said, "Home all
afternoon."

He was embarrassed. "Look, I'd rather meet you someplace else. How about under the Washington Square arch?"

"Well Christ Almighty," she said. Paused. "Well, all
right."

They met. She gave him a wan smile. She was not
wearing lipstick; he had forgotten how her paleness needed
the blatant red of lipstick, except when she tanned in June.
But the tooth had been expertly replaced, and apart from a
peculiar stiffness of her face, the cautiousness of fatigue, she
was a girl to make men turn around, shake their heads, and
ask themselves if maybe. They strolled; she talked vaguely
of having broken with the Wazuli—"and all that scene, you
know, man"—and trying to write.

"How are you making a living?"

"I said I *write,* man."

"You're publishing things? What?"

"I wrote that article on hypnotism, you know." (He
did not know—how could he?) "You know I left it there
at that magazine. I never read the magazine so how should
I know what they did with it?"

At last, more and more uneasy, wanting to call his girl,
thinking they should set the date for soon, he demanded
bluntly, "I didn't think you really wanted to see me. What's
on your mind?"

"I got these letters from your wife," she said.

"What? My *wife?* You mean my former. You mean she *wrote* to you? Lately?"

"Yes, sure, didn't she tell you?"

This exasperated Frank. Since he went frequently to Cleveland to see his boy, he had frequently to see his former wife and he hoped for level dealings with her after all this time. He didn't like the idea of pen-pal exchanges between Lenka and her, those two distant chums.

"I'm worried about her," Lenka was saying. "That's why I thought you should pick up on these letters, see. You should fall up and look them over, you think?"

Yes, he thought. They walked across to her apartment on Christopher Street, a hall smelling of cat and a lazy custodian, mailboxes unmarked and flapping open, the locks broken. Lenka lived on the top floor. "I like air," she said vaguely, "I don't mind the walk up." She liked air, but the windows were shut and there was a choke of attic heat, close, hot, unclean. She called the place her pad and she actually had one—a thin mattress on the floor, with a cotton spread covering it, fresh from the laundromat but unironed, and orangish foamrubber fat peeking at one corner. He remembered once making love to her and the sudden shock of four paws, a jealous cat leaping onto his back. She still had cats, but different ones, a pair of kittens. He wondered if the Unholy Wazuli and the temporary visitors had minded the cats. Lenka was moving against him, putting her head against his chest, arms limp, not moving now.

Frank stepped away. "Those letters."

Pouting, she went to a cardtable and looked through a pile of papers, old copies of the *Times, Down Beat, Variety,* a row of paperback books leaning against the wall. A split-spined copy of *Zen Archery* had a letter marking her place, but Frank would have recognized the handwriting. This was Lenka's hand—an unmailed letter.

She shrugged. "I guess I threw them away. I kept them around, but I was cleaning up . . ."

He wanted to laugh at the trivial, stupid, insane lie. Of course there were no letters: his former wife was as done with him as he was done with her. What possible advantage could Lenka gain in making a fool of him like this?

She may have invented a foolish lie, but she recognized the glare of contempt on his face, and in her life of now a quarter of a century, she had learned only one way to answer the judgment of men. She slid against him, on her face a mixture of coyness and dread, a flirtatious halfsmile, a slinking catlike practiced leaning against him, and her eyes filled with tears as she shut them, tears balancing on the wetted lashes, slipping down her cheeks. "Frank," she said haltingly. "I stopped remembering for a long time, I don't know, things were difficult, I thought you were too angry . . . But I've been remembering . . . That's why . . . Forgive . . ."

He put his arms around her, held her to him, but with confusion more than either amorousness or tenderness. He stretched, feeling her light hair against his chin, looking out over the small hot gray-and-brown room. There was a pile of 45-speed records: jazz. Probably the Wazuli's legacy. She lay her head against his chest and waited, but waited cunningly, her body rising and falling with exaggerated breath, fitting itself against his. He felt desire for her. Then he thought of the letters she had written to his wife, and the letters she had just now lied about, and suddenly, as he held her, she had turned her head up and wanted to be kissed, and his most vivid fantasy was this one: *She was unclean.* His uncurbed dread ran toward a muddle—deceit, illness, secret pity, slime, retribution. Not knowing what he feared, he thought only: filth, cunning, running filth, blotches, sores. Because he could not bear her sorrows, he thought:

Deceit and cunning and disease! Her lips came open, slightly wetted, and her breathing stirred imperatively on his face. She was rubbing up against him, trying to make him kiss her, because it was another trick, like writing to his wife, like telling him so many lies; yet as before in Cleveland, she really wanted someone, wanted him, wanted the good comfort of love; and she also wanted to be kissed because she had a disease to give him.

He pulled away before their mouths touched; her nails clawed along his arm, shredding skin; he fled, hearing her sobs at the open door as he careened down the infected stairs and onto the free air of the street.

This was already long past the end, of course. But logic does not apply when a needful man has received love —even false comfort, false love. One more time, with the permission of his new wife, Frank telephoned to find out— what? How she was. He received the crisp mechanical answer: "The number you have called is not a working number. This is a recorded announcement. The number you have called is not a working number. This is a recorded . . ."

It would be useless to go to her apartment, but he went anyway, and then to the post office; but no place, no way, was he able to find a forwarding address. She was gone. Finally she had disappeared from his earth.

His wife, who was now pregnant, shrugged with a certain amount of satisfaction and relief. He kissed her, grateful because she had been easy on him about Lenka. "But she did me a favor, Frank!"—the sweet logic of the practical wife. "Otherwise you might still be in Cleveland. Rub my back, will you? No, just hold me."

On the side of life, he was stroking and comforting this dear person who carried his child; she lay her head against his shoulder with a worn, anxious smile; there were only a few more weeks to wait. But as he touched his lips to her hair, lightly moved his lips on her forehead, he could hear the angel on the other side of oblivion questioning that other girl, who bore no mark or sign of him: "Lenka Kuwaila, what about Frank Curtiss?"

And she rendered her verdict: "Well, you know . . ."

Love and Like

He got to Cleveland rather late, telephoned his wife from the terminal, and asked if he could see their children early the next morning. She seemed easy and friendly and said sure thing, of course, why not? He sighed when they hung up and he stared at the telephone. Maybe his absence really could work to level things between them.

Why not? as she said. They had loved each other for ten years, or rather, for a part of those ten years impossible now to calculate. He remained sitting in the telephone booth. He was a young man with a thin, almost boyish body and a large head, heavily muscled at the jaw. On his face he wore the haunted, eaten look of a man whose accomplice has betrayed him. Whether his accomplice was his former wife or his conscience was not yet clear to him. Conscience was still talking to his wife: We didn't make it, kid! And he was remembering one of their last quarrels before they gave up, when he said, "We'll try! We'll try!" And paining badly with those fragments of the past, he heard again her quiet reviving words: "We'll try, darling."

If they had finally made out, it would all have been remembered as the progress and process of love; with failure it could seem all bad; he was determined to hold in retrospect to a mixed verdict—some pretty, some unpretty, and nevertheless the long Sunday afternoon habit of lovemaking spoke for a true intimacy. The hardest, most essential responsibility to a dead marriage is to preserve the ripe strength it once had. Must have had, must have! So without love now, if that's the way it was, why couldn't they simply like each other for the rest of time? Not just for the sake of the children. For the sake of themselves and what they had become through their marriage.

All this was a resolution. Done.

Then he fished for another dime in his pocket and called Sally. Okay, it was late, but wasn't she glad to hear his voice? She laughed sleepily and asked him how he could doubt it. She was sleepy was all. She had been thinking of him. All right then, dreaming. He could come right up— would it take twenty minutes? For splashing some cold water and getting good and waked and dressed.

"Don't bother," he said, and even in the telephone booth, under the falsification of wires and electricity, the laughter brought her back to him with all her soft, warm childlike sleepiness amid the fragrant bedclothes. Sally's face was devoted to laughter, especially the very blue, waiting-to-smile eyes—those eyes of a blue which could give him what a strong awakening on a morning in the country gives, courage and appetite and great belief in the future. The morning he left, she had made breakfast for him, hotcakes with butter, sweet syrup, three kinds of jam— mostly he remembered the sweetness and much melted butter. With his mouth stuffed, he shook his finger to warn her that he had something to say as soon as he could swallow.

"What's the matter, darling?"

"Oh it's good! It's so good, Sally!"

And the lashes fell over the brave summersky eyes. She was timid despite her laughter's deep abandon. "Then why do you have to leave Cleveland?" she had asked. The question cost her heavily. Without me? her paleness said. The unsmiling blue eyes were trying to force his reply: Then why don't we . . .?

Unspoken questions were, as always, the ones he felt he had to answer and precisely could not. Therefore he had spoken in a tone of stubborn exasperation. "Because my wife lives here. Because it's too soon. Because I have to." He reached across the debris of eating to touch her more gently. If he could tell her, he would. "Now, with you here, Sally, it's all right. Right now. But I can't tell you about my wife and what she did to me. What she does! What she still does!" he cried out abruptly. His heart was pounding and the good of the breakfast was gone. "And the children —I still can't imagine any other life than being their father—"

She was looking at his hand on hers with a curious withdrawn attention.

He said quietly, "Maybe I just haven't found the way to love them without loving their mother. Maybe that's it and there is a way."

His wife made him need Sally; if only she could free him entirely for Sally! This way, entangling him in her wrath, she hardly let him know who Sally was. He had to find her in a long history in which she had no part, past a furious, gyring woman, after outrage and love gripping each other as do alloyed metals under heat and pressure. Let Sally make him pure—as he never was—let Sally make herself felt!

But her eyes were answering nothing, were asking him: And why can't we? He realized that she had not heard him at all. Everyone is sometimes made deaf by intentions. He might as well have been brutal: And I just don't know about you, either, dollface. Seems as how I met you someplace before.

Now he shrugged and felt the damp shirt moving on his back. Every time he said the word "wife" she should interrupt and say, "*Former* wife." Shaper to Shaper—*over,* he decided, ferociously willing it as if he were passing a message by radio and the battlefield made communication difficult: *Over!* He had just finished writing a technical manual on the care and operation of a new, improved, long-range walkie-talkie. In Cleveland he had worked for General Electric on instructions for the installation of intercoms in language any mechanic could understand; in the identical off-white New York office to which he had arranged a transfer, under the same Armstrong Cork soundproofing, with thousands of little holes conking, stunning every whisper of distraction, he had labored with a Signal Corps semantics expert on further explanations of how to keep contact open under conditions of stress. "Limited contact under conditions of vital stress . . . ." He was making mass poetry for five-stripe sergeants who don't like the word *war*. It was a career for a careful explainer. But now over to Dan Shaper, please!

Deciding: Condition of stress not total chaos if receiver flashes emergency transistor filters out static toward coded meaning (see Fig. 3). Put into heart's English. Also see resources of regret, hope, and desire for possible decoding toward good conscience.

2

At seven-thirty the next morning he was running up the stairway toward his daughters. The buzzer had admitted him; the door to the upstairs flat was open.

"Paula, honey!"

"Hello, Daddy. Mommy and Cynthia are still sleeping. I knew you were coming. I got up and took my own breakfast. Wheaties and prunes and a pickle. Mommy says I can eat what's on the bottom shelf of the fridge and that's where the pickle was. Hello, Daddy."

Exactly what he wanted always, this time Paula was a six-year old lady sitting on the couch. First she rang the buzzer to let him in, then she returned shyly to her place to wait for him.

"And I knew you would be coming back today because I counted the days," she said. "You said thirty. You promised." She was quivering with excitement beneath the formality with which she had vain hopes of hiding herself. A month is even longer in a child's life than in her father's. He took her in his arms and she said, "I'm *glad.*" Her eyelashes were wet when he kissed them.

"I'm glad to see you too, honeybear."

They whispered together gravely to keep from waking the rest of the house. He felt strong in his monthlong convalescence. He forgot that he had slept only the sleep of the recently divorced, that is, no sleep but that profitless, dream-jammed one of might-have-been and exhaustion. Paula gave him her news. Not only had she lost a tooth, but also the ragged edge of the new, grownup one had begun to appear. He looked and saw. At her command he appreciated it with his finger, too. They were interrupted by another child, running scared and barefoot to join the celebration, four-year-old Cynthia. Disappointed, Paula bravely permitted Cynthia to catch up with a minute of greeting.

Then he pulled them both onto the couch beside him, still bed-warm in their summer pajamas, and so were they three sitting when his wife came out. She had heard them, stayed a long time in the bathroom, and emerged only after satisfying herself that she was sweet and alert and nice to look at. He was very much aware also of how he looked to her with the two little ones wriggling close to him.

She smiled and said, "Hello, Dan." Her hair had been cut in a new fashion and fluffed out to make a soft frame for the delicate bones of her face. Her brow, finely marked by frown lines, seemed wider now, peacefully expectant. What happens to a young woman when she divorces? Aren't her eyes puffy in the morning any more? Where does the blue lymph go? Is she no longer stringy and dismayed after the first glimpse of herself in the bathroom mirror? Not this one. Dark, slender, and cool, she was mobilized for love again.

Shaper was pleased by her greeting and—with only a twinge of self-judging jealousy—by her appearance. He put it down to his credit that she was not ruined for the hope of love. His moving out of town had done them both good. Sally last night had started the visit auspiciously. Paula was a marvel and Cynthia a wonder. And now his wife was the decent human being he had almost always believed in.

"Yes, thanks," he said, and they all four had breakfast together, just like a family. Since the first years of their marriage, his wife had barely eaten in the morning, drinking black coffee and nibbling at dry toast and then rushing to the scales, but today she took an extra piece of toast and covered it with butter in order to show him that she could now enjoy food. Well, let her have that pleasure, he thought with a fine expansive sense of tolerance. They both watched the girls munching greedily, proving something to their parents.

Later, while the children played with their new toys, they sat together in the front room and talked, balancing coffee cups on their knees. "It's all right now," she said. "You did right to go away for a while. There were good things, weren't there, Dan?"

"I'm glad you remember."

"I do. I do." Her narrow face with its wide brow wore

a complex expression—frowning, tender, at peace. They
had shared and not shared. They had been satisfied, un-
satisfied. She had wanted, they had both wanted another
child; but (stiff white mouth and tense, silent staring out
the window) she had needed a guarantee that this time it
would be a boy. She had found a doctor in Miami with
fantastic notions about special diets, the power of raisins
and lima beans and times of the month—litmus paper, fever
charts, count the days—and a husband to be applied as an
agent when the alchemical and astrological signs say yes.
Desperate woman! Yet a man can grow to accept a partial
madness when it is the condition of the rational universe he
desires. Desperate husband! (Aren't many people super-
stitious? When she has her son, what difference by what
illusion she was comforted?) But one day he faces the obvious question: All right, there's a fifty-fifty chance, say.
And if it's not a boy? Kachoo—sneezing with boredom and
despair.

And if it's *not* a boy?

As always, his besetting flaw was the one of perverse
hope and pride—the crazy patience of the man who needs
love too much to take the necessary risk of losing it. When
this danger is not challenged, love and like both are
doomed. He had feared to compel his wife to follow his
lead. He would not submit to being dragged along by her
frantic jittering after happiness; she could not follow his
bone-tired, patience-ended assertions of will; for them it
had long been too late for all but knowledge, and perhaps
in love it is always too late for that. The terrible guilt which
he carried with him was a hope, not an understanding: Once
she might have been made to want what you want, if you
had pressed hard enough, and if you had said in time, No,
not that way! Follow me and come to yourself!

The enduring of wrong amounts to an acquiescence in

evil, a sin of active malignance which grew on the body of their marriage like a tumor and, like a tumor, sapped its strength to proliferate in this cruel organism, divorce. When the body is dead and all health irrelevant, only then will the cancer cease. In the meantime, every joy, every lively nerve, every vein of health must supply food for the fibrillar parasite. The dying creature curses its strong heart, its tuned body, because these prolong the agony. Each motive for happiness must be bled dry.

Shaper knew that he had not acted in time.

But finally he had said *no.*

NO!

Said no to lima beans and love by astrological suggestion—and maybe, kid, you're right about wanting to see Doctor Kasdan, he's supposed to be a good one—although he believed in that cure almost as little as he believed in the efficacy of lima beans to induce suckling boy babies instead of beautiful but incomplete girls.

A nightmare. Yet this was the intelligent, accomplished woman who could charm a stick into life. Seething and plausible. She took a cigarette from the box on the record cabinet, very sure of herself, very much the fresh young divorcee, and said, "Dan, I thought about you while you were away. We both lost. . . ."

"Yes, despite everything we've lost a great deal."

"We lost *control,*" she said firmly.

He felt rebuked, but it did not touch his reviving humor. Often she was bad, but sometimes she was steady and knew the way. She was right! He longed to regain this old sense of his wife's rightness. He needed it to go on from where he was.

"I don't blame you any more about that . . . that," she said. "It was wrong of me to be so . . . so. . . ."

This time he did not make the mistake of supplying her words. Perhaps she was testing him.

"So angry, nervous with you," she said. *"Judgmental,"*
—one of those damn labels again, he thought, but nodded
encouragingly. Warily she went on with a speech that
seemed almost rehearsed. He did not expect her to grant
him a confession, but he thought maybe she was making it
in her own way at last and that this could finally release
both of them: I was jealous, and not merely jealous, also
morbid and criminal and made furious by fantasies, until
you had to give me justice for them because you too demanded someone totally committed to you, because jealousy itself is an infidelity which takes a wife from her husband. . . . But she said instead (and who would she be if
she used his words? her own were good enough): "I think
I've learned something. We each learned, so it wasn't so
bad. We probably couldn't have married anyone else, or
anyone better, so why blame each other?"

"Right! We won't any more!"

She frowned and did not hear him. He felt her effort
not to slip down and down into the despair which had
driven him away. It had poisoned him—all that cleverness
turned to making him out a monster—and it had poisoned
her. Rage, like jealousy, is a fire which burns out the future:
she apparently knew it, and the softness in her eyes, even
this willed, desperate kindness at the door to the furnace,
restored her to him as he needed her to be restored. Then
they could both go on to love again, not merely beyond
hatred, but also strong in a practical, difficult friendship.
Perhaps that was too much to ask, his version of her ro-
manticism, but at least it was a principle worth striving for.

"We had some good reasons together," he said.

"What? Oh! Of course! I know, I remember, Dan. It
wasn't just our psychological set, we really liked each
other—"

He grinned wryly. "So it seemed at the time."

She did not admit a poor effort at humor in his enforced grip on the past. "That's the way you remember it and maybe that's partly how it was. I suppose. Anyway,"—with great solemn effort for which he wanted to thank and thank and thank her—"whatever our motivations"—although he winced at the word—"we—yes—Dan—*we loved each other.*"

"Yes!"

And again she retreated. "But it was sick."

"Okay," he said.

And she folded her hands contentedly. "That's what I've learned."

Who's been teaching you now? he wanted to ask. He resisted successfully. He wanted her to understand about the passive faithlessness of the woman who expects her husband to be what he is not, what no man can be, who lies with him locked in her lonely dream of perfection, who sees her real marriage by the strange sunless radiance of a dream marriage which is unaltered by growth and event, by this particular day on earth or that one. Absolutist! Idealist! Romantic! These had been his epithets for her. And you can't make yourself into Eleanor of Aquitaine and me into a troubadour by nagging me for talking with a girl at a goddamn party! All right, so I didn't, didn't, *didn't* light your cigarette! So neither of our children were boys!

He managed. He said nothing.

The admissions she had just made were an extravagant yielding. She felt loss, they meant; relief and giving up pain could help to teach her to praise life, and when she could bear the din of pleasure once more, she might even be grateful to him. Together they had exorcized childish ways—the lesson was nearly fatal; they had also learned and practiced love. Once free of each other, they could go on with this lifelong music.

But how stiff she still was!

Nevertheless, in her own way, calmly, gently, and much sweeter than his secretly unleashed judgment, with but a slight stiffness of the mouth, she went on. He was impressed by her rapid peacemaking, so soon after the tears and threats and furious thrashing. There was a deep quiet note of loss despite the artificial speech. He listened: "It was inevitable. You were my mistake and I was yours. But neither of us is *bad*, and we could have married really bad people, real stinkers—so if we know it was inevitable. . . . Dan," she concluded rapidly, with a flush, "I said things, did things. Now I'm sorry."

She was in misery. He wanted to comfort her. Then she straightened up with a strong glance of resolution and touched her hair. "I'm sorry," she said.

"I'm sorry too, kid, for all I did wrong."

Apologies and pride and gratitude. Shaper felt a reviving flow of tenderness for her because she said *stinkers,* and maybe even thought stinkers, and not that cant of hers, *destructive personalities.* They sat very still, in a heated blush both of them, their shame almost a courting shyness, and they listened to their children splashing in the sink and laughing. An odd music for courting. The children were his laughter and hers; her body and his were met on the children as they had been entangled in each other. All this willed and anxious sweetness between them might finally give him Sally, give her whomever she wanted, and not merely send them raging after others. It could be the final creative act of their marriage—the two of them educated by their errors, not bound to them, freed for love and not greedily clutching at it. They would always have Paula and Cynthia together.

Once, on the day when their lawyers had first met, before this resilient stupor with which he shielded himself had settled in, he had cried out in this room, after they had both put the children to bed and he was facing her, ready to say goodbye, when he was at the door with all the unfinished business of their life meeting him in her huge hot eyes: "We didn't make it, kid."

"We tried. We tried."

"We tried, honey."

And they had fallen into an adulterous passion, still unshaken in their will on divorce, the adultery made painfully sweet. He remembered it with shame, his eye suddenly prickling and aching, and saw himself again covering her with kisses, forcing her mouth open while her body bent backwards, arched, received him. She had given herself without a word, moaning, and then he had fled like a thief.

Now he was merely quiet. The ache in his eye was an unheard sound, an unseen tremor of desire.

Still they would always have the children together.

He felt the day's heat already sweeping in and looked about for the fan. In his reticence in this familiar and very unfamiliar house, his and not his, he obeyed the stricture she had once made in anger—don't touch anything, nothing is yours any more! (Nothing but the children.) "Put your hands on me and I'll get an injunction," she had said the next day. It was her only reference to that strange, silent last lovemaking. "I'll slap a court order on you so fast it'll make you dizzy."

"Okay, kid, do you really think I want to touch you?" And that time his eye had not ached, not seemed invisibly swollen. It was the end. Almost comfortably he believed in playing out the rest of their career together without the danger of intimacy. Of course he was wrong, but something of the comfort remained in his waiting, his planning, his cautious observance of the new rules of tact and courtesy. It was only the children he needed.

She had rearranged all the furniture, painted, covered,

hid, and replaced, so that the house could begin anew. He recognized it as he recognized her, from a distance, from a long time, from a dream of voyages. She had planned it that way. Fastidiously he had been plucked out of her skin and the scars dusted over, so that she could say, *Who? Who?* She wanted him to notice how much he was not at home. How managerial and intelligent of her to begin briskly anew! With what a rush she had retreated from him!

He smiled at her. "You look very well, kid."

She turned and pressed her lips together tightly. In pain she had a large mouth—childbirth, bereavement—he had been there with her; anger was a small one which sent him away. By the resenting white line at the corners of her mouth, he recognized his wife, the one who had first wanted him for pride in what he did—others wanted him, he was not like the herd of college boys; then wanted him to do nothing that did not include her, that might make others covet him; and then when they were cozy in a common, including misery, rebuked and rebuked him for his failure to be her romantic ideal. O father she lost, O son I did not give her, how amply I was repaid for trying to replace you! What foolish pride that thought this abstract hungering of hers was desire for me! Impossible victories that I wanted!

Now thanks to that bloodless thin line and the stiff tremor of her response to his word for her, *kid,* he felt entirely at home. It was almost like the last years of their marriage again.

She reached for an envelope in her purse. "You forgot to pay my dental bill. It dates from before our settlement," she said with her marvelous cool telephone voice, "so of course you are responsible. Dr. Jonas' secretary called me about it and I said you had probably forgot. I said I'd give it to you personally when you got back to town."

He took the paper, put it in his pocket, and called like

a drowning man, "Paula! Cynthia! Let's go outside, would you like that?"

They came screaming with pleasure into the room and he believed that, yes, he could still keep his grip on the green feelings he had brought in from his month away.

3

He liked everyone, even his wife. Perhaps he loved no one but the children—he was so diminished by the belly-ripping, face-clawing final year of marriage—but he felt a reviving and undiscriminating benevolence toward the world. Plus desire for Sally, ah, that's important! It was recovery from an illness. When he returned to his hotel after leaving the children for their afternoon nap, his thoughts wheeled around to Sally, and they were imbedded within a silly glow of sympathy for everyone, irrelevantly, from the desk clerk with sinus trouble to the Japs at Hiroshima. Symptom of convalescence. "Key, please! Hot enough for you?"

He wanted to share this precarious perch on health. Sally had agreed to drive out to Chagrin Falls and go swimming with him. The first time he took a girl swimming was important to Shaper. It's a risk and rousing. You run the challenges of dirt, ants, and fatigue; he took chances on a cold noting of his skinny body in boxer trunks, the scatter of hair and the ropes of tendons and no strong rhythm of distraction. Enjoying the happy vanity of a lovely object, long used to triumphant waiting, Sally might have an eye for some tumbling beach athlete, not Dan Shaper with his glasses and his bony knees. Admire, admire me! her every movement had been saying to him for months. He had done it well. Was that a guarantee that she would love him?

No matter, he thought as he shaved in his hotel room;

I don't want love now, I couldn't take it yet, what I need is just what Sally is giving me. Why worry about categories? He remembered that warning song: "Silkless silk and milk-less milk! Love oh love oh loveless love. . . ."

Fully dressed, he lay on the bed, organizing himself to meet Sally, feet straight and toes up, watching the hand of the clock move down to two. These few minutes of rest were necessary, despite his driving heart, after a morning spent with his children, seeing in their faces the intermingling of his wife and himself, feeling her breath with his gesture when they talked, his forehead with her dark, thick-lashed eyes when they laughed. Their eyes when he rolled on the floor to play bus or airplane as they had during the easy evenings of their babyhood (they remembered, they demanded it)—they wanted him to bathe them again, as he used to—and their mother's eyes, the tragic pouched eyes of the beauty unsuccessful in love. And then the solemn politeness all around when he turned them back to her.

One minute to two! Think of Sally—fullbreasted and fullhipped, blond, frequently amused—how lucky to be all those things that his wife was not! And Sally had her own secret sources, too! He remembered the yearning of her response to his first, long-delayed kiss, when in the renewal of timidity, the return to boyishness brought on by the long illness of his marriage, he had quite simply been afraid. No, it took wisdom to be full and warm like that. Her hand on his back was deep art, her weight on his shoulder was Plato and . . . and . . . Sally, not Plato! No romantic ideal! She did it for herself and for him.

Lord, ten after two already. He must have dozed. He threw swimshorts, towel, clean clothes into the blue Air France bag he usually carried for tennis. He took a taxi to Sally's apartment, where she was waiting for him at the entrance. She had no need to keep him waiting; she didn't play that game any more—she felt his need for her and forgot to protect herself. She said: "Darling! It's such a beautiful day for us!"

That was intelligence, wasn't it? Her own marriage had been a revolving door, in and out with practically no noise or loss of heat, but she probably knew more about it than he suspected. Surely she knew more than she would tell. And she had her own automobile, a blue Ford convertible, to which she just automatically handed him the keys—that too made her clever and deep. Like all American boys, he had dreamed of girls like her with their blond heads thrown back against the leather seats of cars like these. . . . That it was her automobile only gave the joke a turn. Once he got over the divorce, lawyers' fees, travel costs, the rest of it, he too would have the open car which his wife had always thought too dangerous, bad for a dry skin, impractical.

"Why didn't I think of picking you up at your hotel?" Sally asked.

"Never mind, just move over and sit close to me."

"Are you a onearm driver?"

"Like to be."

"Then I'll put a knob on the wheel for you."

Wryly he submitted to his retreat toward college-boy pleasures—the blond, the convertible, the exaggerations of flesh in erotic gaming. Well, he would tolerate himself, he would come out of it. Let the submerged fantasies see the light, why not? Sally was there waiting, and more than merely *the blond*. She was Sally. Her silent smiling said that she was with him part of the way at least.

And they teased and played while he drove under the hot August sun through a part of the city, a part of the suburbs, out to the private country lake he had chosen because neither of them had been there for years. They paid to enter. On a weekday like this, they had the short clean beach almost to themselves. When they met on the beach after dressing, he submitted to a moment of shocked, almost unpleasant awe at her perfection of body under the blaze of sunlight. Beauty is pitiless. She turned under his brooding with a model's pouting halfsmile, her eyes blank, self-regarding, retreated into vanity. This must have been an old girlish habit. He hated the thought of her searching him for flaws, as he was now doing to her; but he needed to be looked at with pride, too. The different male and female ways about bodies would protect him, no? And hadn't they already begun the long study of each other in the close and secret dark?

Different, different.

She was a marvel, and that they both knew it somehow widened the space that had been closed by their first tentative lovemaking. A monument wants a pedestal.

Then she turned and ran, elbows pumping, toward the water. He caught her and they went in together. They laughed and spluttered, and she began swimming, and he caught her again. "Let's go out to the dock," she said. She swam poorly, splashing and puffing; he swam well and easily. Sally's wisdom! When he helped her up onto the outer dock, she was no longer a monument. She leaned on him, gasping a little and laughing. He kissed her shoulder with its gleaming, running beads of water. She nipped his hand with her bared teeth.

They lay a long while under the descending late afternoon sun, stretching against each other, talking at intervals, listening to the few shrill voices back on shore. He spoke a little of his wife. He did not speak of the children. "Just smile," she said sleepily, her face close to the hot white-washed boards. "I don't want you to worry about a thing."

He stopped worrying. He put his arm on her back and

rubbed the strong articulations of her spine until his fingers ached. She smiled, saying, "More, more, more. Ah that's nice."

She was very young, overproud of her body in the suburban way, just beginning to get past using it as a weapon instead of spending herself through the splendors of flesh. But she was learning, she was. And if her beauty alone had frightened him, could he ever have borne that rare loveliness which comes of beauty joined to a proper sense of its being? No, thank her for limitations. And she was learning to spend herself freely, too. And with him.

At sunset they sat up to watch. She leaned on him to share the radiating warmth of her body. They approved of the sky. He missed not seeing the children this evening, but he needed Sally now; he would go to them again tomorrow. With a fine sense of no hurry, no hurry for anything, they waited until the sun was gone.

But the swim back to shore made them furious with hunger. She suggested buying Chinese food and eating it at her apartment. They drank a great deal of tea and nothing else. The sunburn began to show on her face and arms. She put a stack of records on the machine. They made love slowly, patiently. "Why are you smiling?" he asked her, and she replied: "Why are you smiling?" He explored a generous body with its slowly stirring languors and bold risings to the touch. She explored whatever he meant to her. "Why *are* you smiling, now tell me!" His hand had discovered, with the sense of regaining a fine lost memory, the crisp, crinkly, blond hairs of her secret places.

They gave up talking. They loved each other until they both felt as light and pure as driftwood, and then all tumbled together they slept.

4

Paula, who was six, said to her father, "Mommy says you don't love her any more."

Her father, who was thirty-two, replied, "No, but I like her."

"But, but," said Cynthia, who was just four. "But can I go out and find Gary?"

"Why don't you stay with me for a little while?" her father asked. Dismayed by his querulousness, he repeated the remark in another voice. "Stay here with me. I have to go back soon. Anyway," he added, "it's almost bedtime."

"Okay," said Cynthia, resigned. She was a very small child, pouting and serious, with overbusy limbs. She paced back and forth on the long, low, especially constructed, "contemporary" couch which her mother had bought partly because her father didn't want it.

"But *why* don't you love Mommy any more?" Paula insisted. "You always told me you did."

"That was b-b-before." Her father stammered for an explanation, dulled by knowing that there could be no valid one for Paula. "I tried—we did—I wanted to. We just weren't happy together. You know how that is, Paula."

"No," she said flatly and firmly.

"We have to live separately. It's like when you and Cynthia are tired and quarrel. We put you in separate rooms until you feel better."

"When are you and Mommy going to feel better?"

"It's not exactly that way with grownups." The sly innocence of Paula's question brought his hand out to touch her pleadingly; he wiped away the smudge of dirt on her cheek. She always made herself up with a stroke of dust as soon as possible when her mother washed her face. Cynthia, humming to herself, was listening with a smudge of prying watchfulness across her eyes. With a premature false security, the two girls frowned for serious discussion. The children of the divorced are engaged too soon in love as a strategy. Joy recedes before strategy; these children are robbed of their childhood. The huge brooding of possibility which human beings have at their best comes of the long passionate carnival of childhood; no fear of cost down this midway, just another and another breath-taking joyride on the great rollercoaster! and another quiet gathering-in of food and rest—it should be. It should be a storing of unquestioned certainties for the infinite risks of being a person. But instead, instead. Heavily Shaper touched the two girls as if to make them child animals again. It was not right that a father should feel this hopeless pity, and this need to enlist his daughters in the harried legions of rationality: "Here's how it is with grownups—"

"You mean Mommy and you?"

"Yes. Yes. Now listen. We feel better living in separate places. We're going to stay like that. But we like each other, Paula, and we love you and Cynthia. We both do."

"But, but, but, but," Cynthia sang, carefully wiping her feet on the pillows. "But heigh-ho, the derry-oh, the farmer takes a wife."

"Cynthia," said her father, "you shouldn't. Take off your shoes if you're going to play on the couch. It wasn't made for children."

Cynthia looked at him silently and, scraping the fabric, slid down beside him. Paula pulled between his knees, fighting to get closer than her sister. She began to suck her thumb. Her father pressed his lips together, resisted the temptation to remove her thumb from her mouth, and instead lit a cigarette. He decided that perhaps his silence would oblige her to remove the thumb and speak. It did not. At last he said, "I want you to understand. Mommy wants you to understand, too. Even though I'm not going to be

Mommy's husband anymore, I'll always be your father. I couldn't change that even if I wanted to, and besides, I would never want to. Don't you want always to be my daughters?"

Sucking busily, Paula said nothing.

Cynthia announced with a grin, "But I want a daddy who loves my mommy. I think maybe Uncle Carl, he loves Mommy—" The look on her father's face told her that he was not enjoying her joke. "But I *know* you're my daddy for real."

"I am. For real."

"Okay," she said, bored with the discussion.

Paula looked at her wet and slippery thumb, considered putting it back, had another idea. "Why doesn't Mommy say hardly anything to you no more?"

"*Any* more," her father said. "I already explained. Because we don't get along—just like we don't let you and Cynthia talk to each other when you don't get along—"

"But we do anyway! But that's only for a few minutes! But it's not, not, *not* the same thing, Daddy!"

"No," he said, "you're right. It's really not."

"Then *when?*"

"When what?"

"When are you coming to sleep here again?"

"I told you, I already explained. Mommy and I—"

"When you went away you said you'd come back to live here in a few days."

"Well, we thought maybe. I hoped. But it's worked out this way instead. Now listen to me, girls, it's not really so different. I see you very often. We go out together for milk shakes. We're just like before."

Silence from Cynthia. From Paula, coldly, suddenly with her mother's precise articulation: "It's not the same, and you know it."

"Okay, you're right, it's not." Her recognition of his

hollow heartiness made him flush. She cut right through
what he said. She remembered very well that he had been a
part of the life of the house and she did not like her new
sense of the house. He said, "I guess you're right, Paula,
but that's how it is. That's all. We don't have to talk
about it."

Silence. Then:

"So you really don't love Mommy any more." But she
was a child again. The moment when she spoke with her
mother's voice had passed. "Daddy," she said.

He resolved to go through it patiently once more. "No,"
he said, "and she doesn't love me. But we like each other,
and we love and like you, both together, and we always will.
You understand that, Cynthia?"

"Okay," said Cynthia.

Paula was sucking her thumb again. Her mouth was
pulled around, working and bothering, as if she were trying
to pull the skin off. She might be learning to bite the nail.

From the back of the house her mother walked toward
the living room where the two children and their father
were talking. She said hello, picked up a book, and returned
to the bedroom. This meant that she would like him to
notice that his time was up. A brisk, dark young woman,
she was freshly showered and very pretty, although too thin.
She wore a housecoat, but a girdle under it, stockings, and
high heeled shoes. Obviously she wanted to get the girls to
bed early because she was going out.

He began to say goodbye to his daughters. He reminded them that he would come to see them at noon tomorrow. Cynthia threw her arms around his neck, laughing,
and demanded: "Bring me something, maybe a surprise!"

"If you like," he said. He had a sick lonely weakness in
his stomach of something not yet done, not possible.

"Do you like me, Daddy?"

"I like you and love you, Cynthia kid."

Paula was rubbing her face against his hand, the thumb still in her mouth. He lifted her to kiss her, saying, "And Paula too. Now goodbye until tomorrow."

As he started down the stairs, Paula stood with her swollen thumb dripping and shouted after him: "Oh how I'm sick of those words love and like!"

5

The next day there were fresh flowers in a new vase on the coffee table. His wife was cool and abstracted and the familiar house could not have looked more strange to him if he had returned to find it filled with angry, overheated growth, like an abandoned greenhouse. Even not considering the flowers, the entire room spoke to him with faint whispers of disarray about how his wife (ah no! *former* wife!) had been out late and importantly that evening. A wrinkle in the carpet informed on her. The piled pillows on the couch were his witness.

"The children are having lunch," she said. "Would you like something?"

"No thanks, kid, I had a late breakfast."

She hid a small yawn behind her hand. "Me too." The yawn was excessive. It was more than required. She was putting it on with a trowel. Well, still, this was very much better than the hysteria with which she had sent their marriage into darkness, like a couple trapped forever at an abandoned Luna Park in the spinning, jolting cars of the Bug. Of course, this had its own special touch of refined cruelty, which merely went to show that she still depended on his feelings for some of her satisfactions. "Sit down, please," she said.

"Make myself at home?"

She smiled tolerantly. He wondered if she had any imagination for how it disturbed him to visit the place which had been his home, which in some way still was, which was so mysterious, like a room dreamed of and then found and then you're suddenly unsure of whether you really dreamed of it or only now think you did. Of course she understood; she had worked the house out for herself, and had a right to; but any imagination past this redecorating, working-it-out variety requires sympathy. When he looked up at her, she was still dressed in that social smile. Excessive!

"Some coffee?"

"No thanks, really. How do you think the children are taking things? My being away. Visiting. I was wondering if maybe I shouldn't see them too much when I'm in town. You can't make up for the normal daily—"

"Yes, overstimulating them."

"Too exciting," he said, giving up his thought by agreeing with her.

"They don't show it, of course. It's funny," she remarked, smiling patiently, as if it really were funny, while she explained the joke. "At their age they can't express it, they're too well behaved, they don't have the vocabulary for discussions. . . ."

He gave up listening. He was trying to place himself in this room. Sometimes they had pulled the shades and made love on the floor. He heard her despite the noise of memory. Her mania for psychology had always annoyed him. Jargonizing. And yet, and yet, once when she could not sleep he had held her in his arms on the couch while they quietly talked all night about her father and brother—she could talk English when she wanted to—and she spoke of love and violated need and loneliness. Then they had talked about each other and their own children and how different it would be. Then they had gone out on the porch to hold

hands in the chill spring dawn and watch the lights go on
in kitchens and bedrooms down the street. See, we didn't
need that sleep, we've gained a night on everyone, he had
said, and she had answered: Yes, yes, yes, we have something they don't have. I'll even make you a better breakfast!

"But," she was saying, "I'm afraid they will express
what they're feeling about us now when they get to adolescence."

Another time, after a terrible quarrel—thinking that
maybe with the guidance of their bodies which wanted to
give to each other . . .—more than hopeful, prayerful, they
had spread a quilt on the floor just below where she was
now sitting. They had helped each other down as if crippled,
slowly, slowly, and then safe on the floor, had flung all their
strength into the cruel struggle to possess, a lurching grind-
ing grasping assault on tenderness, and her head thrown
back and her mouth open so that he could not see her teeth,
only a dark place and a pulsing groan issuing deeply from
within it, and then fiercely she closed and bit his shoulder
and the cry, *You did it—you did it—you did it.*

What?

Oh love, love, love.

Would the rock be there the next day for rolling up the
mountain?

He blinked and straightened his shoulders in the heavy
inert grip of sweated clothes. Now was now and his former
wife was talking. Now was also then, but his former wife
was speaking. It was now ten summers for them. She had
something to tell him about their children.

"—with sibling rivalry," she was saying. "They're beginning the latency period."

"Oh yes, yes." Didn't she remember how he disliked
those words? What was she trying now? He went into the
kitchen for a glass of water. The children made him re-

hearse what they would do together after lunch. The park and the swings and a milk shake. All the milk shakes they could drink.

When he returned she was sitting calmly in her chair, hands folded together, with a subdued halfsmile on her face. He recognized her analyzed smile, the one she reminded herself to slip into when she talked psychology. That little smile cost me a year's pay. Okay, go easy, he told himself, it's only a year's pay. A convertible plus gas and insurance. A while in Europe. It's a funny nice little darling of a smile, really—all sympathy and comprehension and let's-be-mature-about-the-infantile-phase. No joy, no teeth either, but it's still better than the screams, much easier on the neighbors and a good deal easier on me.

"Did you visit Pete and Ellen last night?" she asked.

It gave him a little malicious pleasure in his turn to let her know that he had not been lonely, that he had not even gone to see his best friends in Cleveland. "No, I had something else to do. I'll see them in a day or so. I called them."

They were both silent. All the maneuvering and rivaling warned him. He was doing nicely, but better get the kids out soon, get out quickly. If she felt his strength of distance, if she sensed Sally and stopped being nourished by whatever it was in the room, the flowers, whatever it was, things might go poorly again. He followed her eyes. Three novels by Evelyn Waugh, new in their jackets, were piled on an endtable. A quick twitch of grin crossed his face. He had never liked Waugh, neither had she; ever since college they had taken literature passionately and together, even after she had begun her long crush on the bound volumes of The Psychoanalytic Quarterly. Now the little pile of Waugh was a roadmark meant to state: See, I've come under someone else's influence. I'm reading the books *he* recommends, doing the things he. . . . It amused Shaper, but when he

finally spoke his voice was husky and he had to swallow and
it still didn't clear. "I talked with Pete," he said. "I suppose
I should go out there."

"Yes, if you're not too busy. Really, Dan, you don't
have to be afraid about our friends. I wouldn't spite you for
the world—"

"I'm not worried. They know me. I mean to see them,
but you know how it is, things come up, I'm only here a few
days."

With a thrill of satisfaction, he felt the balance swing
over: I'm giving her now! She's getting it! This while he
knew how much she pained only by how she goaded him—
so rusted together are the ways of untying man and wife.
And this all the while that his eye began to ache, that he
asked himself a fleeing, trespassing question about how he
could expect to hold his job while committed to this con-
tinuous deep marital work, that he suddenly saw a tiny receding Sally fretting and scowling and making up her eyes
and mouth three times over because she was jealous of his
quarrel with his wife. Sally's moods were reflected in heavy
ways with her lipstick. His own lip was sore inside where he
had bit it. That was his wife's habit which he had borrowed.
Divorce, divorce! he thought. Let us be divorced in the flesh
as we are by law!

She was watching him shrewdly. She knew him. He
could keep the bitten lip from her, there was no way she
could palp it. It was a contest to hold secret the hurt eye
with its invisible throbbing. And then Cynthia ran up and
put her hands in his pockets to see if he had gum.

"Get out, Cynthia! Go wait for your daddy in the other
room. Paula has enough sense. Can't you see I'm talking to
him?"

Like successive waves of fever and chills, chills and
fever, his tenderness for the children, who resembled both

wife and him, gave way to hatred, hatred, cold disdain for
this woman who forgot so much, who destroyed so much.
And then a sharp new ache in his eye, flicking all the way
up into his brain, no, just the sinuses, no, cruelly into the
brain: Maybe I should just have given in. Maybe I should
have taken it on her terms.

No, no! He wanted to turn off one whole side of his
head. The eye had a furious life of its own. He warmed it,
comforted it with his palm. Bent to it for an instant, he
looked up again strictly. "You don't have to sit here if
you're busy," he said.

"Oh I don't mind, Dan. And besides, there really are
some little things we have to straighten out."

"Well, thank God most of that is over." And he added
meaningfully, "We don't have to quarrel any more. We can
concentrate on the children. We can be friends."

"Yes, of course, but turns out there are some other
expenses—"

"Oh please, no, kid."

"Yes."

"What do you mean?"

"Some other little things. It's complicated raising children under these circumstances, all alone—well, never
mind. Let me see. Not just Doctor Jonas, but—"

"What? That again? I won't bother pointing out about
that one bill, but as to any others, you know very well—"

"*You know very well!*"

"Please don't be sarcastic. Let me finish." But she was
staring at him with her enormous eyes turning black—as
with anger, as with love—the pupils dilating and thick con-
gested hate squirting like black arterial blood from a deep
wound over the thin face. He struggled to be without memory. He thought again (how many times like this?) that if
he could keep calm, keep easy, maybe she too would make
the effort. He said in a low, forced, effortful voice, "You

know very well that our agreement states that you meet all expenses out of the check I send you every month. There's no other way to do it, kid—"

"Don't call me kid! I never liked it! Your idea of an endearment!"

He went on stubbornly, quietly, "You know what my income is. I don't even. . . . Well, I'm not complaining. But there's nothing more to discuss about money unless I fail to send you the check some month."

"Kid! Kid! You still want to call me kid, but if one of your children needs some special care, what's it to you—?"

"What's the matter?" he interrupted, frowning. "*What* special care?"

She mimicked him with ungainly, ferocious sarcasm. "It's not in the agreement. . . ."

"Are you going to tell me? Or is this all nonsense again?"

"I want to send Paula to the Bainbridge School."

"What for? We—*you* can't afford a private school like that. Anyway, what does she need it for?"

"A fatherless child!"

"Is that my fault? Did you want me? Did you *want* me?"—and he felt the harsh sting of self pity like dust at his eyes and he shook it out angrily. "Didn't I fight to keep us together long after any other man would have run off or gone batty?"

She tapped her foot and did not answer. He had a suspicion than he could peel off her skin now and find a genuine, very satisfied smile, but with a forced calm—like his —she began patiently to explain. "I've discussed this with several people. The Bainbridge School—"

"I'll tell you just one thing: I don't have the money."

"—is oriented toward difficulties, special problems, broken homes—"

"Oriented, oriented!" He called out the word as if it

were a verdict brought down upon her. He stood up, shaking. He had a throbbing frontal headache just behind his eyes. "Please let me get out of here, I've got to get out," he said. "Let me take the children and get out for a while. The little thing we should orient ourselves to is orienting ourselves toward not talking like this when they're watching."

And they both turned and admitted the presence of the two, very quiet, very thoughtful little girls. "We were just talking," Shaper said weakly.

Shrunken and bent, all the pleasant civilizing of their time of separation scraped away, his wife managed to wipe the children's faces for their walk. At the door she turned to him and said severely, "When you come back, please leave them downstairs to play for a few minutes. I want to talk with you alone."

Blackmail! In order to see the children, in order to keep her from trying to rip him out of their lives as she had ripped him bleeding out of hers, he had to find some way of settling into a decent habit with her. The headaches that were already a tradition of their arguments made him almost blind in his left eye. He counted on her not interfering with the children—at least for this her psychology supported him—but he suspected that she wanted to think of him as an ideal monster, and then she could reason that for their own good they should *relate, transfer, orient* to some other man. Her words! That damn vocabulary! Lousy blackmail! He tried to soothe his eye by cupping the palm of his hand over it. Blackmail!

Within the dynamics of her romantic, absolutistic passion for the ideal, each failure between them had to be complete and each small difference total war. Symbols had become reality, reality had become a great abstract, timeless, and predetermined sign; her energy was bent furiously on making reality over in the image of her idea about it, even at the cost of destroying its value as reality. (She could not measure the cost. Cost is not a part of heavenly systems.) This way of life has a kind of internal logic, perfect and unaffected by experience; there was no opposing it. Once her husband was defined by her needs ("It happened to me when I was immature"), there was nothing he could do to become human again. Even yielding to her—that most human of acts—enraged her because it violated her idea about him. She hurt herself, and could not stop, and threw herself and the husband she once loved and anyone else in the way (including their children) under the clanking treads of the interlocking syllogisms by which she lived: Good and Evil are pure; the ideal exists only in heaven; my husband is here below with me, on earth; therefore he is evil. I must have perfection; I do not have perfection; then this is hell I live in and I am damned and I will destroy, destroy, destroy. . . . Still, someday, O someday I will find pure virtue in a man! He must exist because I can imagine him. I need him right now! I deserve him, I call him, I insist on him! I am pure, I have waited for him, this other creature has no value because see the way he shrivels, vanishes, like a bad idea! I will prove that he does not exist by making him recognize it himself.

And so silly, smart novels. And bouquets of roses in a cut glass vase. Well, if he knew how she was getting at him, he should be able to get out of the way. And he didn't have to display Sally, either.

6

Fortified by wry self-congratulation at his assent to whatever she now needed in order to do away with him, he could turn his back on her judgment and go to another. He did not believe in magic; her eyes could no longer make love to him, make harm for him, uncover into life that which was only recently buried but quite dead, and down the dust came sifting fast. It was done. There were the children left, for ever and ever the heirs. He would shower again and scrub hard.

But always there returned the tangled memories which dragged him off the straight road leading from life into the violent death of divorce and back into life again. Their children were not the only heirs, the only judges. It would be useful simply to hate her until he forgot her. It would be fine to despise her. Pride! But when he had almost succeeded (for example, in a sweet moment of fuel and money while having the oil checked in Sally's car), abruptly his greedy feeding on resentment came back to him, his joy and suspense before what she would do if she discovered that, for almost a year, there had been another girl. She needed the lesson; he had almost told her himself to let her know how he too might be lonely. . . . But recognized his cruelty. And remembered that the night before she found him out, she had risen to his grief and guilt to comfort him in what she took for a passing depression; there had been a miraculous access of tenderness and gratitude, and she had said, "We have the best little kids in the world, I know it, Dan. I'm sorry about the boy, I know it's foolish. Be patient with me. Care for me."

And then the next day the gossip came round and she had confronted him and he had thought, Let her learn, let her burn awhile. We've tried everything else.

Divorce time, wake up! It was time to move past his malice and her answering sweetness, past his yearning and her vindictiveness, past their other swinging meetings and partings, and years of it, common efforts, successes, bitter ultimate failure. While she talked, talked, talked, harassed him, practiced meanness, he could still find the silent regret

faraway—deep in her eyes—apology, helpless apology—
and yet the two of them could not settle together into firm
admission of it. Her regret and her ancient willingness to
love were resin-soaked roots. She consumed them. She refused to look at them. So be it, she seemed to have decided,
abandoning her will with relief, and threw the uncured
wood on the fire; and the destruction of what she most
needed to grow from gave a wild hissing edge to her sarcasm, "I do wish that you would please stop calling me *kid*.
Customarily that's for the children of goats. I seem to recall
that I have a name."

Arson. She still remembered something more than that
from him. On her face—as the lover in the morning finds on
his darling's face the marks of their excess together during
the night—he saw the brand of her secret self-appraisal,
secret wish that it might be otherwise. It was like that thickness and slight purpling of eyelids in the morning after the
flesh has made fantastic avowals that moments do not die
(even as the moment is dying), that what the intentions of
lovers have brought together no God shall sunder (even as
spirit and life notify us of matter and death). Who desires
what they had now earned? She had wanted to want only
him. To him she had cleaved for everything, rest, trust, energy, hope. "But I need a son, too," she had said. "Lots of
women have sons. No one is perfect. I want *your* son, Dan,
no one else's. Why can't I have the one thing I need?"

For everything, for too much.

As he recalled his chill judgment of her fever, the summer and the city spun crazily around him and he thought:
It is as she says—all my fault, all! I was bored with her because I could not admit my need of her, because I feared
that her weakness excluded me and she could do nothing for
me. I took for boredom my dull despair of touching her
without the qualification of a son, of receiving what a hus-

band asks *without qualification,* so that I determined to need nothing at all from her and to build a life which did not depend on her. I sought to harden myself by freezing. Monstrous!

"You're a monster," she had shrieked when he admitted that his strength to indulge her had come from a little student at the Institute of Music.

"It didn't make any difference then. You were thinking about your skin, your waistline, your father, your analyst, your fantasies about a son—you didn't really care what I—"

The war again. Go! He leapt from the transport. His parachute was tangled. Other bodies hurtled free, mouths open, teeth bared, roaring with effort. They relished the free tumble into space; for him it was death. "Monster!" He plummeted. Didn't he have the same rights as others? No. He would be a sickness of gore on the earth below. "Monster, monster!" And then it came back to him, first with a belly-jerking violence, earth and life crashing up toward him as the parachute caught, opened, and he gasped, and then he lazily swung like a pendulum on a great clock: I am not a monster. Nor is she. But I am not, either.

He went to Sally that evening with something which he knew was not love, but she thought it was. Surely she was not really deceived; his need of her was what she needed, and love an irrelevance. Nevertheless she showed her doubt in ways that made it harder for him—her anxious trick of brushing and rebrushing her eyelashes with mascara, her rather heavy step into the kitchen, giving him a glimpse of the thickened waist to come, the overbright, slightly foolish, false glee of her smile, responding to uneasiness by an American piece of advice, *Keep smiling!* She came back with coffee, a glare of teeth, blond eyelashes on which he made out tiny beads of blacking.

He asked her to take off her makeup and she did. His chill calculation shocked him. He wondered if his wife had so shot his nerves that all he could bear now would be a sweetly boring girl, worried only about pleasing him and getting the shine off her nose with the right shade of powder, a lover of musicals and of her beauty sleep—and of pleasing him! That quintessence of desirability! She watched, frowning. He grew tender and regretful. What could he ever do for her? She meant to be good to him. She studied him silently, unreproaching, with the pallor of the blond girl without makeup under bad light, and she suddenly seemed very beautiful, the most lovely woman in creation. He switched off the lamp and they moved toward each other in the dark.

When they lay down together, she said something which surprised him. It was trivial and familiar, like the breathless delicacies of undressing, and yet it was a trouble that she should cry out to him with words that seemed merely taken from a popular song: "Oh put yourself close to me baby."

How he wished for her silence then!

Afterwards he realized that the shock of vulgarity came not from her words but from his considering and judging her without interruption. He stroked her hair gently and felt sorry for her, for him. Someone was using someone. Somebody was somebody's weapon. There, there. "Sally, darling, I'm not good these days," he said. "I used to be, I want to be, but I'm in trouble."

"You are, you are, don't worry, you are good."

"I'm in bad trouble. I'm afraid. Nothing's clear any more."

"It will be, don't worry. You just need time, Dan. You make *me* happy."

"Do I?"

She put her finger on his mouth, shh. She wanted to sleep. He dozed too, asking himself, Why don't I ever think of her until I have to? That first day and the swimming was an accident, the false health of fever. Not right, not right, though I take my breath from her hair.

Then he slept.

In the middle of the night he woke with a start, with a sense of flapping inconsequential interruption, as if a cat had jumped onto his back. He lay staring into the murmurous dark and fearful of the dream he could almost remember which had awakened him. Oh yes, yes. Forget about it. He had been falling without a parachute for years and years. He did not crash to earth; he diminished. The starving man could not take food—even the thinnest broth was an agony to his constricted body.

The air conditioner threw its chill breeze into the room. Gradually, very slowly, reluctant to disturb the fine integrity of her sleep, he began to stretch against Sally for ease and new rest. She was warm, spreading, slightly curled as she lay. He pressed against the softly sleeping girl. He put his hand over her back and moved it down through slopes and valleys. She stirred and their mouths were breathing and feeding into each other. In a few minutes he heard a hoarse voice, his own, saying, "Oh come to me baby." She gathered him in.

7

The last day of the visit. Shaper wanted to store up memories of his children so that, like a camel, he could survive away from them through a season of drought. Yellow-eyed, lurching, he was still not a camel; he could not live for oases; he could not carry Paula and Cynthia in a hump. Still he had hope. Although it was already several days past the end for his wife and him, he believed that perhaps they could manage one more meeting for the sake of the children.

Sally gave him her automobile to drive out to the house. This time the mild luxury, moving through traffic in the sun with the top down, failed to reassure him. He found himself singing an old Louis Armstrong blues tune:

> *From milkless milk*
> *And silkless silk*
> *Love oh love oh loveless love*

On an impulse he stopped at Peter's, found him home, and asked him to come along. "My wife and I will both be on good behavior with a third party present." And he looked away. "That's the way it is, Pete. Sorry."

The children were shy; they knew he was going. They had no practice in goodbyes. For them he was already gone. Paula gave him a drawing of flowers and the sun to put on his wall—"where you live, Daddy." The sun was sticking out its tongue.

As the subdued and uneventful visit ended, it occurred to Shaper that Pete might find his insistence on having a witness somewhat melodramatic.

"Goodbye," he said to his wife.

"Goodbye," she said.

"I hope everything goes well."

"Have a good trip back."

They shook hands. Peter looked embarrassed. They went downstairs. Shaper glanced back from the driveway and at the same moment two things happened: The children came out to stand on the upstairs porch and his wife came running down the stairs. She paused, breathing shallowly, before Shaper and Peter near the door of the automobile. She put out her hand with a slip of paper in it. "I enrolled

Paula at that school," she said softly. "I forgot to mention it. Here's the bill."

He drew back and tried to look merely puzzled. "You know I'm not supposed to. . . . I can't pay these bills. We already decided about that."

She held to the low tone, but there was a stir and hiss in her voice. "Who decided? Who? Who decided?"

"Look,"—and he was pleading although he knew this was the wrong way to move her. He had only found a steady right way when he was sick and needed her out of helplessness. It was the only way he could count on for sure. It was no way by which he could live. "Look, I sent a check for that dentist's bill, although you were wrong about the date. It came after our agreement. Now please try to understand, there's got to be a stop."

"A stop to what?"

"We have to start living the way things are. We have to adjust. You've said it yourself. Money shouldn't get in the way now. Our lawyers—" And he watched the pinched face and the black, swollen eyes replacing that bright young divorcee which was her pleasant role. He had hoped, but once more he misjudged her. Through those inky eyes, through the cloud of hate with which she blinded herself and poisoned him, she would not see what they had sometimes been for each other—she never saw that any more; she would not see the neighbors, she would not see Peter, she would not see the children. "Kid! Listen to me, please!" And he had no words to force her to remember how they had held hands and strolled in parks, and tenderly made up many quarrels, and congratulated each other that the girls were a fine combination of the best in both of them.

A stop? Her lips were saying, working within, white and diminishing.

"Listen, please, *please,*" he said, "you have to under-

stand how things are with me now. I live in a room, don't
you understand? One room. I'm not a college kid, I'm not
used to it any more. One furnished room, do you hear me?
I save my money so I can fly in to see the children—"

"Then don't do it."

"What did you say, kid?" He leaned forward, trying
to see her. "I'm sorry, I didn't understand."

"I said stay there. Get yourself a kitchenette. Don't
bother coming in."

He held his breath. He was peering into a night and
his eye was tired. It throbbed and he wanted to comfort it
with his palm. It seemed very important this time not to let
her know about the ache in his eye. He straightened up and
said, "Look at me. Look at us, kid." His eye wanted an
eye to return its gaze.

"Just don't bother," she said, as if her mind were far
away with household thoughts. "Stay away. I could spend
the money. Who needs you here? Don't bother."

She drew closer to him with a little smile on her face.

"And I may as well give you one other bit of information. Why not? Since you're leaving again." She spoke this
last phrase slowly, as if it were particularly important. He
recognized the angry wenchy smell which her body gave up
when she could no longer hold on. She said: "Now I feel
like a woman. I've found a man who knows how."

In the first moment of almost prudish shock, he felt his
face being fixed in a skeletal grin. "That had to come. The
list is complete. Okay. All right." But the grin spread un-
controllably, attacking his bones, dissolving the sockets of
his eyes.

"It was no good with you. Your fault. It was never any
good."

"All right," he said, "congratulations." He turned to
Peter. "You hear? My wife was a virgin all along."

"Yes," she said, "that's about it. I told Carl, too, how I was never touched. Since you're going away again, you might as well have this to take with you. Nothing. Never anything, though I tried to make you believe . . . . "

Their children were leaning over the railing to peer down on them. His hand flew toward his eye; he stopped it midway and put it down. He said: "All right, there's no point in discussing this either, is there? Our lawyers have it all settled now. We paid the lawyers to do this job for us."

"Lawyers!" And it was done. Something new had been released, and in public, in the summertime, with people coming out on their porches or peering through the screens to listen and saying *a shame* and smiling to themselves. "You want lawyers to raise our children?" she shouted. "That's your idea of a father?"

"All right, all right," he said in a low hoarse voice. He held himself stiffly, shaking with fury and disappointment. "Can't you control it? All this nonsense. There are people. You're doing it on purpose, kid, don't you see?"

She screamed as if he had struck her. "Don't call me kid! Just get out of my life!"

"Okay, okay." He turned to climb into the car. Peter was already huddled miserably on the seat. As he moved behind the wheel, he felt an almost physical eruption, a brutal crack in his throat, and the word came out, "Fishwife!"

"Corrupt! Corrupt!" she was shrieking at him. "Get out of my driveway! Go! Corrupt! You never cared for me or your kids—*children*," and desperately she sobbed the correction. "Or anyone but yourself! Get out of my life!"

That was how, standing silently together on the porch, the children saw him last. He was being chased by their mother's rage.

At the corner he pulled over to the curb and asked Peter to drive. "I'm not in control," he said, shivering, and went on as if this were the total explanation. "It was what broke us up. I had to stop, I couldn't be run by her temper. Once I saw Paula watching me back down like a fool just because of that look she gets in her eyes—you saw it, Peter —when she can't be reached. When I saw my daughter judging me. . . . It didn't even help to slap her, I tried that once or twice . . . ."

Peter turned and drove through the long park along East Boulevard. He was explaining, comforting, merely talking. "Well, she has to feel better about what she's doing. She's not the kind of woman who can take ambiguity. You have to be all good or all bad, and you're *it,* man. Once you could do no wrong; now. . . . Well, women are like that. Don't think she's going to be nice for the sake of the past."

"What about the kids?"

"The past has got to be wiped out. Women have their feet on the ground—anyway they call it the ground, sometimes it's our faces—and one thing she thinks she can do for the next man—whoever he is, I don't know if she's telling the truth," he added hurriedly, "is just wipe you out. That way she gets to be a girl again. She said it plain enough. For her you've got to be pure mistake, friend, and nothing else. Evil Dan the Bad Young Man."

"No kindness at all? That's how I'd like to be. Let me tell you something: When we first decided to separate we both wept."

Peter shook his head. "She told Ellen *you* cried. She said you're maudlin. She said you held her hand until it ached. Make up your mind to take it. Women—" Did Peter believe what he was saying? No, he was tuckered out and embarrassed and his mouth was uttering for him the cynical clichés about women which men in club cars tell each other. It was what he thought Dan wanted to hear. He may even have believed it true at that moment, true because it sounded familiar, and with a deep breath of fatigue (he thought this was sympathy) he again spoke what he took to be comfort to his friend: "Women," he sighed.

"But doesn't she look all yellow, sick? Her skin that color and those enormous black eyes. Yellow, sick, and mean. She used to be so pretty. She still is. Oh she hates me!"

They both fell silent. When Peter felt that he had done his duty, he asked to be dropped at home. He needed to get away. He loved his own wife; he felt as disconnected, tired, and jittery as if he had been casually unfaithful to her. Naturally he resented his old friend for bringing him to this possibility, and also—because his wife was surely his best friend—he resented Dan for eliciting his jovial male cynicisms. And within, too, he felt a thrill of pride: not for him this failure! This is the pleasure we are said to feel at funerals. And at a still deeper, more solemn place, because he was a good and kind man, he felt regret for his friend and also knew something of what was happening to him. This sense came up through the barriers as discomfort, as a desire to squirm: I can't take it, I want to do my duty by you, Dan; I want to get away. He had his own wife and children to play with on a fine dry summer afternoon. Ellen had asked him to do some shopping.

8

I held her hand until it hurt her! And what a bore she was with her whining and her headaches and her suspicions! Suspicions!

Better. He used his old ritual for remembering himself into gratitude for freedom: her nagging, her picking at her face in the mirror, her stiff jealous mouth with the white lines. Sure, finally he had given her cause for jealousy, why not? But first he had warned her that she was making him lonely when she stood before the mirror, plucking, squeezing, hating herself, dreaming of miraculous sources of happiness—her father fantastically restored to life, a baby boy instead of girls, an analyst who really understood and *said* something.

> *With dreamless dreams*
> *And schemeless schemes*
> *Love oh love oh—*

It was fine to be driving Sally's car with the top down. She was waiting for him, and she would be all health and dazzling smiles, unskilled in moping, untrained for meanness.

But don't you have to take a woman from strength, not weakness, if you are to give her anything important and receive anything worth taking?

And after his ten-year marriage, wasn't he too distant from Sally to bring her anything but that cheating desire, the need for comfort? He had loved his wife despite everything, he knew he had, they had been young and unmarked together, he insisted on remembering—and he did not love Sally. He made too much of the hot pity of bodies. He had thought to find love by loving, but instead, at length, filled with crazy pride, he had discovered sex. The solution was as ineffective as the discovery was unoriginal. Like his wife, he made too much of things.

When what he needed to save his life was simplicity, a bare white room and sleep, restoring sleep, how long could greater and greater complication soothe him?

Didn't that mean only trouble to come?

Perhaps. He parked Sally's automobile on the street before the massive, teeming apartment building—luxury

circa 1928—in which she lived with her closets full of
clothes, her mirrors, her pink-feathered slippers, and her
music-to-dream-by. But if he couldn't allow himself Sally,
that beautiful and perhaps silly girl—yes, he should say it
out, maybe it's true—he might be unable to prevent doing
what he had too often already considered. He had stood
caught in the middle of his furnished room and thought it
through. He had first been indulgent, then shocked by the
persistence of the idea. Apparently it was one to reckon
with.

He went up the long walk to the stuffy, over-decorated
entrance, found her bell, and rang it. Could Sally stop his
idea?

As he often did, he tried to think of what would happen to the children. That was a puzzler.

A Tale of Two Husbands

It was like giving up to a boyish dream. The lovely Swedish girl offers herself to the lonely stranger on their second day out from New York, in stormy seas, just before the dim gray dripping vision of Halifax rises into view through his porthole.

"Everything okay?"

"I am so happ-y. Vy? It is not wrong?"

"Of course it's not wrong to be happy."

"Frank. Frank. Um—you like to see land?"

"You don't have to talk, Gretta. Want an apple?"

Then the *Saxonia* docked, took on two groups of French Canadians, one of ancients and cripples bound for Lourdes, the other making a pilgrimage to the Café des Deux Magots, and moved off again into the irongray North Atlantic waters. It was nine days to Le Havre, and then a few hours on the train down through Normandy, and then Paris once more. But in the meantime, Gretta saved his life; that is, she raised good cheer between them. She gave him a remedy against seasickness that makes you sleepy without dizziness. She purred and laughed and burrowed her delighted muzzle in the crook of his arm. She purred about

everything. She both purred and laughed at the look on the
night steward's red Cockney face when he caught Frank
coming out of her cabin shortly before dawn. She was busy
making something of the life of Frank Curtiss, two years divorced, returning to Paris with longing and dread. With his
wife there the other time, he had been happy. Now imperatively he demanded to know if he were still young in Paris.

It was the shipboard dream of the tall blond Swedish
girl, generous and paradoxically cool, except that she was
slight and dark with huge hot demanding eyes and she carried a Swedish passport but told him that her parents were
Hungarian. "Dead in the var," she said, "all dead. Vun
brother he live in Stockholm. So I take name of Gretta and
live in Stockholm. So vy do you make me so happ-y? It is
possible? Vy?"

It was possible because it happened that they made
each other happy (happ-y) while the November sea pitched
the ship and the bored, stupefied passengers played cards in
the lounges and all but Frank and Gretta wondered why the
devil they hadn't found a faster way to get across. Over-
board a man can last six minutes in these northern waters,
and then you haul him up with ruptured veins, bobbing
thick and dead in his lifejacket. But never, never, never to
come out of this sea was Frank's will about Gretta and
Frank.

During most of that voyage Frank and Gretta were
locked in each other's arms with the pure, insatiable passion
of the suicidal; immolation they sought in each other. They
ate, strolled round the wintry decks, tried and did not suc-
ceed to amuse each other by watching their fellow passengers, and went below. They could not stay away, they could
not surface. Death, immolation, the perversion of an ideal
of love timeless and perfect. Striving hearts, knees, nails,
teeth, it was the rage of jealousy without occasion to be

jealous. They had no memory of each other and spoke of no future. It was a claim on this voyage: forever and ever. No musical lights of Manhattan, no greedy Paris, no past or future, no present even—only this fury, then this gliding fading fall into oblivion, this impenetrable waking once more. When he listened to her in the dark, murmuring half-worded sighs in her funny accent, deep sighs, groans, fragmented cries of astonishment in this funny accent, he found his mouth dropping open for an answering surprise. A woman could still whisper so to him, groan, lost for him! His mouth dropped open in the gesture of a child when he wants to open his ears to hear better. Once he smiled because she spoke so easily from the heart, frowning only for the effortful translation into English, "Vy are ve so happ-y? Vy? Should ve be so happ-y, please?"

On ship there is no work, a suspension, rocking ease and solace, much food, drink, strangeness, hope—great invitation to excess. They ate sandwiches. They plucked at each other's flesh to make April swellings and cravings. She touched his shoulder with her lips, saying, "I am smiling, please. Vy is it so good? Should I be smiling, please?"

"Never mind, Gretta. Just smile."

"You think so?"

Finally it turned out that her reason for questioning their happiness was a practical one—she had a husband who would be meeting her at Le Havre. She saved this information for the last day, when land sparrows had already been seen and a funnel of black gulls followed the ship, screaming in its wake. She arranged very simply into English the ideas which Frank Curtiss must get straight: He was not to make too much of all this. She would stay with her husband, of course. She did not want complication. This moment on shipboard must mean nothing when the ship stopped moving. Over. Nothing, nowhere, never. Done.

They must forget each other. Yes, but they must remember (stiff hurt misery set into the lines about her mouth). And half-turning, she looked into his left eye. "You think I am . . . nast-y?" she asked.

He shook his head and averted his face, covering his eye with his hand, and she burst into tears where they stood on the enclosed deck above the heaving coastal seas, and she ran to her cabin. He consoled her one more time; she consoled him. "I am so ashamed!"

"No. No. No."

"But I am nice?" she said. "Vy you not tell me I am nice?"

"Gretta."

"Nice? You like? Please."

"Nice Gretta."

"Here, touch. I am sore here from loving you."

"I like nice Gretta."

But sorrow, lust, playful extravagance, good sleep, none of it endures. As if deeply obedient to her declaration that he had no rights on her in harbor, on land, after their passage, his desire for her left him utterly when the ship was anchored during the night before disembarkment. The great motors shuddered, stopped, the vibration and dim work noises echoing through the half-deserted cabin class deck ceased, they had somehow to pass these last hours before filing out at dawn. At the ship's party, within sight of the spread haphazard lights of Normandy, a degree of November gaiety had finally taken possession of the small group of passengers. Frank sat up late, muffled in blankets on his deck chair, until the bleak dance racket had ceased. Motion had given him a sense of going somewhere; now he was becalmed. Some of the French Canadians, who had sprawled seasick for a week, now came to life, and two young men, arms about each other's shoulders, swung back and forth, shouting, red-eyed and drunken, "Nous sommes en France, mon vieux! En France, mon vieux! C'est bien la France!"

Frank climbed down to his cabin without caring where Gretta lingered or what she was doing. She was probably packing to meet her husband, or sleeping to meet her husband, or like him, just waiting. He entered his cabin. The core of an apple he had eaten after dinner was still in the ashtray.

No, no, he would not try to find Gretta now. He would let her figure how to be pretty for her husband.

Then becalmed, dimwitted, strange to himself, there followed one of those terrible nights that come to a man perhaps once in a decade. It was not insomnia: it was a state midway between wakefulness and sleep, in some indeterminate suspension, as the ship was suspended between the sea and Le Havre, or between New York and Paris; between his habits back home and his memory of unique joy in Paris (he had spent a Fulbright year there, freshly married, still wearing his Army woolens and plump with good health and hope and sure he had whatever pliers he needed to open whatever crate); he lay on his bed fully dressed between the Paris of his twenties and this unknown new Paris, between expectation and suspicion, between justification and judgment, between the ragged, destroyed, oxidized life he had abandoned like the apple core and. . . . what? A nasty little future? A nostalgic drifting into middle age like those wrinkled, boyish American wanderers found setting the style of the chic bars of Paris and Rome?

In New York after his divorce he had first imagined himself in love with a folk singer with artificially high breasts and a childish way of holding her arms when she walked, hands higher than elbows, wrists dangling. Then there had been a woman divorced like himself, with a child the same age as his, who eased him of troubles and was a pal and buddy to him and brought him back to good bed life; but finally she lay down the law about marriage—she thought too fast for him. Then there had been. . . . But there had been too many, all wounded like himself, childish and hurt, fleeing, unregenerate. And then he began to wonder if he had ever known what love is, or only what it was to be in love—or the reverse—or if it made any sense to want to *know* about such things—or. . . . And so he had decided to escape knowledge by finding happiness where he had once found it, understanding very well that it had no more to do with the place than it has to do with definitions and assurances. (This Must Be the Place, several generations had said about Paris. Now they were saying about psychoanalysis or Zen Buddhism or the Hi-Fi and the MG: This Must Be the Place.) In this life, he thought, there are more jerks than sudden stops, and I seem to be one of the jerks.

Nevertheless, Paris had been his Place. He promised his son that he would be back in three months. He took a leave from his job, borrowed a thousand dollars from his father, sent the check for his child support three months in advance (the Pay-As-You-Go plan), and got a second class cabin at $170 each way, the price of tourist class, because he had twice made love to a girl whose daddy turned out to be an official of the Cunard Line. This extra prize in the box of crackerjack had seemed a favorable augury. Miss Cunard Executive's Daughter (four years at Bennington, seven years with a Jungian, freckled shoulders, grateful for small favors) promoted him merely from Tourist to Second because he did not like travelling with the stupefied, overfed, luxurious first class passengers. Instead he was stupefied and overfed in modified, secondary luxury.

Now he lay on his bed, smoking, trying not to see the apple core, asking himself those circular, futile, primary questions: Where? Whither? Why?

For whom do I live?
For whom?
For what, O Lord?

The answer to all these appeals seemed to be: *Myself; I live only for myself;* and the appeal to God was a manner of thinking which came upon Frank Curtiss despite himself when he was tired, ill, or depressed. It had nothing to do with belief. He said *O Lord* when he had the gripes from too much fried food or too many metaphysics. It meant nothing. But he meant to himself right now: *I live only for myself and don't get the good out of it.*

For a few days, while that apple, a farewell gift from a friend, had lain rosily near his mirror, he had almost believed that the for whom and for what might be Gretta; but of course it can never be a Gretta, the Gretta of fantastic collisions in corridors, whether she turns out to have a husband or not. That the whither and why can be a Gretta is the delusion fostered by the blessed schemes of flesh. Pleasure, he reminded himself, must not be confused with love; and even if pleasure leads to love, love itself cannot be confused with a way in life. Frank knew too many devouring couples, loving each other, very conjugal indeed, destroying. He thought of his former wife, now married again, trying to build Fortress Marriage against all the lack of savor of her life.

How do you spell Chicago?

Chicken in the Car and the Car Can't Go, CHI-CA-GO!

There must be something more than this democratic powerlessness. The desire to unite two bodies must mean something more than two bodies crammed together in bed, discussing for dear life, debating whether to buy a Pontiac or a Volkswagen, planning barbeque pits against the anxieties of lives which do not enjoy work or the prospects of the times. The moat around the tri-level ranch-style fills up with stagnant shishkabob. Something more, O Lord, something more. Can a man book passage alone toward that something more? Does the hermit have the right to go into the wilderness with lightweight luggage, stretch hose, Dacron shirts, wash-and-wear conscience, complete information on contraception while in foreign land? A handkerchief, washed and stretched against the mirror, will dry practically creaseless overnight.

In his school days Frank Curtiss had studied and worked solemnly, and in these years of his thirties, as can be seen from his thoughts, he coasted on his wits with the same solemn lack of joy. His privileged laziness had no ease in it. Only when in love could he wallow in laughter, fly the coop. But he did not have to be caught to come back to his rules. Control, detach, cut the risks. He gave up of his own accord and returned abashed.

He lay smoking on the mussed bed, trying to keep from seeing the shriveled apple core in the little light above his sink, trying to recall the motion of the ship and not even detecting the lapping of water now as they lay in harbor and awaited the morning. "C'est la belle France, tout le monde! La dou-ce France! Nous sommes en France!"—a dim drunken voice through the corridor. "Je suis francais moi, francais de Canada, les vrais!"

How was Gretta passing this last night aboard? Perhaps regretting? No, packing. That afternoon he had touched the lazy sprawl of underclothes on the extra bed in her cabin. She had shared the silken luxury of her suitcases. Then she had told him, showed him her ring, that famous plain gold band which she had kept with some souvenir American nickels and dimes in her purse. No, surely not regretting, too busy for that.

He drifted down by force of gravity.

He touched nothing on the way.

He lay like a stone in the forsaken center of night.

Then mercifully the steward knocked to tell him that early breakfast was being served in the dining room. He found Gretta sitting over black coffee, her hands embracing the cup, her eyes smudged by fatigue, her face wan, her teeth as bright as ever when she smiled. "Ve eat breakfast to-gather vun more time?" she asked. "Yes? I say I am sorry, no? Please?" But she had begun without him, of course, eggs and toast and jam, needing food for the two ordeals ahead, passing through customs and meeting her husband.

It happened that she performed these duties at the same time. Alfred Bergston, a Swedish consular official in Paris, had obtained permission to meet his wife in front of the long low tables where the voyagers waited for the customs agents to fluff hands through their belongings and scribble in chalk on their baggage. One of the young Canadians who had shouted his joy over being at last in France leaned liverish and sick against the wall at the far end of this room. At the moment when Bergston appeared, Frank was standing with Gretta making a last silent farewell, wistful, haggard, intimate in the cold light of first morning in port.

Gretta presented her husband to Mr. Curtiss. Mr. Curtiss had been at table with her during the trip.

Frank mastered the rules of this ridiculous situation. He replied with absolute calm, feeling proud of himself, and noted that Gretta behaved with absolute calm, and was ashamed for her. She knew her way too well. Another victory she had taken from him! It was too easy for her.

But Alfred Bergston looked quickly at Frank's outstretched hand, touched it, and began speaking rapidly in Swedish to his wife. He looked neither at Gretta nor at

Frank as he talked, but rather at her open suitcases, as if
they told him all he feared, all he needed to know. With an
involuntary shrug Frank excused himself and went to stand
at the table where he awaited his turn with the douanier. In
the distance across the hall he could see, in slow motion, the
stiff conjugal gestures of tenderness between Gretta and Alfred Bergston, who was exactly one type of Swede—large,
pale, heavy, handsome in a small-eyed and thin-lipped ski
instructor's way, except that he was a bureaucrat and not a
ski instructor, so that he was going to fat in jaw and but-
tocks and there was a crease of flesh overhanging his collar
and other creases stretched across pants that had fit him
better last year than this year. He must have found Gretta's
southern darkness marvellously fetching when he first met
her. He was wearing a fine black sweater over an open-
necked, excellently laundered white shirt, black flannel
trousers, English shoes with a purplish shine on them—very
much the Scandinavian sportsman, casually elegant, "très
fort pour le fairplay anglosaxon," as befits the diplomat of
a great neutral.

And then the customs man said, "Ouvrez, s'il vous
plait," and Frank tried to open a stuck lock and succeeded
in forgetting Gretta and her husband for the time. Soon
they were gone. Bergston had driven up to Le Havre; Curtiss took the train; there was no reason ever to meet either
of them again.

But meet they did. They met first at the Théâtre de
l'Atelier, in that pretty little candy square in Montmartre,
where Frank had gone alone to see a long-running farce
about a clerk who rebels against The System, in and out of
bed, in familiar French boulevard fashion—a mixture of
sad jokes, pretentious cynicism, and cheerful impotence.
Bergston nodded to Frank, as if they were casual business
acquaintances, while Gretta blushed and turned away. She

asked her husband to get her some lemonade, he went to
the little stand, she stood four feet from Frank without saying a word. He was intensely relieved when Bergston returned (pink lemonade it was) and they strolled away into
the intermission crowd. Why at long last the blush? Shame
at being seen, all three, like this? Or guilt because poor
Frank was mourning her by going alone to silly, cynical
boulevard plays in that Paris of his dreams? Did she believe
it was for love of her that he stood alone in the lobby? And
was it?

She had better, Frank thought, be a cleverer little ac-
tress or her husband will figure it all out. It's surely not too
complicated even for him.

By an act of pure will, Frank determined never to
meet them again. If his will should fail him, then he would
dodge behind a pillar or a plant. He would hold up a newspaper in front of his face. He would grow a mustache. In
other words, after the play he had two cognacs in a Montmartre cafe on his desire not to see the Bergston family.

A few days later they met in the Place des Vosges, in
the little park near a statue of one of the last Louis, where
Frank was strolling and trying to figure out why he was
neither depressed nor elated by Paris, just *there,* with none
of the gay or the nostalgic magic he had anticipated. Re-
garding these circular ideas looped on the tip of a dead
king's lance, he stood in that formal and uncomfortable
stance of public thought, elbow supported by palm, chin in
other palm. The humid, yellow-gray city was just there. I
am just here, he was thinking, and that's all there is to it. An
ancient bucko with drooping yellow moustaches approached
to ask, "Victor Hugo House. You desire see Victor Hugo
House?"

"Non, merci."

"One dollar American you see Victor Hugo House renowned author of worldwide fame guided tour with explication."

"No!"

And the man was gone, but standing in his place, with Frank's *no* still bleating at him, was Alfred Bergston, smiling, bowing, host at a Smorgäsbord, nodding his head to encourage Frank to say more, refuse fish eggs or cheese with caraway, to deny if he could and dared. Frank whirled, wondering if this deep isolation in which he lived could produce hallucinations, but no, there was the old man, scurrying like a young one in pursuit of client or prey in the direction of Maison Victor Hugo at one corner of the square. And partway along his line of vision stood a lovely dark young creature, pensive, unhappy, with swollen eyes, watching—Gretta. Her husband had run ahead to greet Frank.

"Good day, sir!" Frank cried out with utmost formality, wondering if this were because he knew the man had learned his English from books or because he was the melodramatic cad in a joke which had no reality to him. "I want to see. . . ." he heard himself mumbling, and knew they lost the rest of it as he strode off, trying to keep from running and feeling the straining, twitching muscles in his legs: "The Victor Hugo House." He paid the few francs admission and rushed through, past the bound volumes, the manuscript pages in a glass case, the portraits, the vests worn by, the pens used by V. Hugo, and the dozing guard slumped in a chair. When he emerged, the old guide was waiting with a contemptuous leer marring his face of peaceful senility. He suggested that, although the American monsieur had dispensed with his services, he deserved at least some recompense for supplying the idea of visiting Victor Hugo House. The ideas have of value even in this world brutal and pragmatic, he stated.

Frank returned to his hotel room, threw himself on his bed, lay sullen as a child. And yet Paris had performed no ill on him. And the fat Swede was the wronged man. And yet he wept wronged, childish tears, his chest shaking. Then he felt clear, light, and easy. He blew his nose and went out for coffee and found a pharmacy which sold him eyedrops to clear up the redness of his lids. "It's the conjunctives," the clerk informed him. "One does not need eight years of medicine, plus hospital interning, and no chance to marry or have children along the way to see that it is the conjunctives. Vous vous amusez bien à Paris? Paris c'est beau n'est-ce pas? Tous les touristes aiment Paris," he concluded with satisfaction. "Use these drops at will."

A dubbed western movie to pass the time that night. When the villain's lips were moving to say, "I gotta lay low," a heavy false voice drawled on the sound track, "Je dois rester tranquille."

By this time Frank had presented his letters and paid his calls. He began to receive invitations from friends of friends, acquaintances of acquaintances, and he drifted idly from lunch appointments to apéritif appointments to dinner engagements, visiting the Louvre between, strolling the wintry streets, retreating into the cafés for coffee against the cold and damp. Somehow he was spending more money than he remembered it was possible to spend on the simple life. Somehow he was waiting to go to the Paris he remembered and was not yet there. Paris was still exactly like Chicago or New York to him: the place where he had to meet himself in the shaving mirror.

But this common educational process about the difference between New York and Paris—much outside, the same in the shaving mirror—was not yet over for him; or if it was, the example of Alfred and Gretta Bergston was not. The next time he saw Bergston, in the lobby of the Théâtre

Francais, the man's eyes widened in a kind of curiosity and
despair which could mean only one thing: He knew. He
suspected. He *knew*.

And if he knows, Frank Curtiss decided, it is only
because there was really nothing but anger and cunning and
collusion between Gretta and me. He knows only because
Gretta wants him to know; she let him know. Contrary to
what we are told, a woman can always hide an adventure.
Her husband must be told by someone, and in this case it
could be no one but Gretta. And that meant that she wanted
to inform on him, wanted to hurt him. And that meant that
she had merely used Frank as the instrument to attack her
husband; a tool; the cutting edge, and nothing but a blade.

Frank's face was massacred by his new habit of an intense active boredom at shaving. He stood before the mirror
and raced through the process, nicking himself frequently,
stopping the bleeding with pieces of Kleenex which sometimes stuck to his face until he felt the stares in the lobby of
his hotel and ripped off the scraps of paper. There were little
spots of blood measling his collars. He hated to shave. He
hated to stand there, waiting. This winter his pale lean head
looked almost blue with fatigue. He should find a sunlamp;
he should buy vitamin pills; he should improve his color.
He should think healthier thoughts in November, learn to
like yoghurt, buy a nifty new pair of shoes.

If Bergston knew, then Gretta wanted him to know.
Frank's memory of pleasure was over. There was no possibility of constructing the nostalgia of the shipboard adventure on the *Saxonia*. He was, as a musician friend put it,
drifting in Adriftsville. Like the porthole through which
they had gazed, he had been merely a part of the view for
Gretta.

One bleak afternoon he took a bus to the great Père
Lachaise cemetery, where Rastignac had stood looking

down at Paris, shaking his fist at the city and crying out,
"It's between us two now!" He went there, and strolled
among the dead as if to try his luck and meet Alfred Bergston by the willow over the grave of de Musset or at the
broken bottles which sprinkled the grave of André Laporte,
"Inspector of Bridges and Roads." But of course Bergston
never appeared. This was no magical persecution. People
met by accident all the time in Paris; Bergston was not following him. A light sleet had begun to fall and his shoes
were mudlogged.

Now he was convinced, as he lay again in his bed in a
hotel with sweating walls and hot water for an hour in the
morning and another at night, that Gretta had merely calculated all the while and the flailing heart which she had
pressed against his was a trick of metabolism. She had been
a wife all the time. She thought only of her fat blond husband, thought of revenges against him, true; but thought
only of him. She had not been the facile Swedish girl, taking
her amusements as they came, but he had been easy, American, used, a pushover.

He convinced himself that the meetings with Bergston
were accidental, and then they met at the American Express, which lay on Frank's daily route—mail, a drink of
water, a look at Americans dragging their fun around.
Among his letters was a note on Kingdom of Sweden lega-
tion stationery:

Dear Sir:

I must speak with you about an important matter.
Urgent and vital importance. I will meet you here.
Alfred Bergston

I'll go to Spain today! was Frank's first thought, and he was
still making resolutions, ready to pack, when he emerged

onto the rue Scribe, where the newsvender huddled under his tarpaulin, to find the Swede in a trenchcoat, hunched, cold, waiting. From the cavern of this large unhappy body came a voice: "I must talk with you, Frank. Ve must talk it over."

Don't call me Frank! You don't know me! Instead he said, "What about? I don't have any business with you, do I?"

And then, when he heard her words, "Oh, please! Vy?" he finally saw Gretta standing in the drizzle further off, moving in little circles on the broad sidewalk, her dark little face beseeching and her hair coming stringy in the wet out of the woolen parka she was wearing. Apparently she had been forbidden to come closer. She walked in little circles, as if caged, and the occasional passerby hurrying through the rain had to walk around her, carefully, incuriously sensing that she might jump in any direction.

"You must listen. That much at least you must," Bergston commanded.

"Talk then. I'm in a hurry. I'm getting wet."

Bergston straightened up and struck him with a look of scorn. Rain and tears commingled were running down his face. "I *know*," he hissed. "She told me everything. How you did things." Frank started to deny, but Bergston put up his plump hand to command silence, and Frank now felt some authority in the man and his gestures. He said: "You push her around, you push her around and kiss her, you make love on her—I know! I am told! It is not the first time. It is not the first time! She is a pig, but I love her— I do not blame you, sir, I am a man also—but I love her and I want to guard over our marriage. Please to stay away from her! She is a pig!"

This pathetic, hopeless, brutal man! Frank saw him weeping among the creatures in his pigpen; one of his swine had been stolen. Thinly she was hiccuping, tapping her heel on the wet pavement. "Am I a child to be talk of like so? Vy?" And Frank remembered the whispered *vy?* which he had found so full of praise as the empty hours went round with the two of them in each other's arms, setting depth charges—*Oh vy do you make me so happy, vy?*

Like liquid flowing through a membrane, his feeling for her had drained toward pity for her husband. The man wept in the Paris rain, his heavy face a contorted snout, the eyes shut and red while he continued to call Gretta a pig. "I do not blame you, you did not know me, my suffering, man he has desires, he must suffer, it is our punishment on earth, she is lovely to look at, so sweet to enjoy, though she is swine. . . ." Tears rolled down his fat cheeks. The rain and the tears were dripping onto his collar. "Please to leave her alone for me, I beg you, sir. It is not cost to you. She is swine."

At last Frank could bear no more, he felt answering tears starting within himself too, and he burst out with passionate conviction, "I don't know what your wife has been telling you"—he almost said *sir*—"but there's been nothing! Not a thing! *Not a thing!*" It was a lie which he spoke with more blessed conviction than he had ever spoken the truth, and with this conviction came certain knowledge: It really was the truth. As they struggled and cleaved across their beds on the *Saxonia,* there had been nothing at all.

"Frank! Vy!" Gretta cried, this time disobeying and running up to the two gesticulating men. "Vy you say this things? How you dare?"

A grimace of satisfaction crossed Bergston's face. Frank was started on a way and would continue. "Oh leave me alone, both of you. Just leave me alone. I didn't do anything to her or you or anyone—" *Vy?vy?vy?* "Everybody leave me alone!"

"Oh don't say! It helps nothing, nothing! Vy?"

But Bergston wore a huge happy grin on his wet face. He was watching greedily from Frank to Gretta, from Gretta to Frank. Frank Curtiss went on denying, saying no, saying *no,* and felt as the true answer to Bergston's smile the slick grin forming on his own mouth. He denied angrily, indignantly, smoothly, and found himself smiling; he felt himself sleek and fat, or wily and skinny, it didn't matter; he did not know what he felt like anymore or what he would see in the mirror when he looked, but he knew that he had entered upon a new role in life, he had defined himself for himself and admitted how much love he could allow. As he abruptly cried out, "No, no!" once more, and spun around to leave the couple still standing together on the corner of the rue Scribe at the Place de l'Opéra in Paris, he saw that Bergston understood him very well, for out of one inflamed eye the man gave him a huge happy, lewd wink.

Jim the Man

He had a basement apartment in the slum still called Hell's Kitchen west of Times Square, two strong legs, a nosy look on a long-nosed face too thin for a man of his years, and a 1952 Studebaker, painted black by himself, which he kept in a lot near the Hudson River for eighteen dollars a month. For his living he composed wheedling letters for a magazine: "Your subscription has expired, and yet world events are moving so fast that no one can afford to be without. . . ." It was easy money, though not much of it and one day soon a machine would be taught to wheedle and replace him.

Sometimes he spent his days wading back and forth through Times Square (the crowds, the crowds!); he stopped at Romeo's on 42nd Street, where amid howling waiters and neon and smell of olive oil, he ate egg plant parmigiana, eighty cents. He thought about being a poet, a movie actor, a lover of beautiful women, a secret operative in the realms of eternal beauty and truth. During the war he had been trained as an intelligence agent (he spoke languages, thought quickly), but his ankle broke under him in a practice jump. Thirteen years later he still wanted to land in Bulgaria at night, his drop cushioned by the bosom of a sweet anti-fascist who would nurse him back to health by singing folk songs and feeding him yoghurt. He was thirty-three years old, too old for all this. At his age Jesus had been forgiving everybody in sight, to the right and the left, and ending his days.

But matters moved faster in those mythic hot climes.

Jim Curtiss had no friends, he had no enemies. He had no one. He had nobody. He pronounced that word: I ALONE. *Eye alone.* AYE ALONE! Sometimes he jostled a certain Puerto Rican girl of the neighborhood up the back stairway and they gasped and rolled on her bed and he gave her Presents because she would not take money ("I am not professional, Jeemie, oooh, do that again, feelthy boy.") On his birthday she too gave him Presents, including a fluorescent crucifix that she had received in exchange for two dollars, including packing and mailing charges, from a radio station in Texas. "For over the bed, Jeemie, to theenk of me." That, of course, is what gift crucifixes from a non-professional are for—to theenk of Conchita.

Sometimes he met, through contacts in espresso shops and the corridors of Art, a girl from an acting school or a solemn, skinny dancer or somebody's jolly understudy— girls named Barbara or Sheree or Mary-Willa. A different girl each couple of months, when he didn't mind the work involved, or he longed to make love with an Actor's Studio instead of a Spaneesh accent ("Like I dig you, mon," rather than "Oooh, Jeemie.")

But if it is fact that I am alone, he thought, really fact, all alone, then I am surely not paranoid for thinking myself all alone. And I do not believe myself the Son of God, although I too am thirty-three years old, as He will be for all eternity. If He were insane in my way, He would never state that he was (is?) the Messiah. Too cunning for that. For certain the Savior would not dwell in Hell's Kitchen with its arosements of garbage outside and cats inside and clutter of ice cream peddlers coming to port with their little wagons in the abandoned coal distributor's hall next door; the Savior would live off Madison Avenue in a duplex, Jim decided; he would garage his car in a heated place; he would make it with the same girl and live happily ever after on frozen pizza and after-dinner coffee for after dinner, breakfast coffee for breakfast, and powdered onion soup mixed with sour cream on crackers when he wanted to have a few friends over for cocktails. No one would drop bottles or soggy empty ice cream boxes through his weeping willows.

So Jim Curtiss could not be paranoid. He believed himself to be merely Jim Curtiss, intelligent, faintly disoriented, incipiently respectable, nervous, quick on the uptake and the putdown, fond of egg plant parmigiana, fanciful and sometimes imaginative. Ow. Ow. Ow. Also very unhappy with his lot and unable to blame anyone.

One day a spirit made his way past the garbage can in the hall and the woman who said to everyone, "Cats— I don't smell anything. Do you smell anything? My cats are trained—*they* don't smell anything," and this visitor silently, discreetly, even invisibly passed the two toilets which served the four apartments on the ground floor. The woman with the cats had no chance to explain to him about the sense of smell. She might as well have argued with a spook about how fastidious and purring clean were her cats—a nobody passed by while she looked right through him and stroked Pussy One and Pussy Two awaited her turn. The nobody filtered into Jim's garden on this hot September evening. Five minutes from Times Square, in a slum flat for which he paid $37.50 a month, Jim Curtiss had a private garden. He nurtured ferns and willows there, a stone bench, a table; plant food and instructions by mail, of course, but green and good, humid, verdant, a private garden almost in dead center of busiest rock-shot Manhattan. He had rigged up a hose on a tripod and was giving himself a shower, wearing trunks. The willows and ferns shielded him from the curiosity of neighbors—why a garden? why?—who sometimes sounded the matter with fishbones, coffee grounds, or bottles in order to express their bemusement and doubt. But when they squabbled in their adjacent pueblos, they had the top of garden to squabble down upon. It gave them an example. Down came an old mattress once, followed by a used woman. She landed unhurt on the mattress, relaxed by grief but bawling. She didn't want to live no more—firstly—and secondly she didn't want to pay for no broken goddam willow up yours tree. And that was final. "Who's got my purse?"

Now the visitor hopped in, avoiding a puddle, watching Jim puffing and blowing under the cold stream from his hose. He took off a straw hat, wiped his face, made whewing sounds, and said, "Dandy little shower you got there—yep—nice arrangement."

"Jesus Christ Almighty," said Jim. "I didn't hear you."

"I didn't make much noise," said the person, "I sneaked in. Which reminds me."

"What?"

"I'll wait till you get out of the hose." He sat plump on the stone bench, removed his hat again, dried the band with a handkerchief, and looked up as a coke bottle drifted down through the verdure of Jim's garden. "Well. At your own time, Sergeant."

At last, dried, massaging between his toes with a towel, Jim said, "Gas company, telephone company, sanitation, survey about cigarette smoking habits or mental health, electricity, building inspector, what? How'd you know I was a buck sergeant once?"

"None of them," said the man, "and I thought you made tech. But never mind. I'm a chap has his own business —here." He handed Jim a card. "EDWARD BRACE. He Chooses. ACademy 2-1937." "That's my telephone number," he said.

"For what?" asked Jim.

"For calling me up," said Edward Brace.

"But what do you choose?"

"In this instance, you. In other cases I make other choices."

"Um—I'm a pretty busy man," Jim began. "Taking a shower, you know, keeping cool, going to movies, relaxing—takes a lot out of a man in New York. I'm sorry if I'm not in a position to discuss any matters of business until the hot weather subsides, maybe in November, make it after the first—"

"Listen," said Mr. Brace, cutting him off with curt pleasantness. "There's a fellow picks up all the old bus transfers on the ground: where do you think they go? I chose him. There's a lady in Brooklyn Heights leans out the window and watches the world go by, so's the world and Brooklyn Heights will know they are there: I chose her. Otherwise she'd have gone by like the rest. There is a power in the universe making for righteousness—"

"You chose it?"

"Not yet." He took back the card and slipped it carefully into his wallet. He cast a long slow significant look over Jim Curtiss as he put on a sweatshirt over his wet trunks, significant (that look on the face of Mr. Brace) of a long slow gathering of Jim Curtiss into his net. A stain of wet spread by capillary action through the lower part of Jim's sweatshirt. A hectic doubt flushed Jim's cheeks, forehead, neck, gills—he looked for a tear in the net.

"I'm not merely fishing with you," Mr. Brace said in

a peculiar mincing tone. "I'm considering. I have you on my mind. It's not for any nostrum, like curing tuberculosis by gargling with cotton. No. Considering. Now they use streptomycin for pulmonary cases."

And he watched with concern while Jim put on his shoes.

"You don't get foot trouble walking around in that canvas? Your arches?"

"No."

"You will have to do a lot of walking."

"I'm ready for walking, if I want to walk. I like walking. These have kind of foam rubber soles, I think it's called extruded rubber. New process. I walk a lot."

"I know," said Mr. Brace. "Would I be here otherwise? All the way to the far west side on a day like this?" He dried his eyebrows by running a finger along the pair. "You too will need to walk the streets of the city. You will find yourself climbing into the chess parlors of 42nd Street. You will visit the houses with garages attached in Queens, Forest Hills, and elsewhere. You will pace the airline terminals and stand in crowds waiting to see Perry Como. You will eat hot chili on St. Nicholas Avenue and take double shots of P.M. at the special price before closing. You will strive against both the Albigensians and the hi-fiers— to the death! Duplicity if called upon by Manicheans or men in sports cars with plaid caps! You will have much to do."

"I sort of like accurate sound in the trebles, responsible cornering, too," said Jim Curtiss. "And it sounds like a large order."

"It would be," said Mr. Brace, "for a man. It is not enough. You will be more than a man. So first change into clean underwear and stretchsox."

Jim Curtiss went into his room and obeyed. It was late summer and humid, when a man can learn easily to obey. No lights burned before his eyes, no bushes, no rocks sprouted sweet water, no son to sacrifice either—just great Manhattan heat and pressure and the bus drivers get even a little more screwy. Better to obey. While he was dressing, Mr. Brace bent, poked out the soot in the keyhole with a matchstick, and whispered through it, "You may be called upon to become a tap dancer. You will surely need to bounce bacon against the walls and tie your shoelaces without bending the knees."

"I shall be ready," said Jim Curtiss. "I shall put my foot against the wall and stretch my back in such a way that I can reach the laces."

When Jim emerged, now in sandals, Mr. Brace nodded rapidly with approval. He asked Jim to turn around. He prodded the pocket of his blue jeans; there was no wad of money. "Mm," said Mr. Brace, as if he had tasted something delicious, reminding Jim of his ancient pleasure in Jello. He had not eaten Jello in years—the way it snapped and shivered. Nonchalantly an appraising eye noted that Jim was wearing an old pink button-down-collar shirt, of a color and fashion that had gone out several years ago. He could not wear it to his office, but it was frayed at the collar, it was dirty, it was torn at the pocket; it was proper for tying shoelaces without bending knees and perhaps becoming a tap dancer, also climbing chess parlors, creeping into garages, stalking Perry Como; walking the city in a certain way, with charmed sacroiliac.

"I feel as if I know," said Jim Curtiss. "You do not have to tell me."

"Of course," Mr. Brace remarked prissily. "If you did not know already, I would not tell you. You are not called and chosen, you call and choose, you call and choose first of all yourself."

"Only logic," said Jim.

"I say no more. We have no need of signs—kid stuff. Logic! Go."

Jim went, leaving Mr. Brace standing in the garden, humming. He presumed that Mr. Brace could escape by scaling a wall. At any rate, he would not starve. He could cry for help or open the door, whichever came easier. He could nibble on a sprig of weeping willow.

First stop for Jim Curtiss was one of the chess parlors above a Fascination, Just For Fun Game on 42nd Street. In these chess parlors a man can play chess all night, even sleeping on the tables between moves, for fifteen cents an hour. Some men climb the long stairway to play chess here because they do not get along with their wives or because they cannot afford a hotel room, but most because they like to play chess and find the fee of fifteen cents an hour reasonable, since it includes tables, chairs, lights, heat, chessmen, board, and a committed stock of partners; also magazines and books on chess and the likelihood of overhearing and exchanging tactical and strategic information. Jim walked in on the end of a game between a tall young negro dressed in a fez and bop glasses and a pigeon-breasted old Jew with a great deal of dandruff on his collar and shoulders, a lesser amount on his sleeves, and a barely perceptible amount on the chess tables. He also had thick glossy white hair. This proved with finality that dandruff is not linked with baldness or swimming in chlorinated pools (providing the old man was not a secret swimmer, secretly bald). The negro, winning the match, was singing in Yiddish. The Jew, valiantly battling without a king, sang "Short Shorts" in a modified rock-and-roll rhythm, and sacrificed his knight. "If Ah don' love ya baby," he sang, "then Mona Lisa was a man."

"If that man doesn't have a king," the negro mused aloud, "then he deserves great praise for playing chess at all."

"I am not needed here," said Jim Curtiss. "Both these men have logic. They believe in the Open Society, the relativity of values in a changing world, and creative chess. I go." He descended.

"Who needs you?" remarked the boy who took the cash at the door. "You come in and walk around, disturb the players, then you go. Farewell."

"Farewell," said Jim. He could not be expected to turn more than two cheeks. *"You,"* he cried in an access of spite, "you have not got logic. Therefore you must tarry until I return."

"I'll be waiting," the youth screamed down the long stairway. "Place never closes. Bring thirty cents next time and I'll—"

But gently Jim shut the door. He did not want to hear the rest because he hated to hate and that blasted Times Square kid got on his nerves. He did not deserve to work in a chess parlor. On the other hand, the boy probably needed the job. He marked it down in his notebook that he would have to occupy himself with the youth of America at some future date.

He set out for his little Puerto Rican friend's pad. Up he climbed the five flights of stairs, in full confidence of finding her ready, since she went to bed early and slept late. She had very little else to do and bed was home to her. The Welfare Dept. and a few lonely souls like Jim Curtiss (used to be) took care of her need for company. "Jeem!" she murmured drowsily from the mussed bedclothes. "Shh. Do not bother me. I am sleeping. Climb into bed, be quiet, shush, and I will wake up after awhile. In the meantime you can—"

"No," he said, "I don't want to."

She sat bolt upright. "You do not *want* to?" She covered the wanting-to places with a sheet.

"I want to talk to you," he said.

She put several pins in her mouth, preparatory to putting them in her hair, and said, "Talk me slowly in English then, since I listen in Spaneesh."

Jim began. He opened his mouth. He tried to begin. He moved his tongue up and down against his moral white teeth, his ethical pink palate; he wiggled his metaphysical tonsils and his Adam's apple leapt, entranced by truth—he said nothing. He found little to tell her other than. . . . other than. . . . "Thank you!" he cried. "Thank you so much! You have been kind! Happy! Wished to make me happy! Yes! I wish you well!"

"Jeem," she said reproachfully, "you wake me up for to tell me that? I go back to sleep now, please." And she popped back down onto the pillow, from which she gave him a wink. He bent to kiss her and the wink nearly broke her eye in two. He barely touched her cheek, kissing her with a mere winged brush of lip against satin face, and the wink whirled round to a flipped lid of outrage.

"Goodbye," he said.

"Foo."

"Be good."

"Foo."

He descended the long stairway, considering that his assignment from Mr. Brace was more complicated than Mr. Brace had indicated or he had imagined. A man does not like to be told foo. *But,* he seemed to hear Edward Brace indicating in his left ear, *you are not a man like other men.*

Still, to be told foo when you have not yet become a tap dancer, kicked a policeman, composed a rock-and-roll hit, smiled with understanding into the night deposit vault of a bank. Still, to be told foo so fluently. It's not only men have feelings in material matters!

The streets were hot, he felt them through his sandals,

he bent and took a handful of concrete and tar. The summer
had burned through and the liquid center of the great
candy city was moiling, boiling, bubbling, and troubling.
Cherries would have stewed on the cherry trees—if cherry
trees. Instead asphalt, tar, grit, tempers, prunes stewed in
their prune boxes. This September in the city was a time of
vacant, overcooked faces and blocked programs for the
future. The juice of both people and projects had run off in
the pot. The eternal children built their eternal cooling fires
on the heaving sidewalks, and fed them with orange crates,
old tires, papers, litter. Somewhere a Chinese waiter was
studying how to put silverware on a table, cracking his head
over the hard ways of western civilization. Somewhere a
diner was getting silverware in his lap. Somewhere bakers
had their hands up to the shoulders in dough, and in their
lungs—dough. They were coughing, they were dreaming of
powderblue Chrysler Imperials with air conditioning optional added equipment. Somewhere designers of optional
added equipment were thinking up new added optional
equipment.

   In order to journey into Queens—surely this was on
Mr. Brace's mind—Jim needed food, and on 42nd Street
there was Romeo's, the cheapest and most agitated food in
town. Red neon—SPAG—orange neon—HETTI—Haircut
75¢ One Flight Up—"Seats at duh countah, you!"—Hair
Parmigiana with Ravioli and Vitalis—PLAY FASCINATION
—red neon—Everybody Eats—This Is Not a Barber College—pots and silver and orange neon—and Blue Suede
Shoes. . . . A clutch of visitors to town clutched each other
by, twill pants on pop and cotton dresses on mama and the
girls. "Ma Baby Loves, in this case and for example and at
eighty-five cents apiece for two, A Western movie."

   Cream in the little dispensers curdled at Jim. Relish
winked. Manicotti wriggled. Time flew.

Jim emptied himself out onto the street, gasping hot peppers.

"Be Good to a Child!" said the poster. "Stop J.D.!" TWO SHOCK HITS, 'CULT OF THE COBRA' AND 'LIVERWURST ON RYE WITH MUSTARD OR MAYONNAISE.' Bishop and Mind Seer Dr. Nagaswami Will—

Jim was by before he could learn the Dr.'s mind and will. Dr. Nagaswami was not a barber college, either. FOR QUEENS SUBWAYS FOLLOW THE (there was an arrow).

Jim followed the (there were both arrows and lights).

Down the ramp; onto the quay; next to the pineapple juice machine. If it were not the right subway to get out to Queens, no matter; he would climb and descend again; he would ascend, descend, ascend until he got to Queens. Mr. Brace bid him go, but for himself he wanted to go. He composed in his head a speech entitled, "The Anti-Bread, by James Curtiss."

At the office they would be wondering about him. No one would be rolling up his sleeves to write the letters to delinquent subscribers. "We have continued sending you our magazines because. . . ." Let them wonder! Let them go on sending them their magazines!

"Individuals, munching bread," thought Jim Curtiss, "are unable to persist in the existence situation. . . . no. The collectivity of small nations and large, within a structure of physical survival, do not find bread to be a sufficient. . . . no. Even supplemented by fish oil, rice krispies, and/or margarine, urban males and females. . . . no."

No, he thought, rolling up his sleeves.

He was on the right train to Queens. "Without any implied derogation of the place of bread and other bakery products in the diet of humans. . . . no."

NO!

He gave his seat to a young man with a tennis racket

and a copy of the *Herald Tribune*. The young man, long bridge to his nose, pink cheeks, three rows of healthy teeth, one in reserve, thanked him kindly and unfolded his newspaper. Jim read the headline on the first page of the fashion section: MAN CANNOT LIVE BY BREAD ALONE.

He sighed and hung happily from his strap. Yes, yes now. The important thing is not to invent new words but to discover old ones. He had found the truth, thanks to Mr. Brace, this youth, and a distinguished old newspaper. Oh fine yes. He endeavored to fix the words in his memory and believed that he had succeeded. He dozed, still hanging. He thought of his friend with her fluorescent crucifix on which somebody hung, of his colleagues at the office hounding lazy or disappointed subscribers, of Mr. Brace staring at the hose in his garden, of the good people of the New York *Herald Tribune,* and of himself. He thought of himself by thinking of those others—or perhaps it was vice versa—he thought of those others by thinking of Jim, Jim, Jim Curtiss.

In Queens he emerged and his easily astonished eyes found row upon row of garden apartments! apartments built in squares around squares! and in the center square was green grass! Thus he also walked among ranch houses with garages and crematoriums attached; gulls screamed and teevee repairmen screamed back; a jet liner made a forced landing on a badminton court; hot were his feet in their sandals as he approached a medieval shopping center which was very gothic, also romanesque, crenolated, shielding archers all in green, their longbows strung against shoplifter strategy and inflationary tactic. Savory young wives, looking in their blouses and leotards like adolescents of either sex, drove up in the Second Car (Volkswagen, used Pontiac, Rambler). Crates of English muffins, non-caloric beer, and toy balloons for the kiddies were loaded for them by happy smiling errand boys, tipped a quarter, and some-

times an extra dime just for wearing an Errol Flynn moustache and caring. Trucks from the great drug companies
had high priority at this corner, delivering sedatives and
tranquilizers; loafy-faced policemen took off their hats,
hushed the traffic, and everyone stood at attention. A fire-
truck shrieked to a halt. Let the house burn while the non-
habit-forming calmatives are installed on shelves. Neurosis
troubles the digestion but feeds the flames.

Jim Curtiss took his place on the sidewalk before the
alley between the drugstore and the supermarket. Preparing,
he recalled the rule for sidewalk spielers—unfurl an American flag. He cleared his nose with a handkerchief instead.
To his surprise and delight, he found his sinuses expanded,
free, and easy. Again many thanks to Mr. Brace! Love
clears the nasal passages, he thought. I must inform them
all.

He began: "Bless you!"

That had nothing to do with it. No one had sneezed.
A few stopped to listen, merely because a lot of noise had
come out of his mouth, a sharp crack, an explosion of
sound. But no one had sneezed. That was not where he
chose to begin. He tied his shoe, waited, and cried out to a
pretty young housewife in tapered slacks, "Yes! Go to a
man's apartment! Yes! You have a right! Go to a man's
furnished room! Go to the back seat of his car! Please! I
ask you kindly! But *want* to do it first, Ma'm."

She listened pensively until he came to that last cour-
teous, Ma'm, and then she recognized the threat in his voice.
"Oh!" she cried as if desperately pinched, and off she
trotted, calling, "Oh! Ouch!"

Tooshay, thought Jim Curtiss. Now for the next point.

A crowd had gathered about him. He took off his shoes
to indicate that he recognized them. He did. He did not
exactly see a crowd: he saw a man with a child in a stroller,

eating licorice, both of them; he saw a mulatto woman with a shopping bag and pale blotches down one side of her face, as if she had almost decided to be white—she had red hair, too; he saw a young man with a green sack bulging with books (as a student at Cornell Jim had carried a green sack bulging with books because at Harvard they carried green sacks bulging with books, also tennis balls); he saw men, women, and children, and a helicopter buzzing overhead as he raised his arm for silence.

"Yes, bless you!" he cried, ceding to an imperative desire to make love to all of them, that talent which it is death to reveal. "Do not go to a matinee, hear me out! Listen!" And he felt a creature thrill of power to his spine— successful rivalry with an afternoon show. Even the helicopter fell silent. "I tell you this: Think! Provide! Recognize fact! Mere love is not enough, either! You may build the finest house with deepest love, the deepest faith in love, the deepest truth and trust, but if you do not make contrivance for discharge of the wastes of life, your dream house will turn into a palace of filth and abomination!"

And the crowd answered him, "We have sewers." And the helicopter snorted, rumbled, made threatening passes. And the crowd murmured against him, saying, "He has a dirty tongue. Wash his mouth out with detergent."

"I have lived long among you," cried Jim Curtiss, "lived in your way, ignorantly, sinning by occupying myself with nonsense, drinking when I was not thirsty and going with women in a lying fashion, taking in movies, buying stock on margin—"

And the crowd muttered, "He must have had an unhappy childhood. Kill him."

"But now I know! Understand! We must learn to touch one another without closing our fists or bending our knees!"

Hushed smiles and comments from the mob. He thought: Pleased that they lie so patient, so quiet. Ready to get something for the athlete's foot—their only trouble sole trouble, soul trouble, get it? Nudge somebody. "Ouch! He interfered with me!"

"I only pinched you, Madam."

"Help! Hel-lup!"

He bawled back at her, "There is a great difference in the honey of bees! Some you buy are fed on sugar! Others drink from flowers!"

And the bells of heaven pealed for him, and the sky opened, and the angels came forth; but the siren of a police ambulance, and the door, and attendants in white coats flying forward with a stretcher to seize him. When Jim saw that one of the police nurses was Mr. Brace he began to fight back; he kicked and scratched and bit; since he was not a man, since he was appointed, he had permission to fight with what he had been given—nails, teeth, knees, feet. The crowd bellowed, but did not hurt him. The nurses grunted, but tried not to break his arm. Jim shrieked, "No! No! No!" three times, like that, and then he was pinned and strapped by broad brown leather bands to a stretcher and Mr. Brace was applying a needle to his arm, saying, "Quiet now, son, nobody wants no trouble from you. Lie down. You snap off this needle, it'll be the skin off your own—"

No.

"Nice fellow. Yes. Lie still now. Okay, *done*."

A madman newsboy was shouting and dancing about him, shrieking, "Man thinks he's Jesus Christ Almighty! Lookit! Man thinks he's J.C. Himself."

No, Jim Curtiss did not think that. No, he was not Jesus Christ Almighty Son of God. He rocked as the stretcher was heaved, up, hup now, into the ambulance. No, he was not even Jim Curtiss. He folded his arms and accepted the hood of sleep closing and darkening over him. He only followed orders. Yes. He was merely another very sleepy fellow in trouble in the city of New York and the Borough of Queens.

Postface: An Aftermath About These Stories

*These stories all aim to be true and
full of joy, or true and full of sorrow, which amount to the same thing
for the storyteller, though very different to him as a man before the story
is written. First he is concerned with
his personal joys and sorrows; then he
hopes to tell a public story, freely
guessing, playing, lying, until that
best reader of whom he dreams cries out,
"Stop! Now I see what you see!"*

It has been suggested that
a note about the particular circumstances of the writing of
these stories might interest a few friends, enemies, and
necrologists. In other places [*Fifteen by Three* (New Directions); *The Living Novel*, edited by Granville Hicks
(Macmillan); *Fiction of the Fifties* (Doubleday); and in
a series of surly and enthusiastic papers printed in the *Hudson Review*] I have written at some length about the forms
of fiction, about the metaphysical purposes of tale-bearing
in our time, about the general differences and connection
between the short story and the novel, and other such matters (musica morbido); as a means of passing the time be-

tween stories, I have also leaned out of my glass house and thrown my quota of bricks (tempo allegro). Here I shall confine myself to a few specific and casual remarks about the stories in this book.

"The Heart of the Artichoke" (*Hudson Review,* 1951) was personally crucial because it gave me a sense that I was now my own man. I had written other stories and a first novel, *Birth of a Hero,* but with this story I felt that I had discovered myself as a writer in some conclusive way. (Of course, this discovery must be constantly renewed, since the self is a north pole which is altered by drifting snows and a shifting axis. But now I believed: *it can be done!*) Partly I was nourished by a happy time in my life. I was finished with school, having fun on the G.I. Bill and a Fulbright, author of a book which had just been accepted by a publisher; I was about to become a father; I was rediscovering the American language by learning French and rediscovering the city of Cleveland by riding a bicycle in Paris. Believing myself fortunate and loved by my wife, oldtime troubles in love suddenly came to life in my head and I found that they were now funny to me; and although no less sad, I could grieve for others because I was now very clearly someone quite different from myself as an adolescent. And different again after finishing this story. And different once more about myself, my parents, and my friends after rereading it.

I wrote "The Heart of the Artichoke" in two sittings at an outdoor café near the Place d'Alesia, keeping an eye on my bicycle parked at the curb. My book editor tried to place the story with a number of well-known magazines, but it finally appeared in *Hudson Review,* then a new quarterly with which I have enjoyed a pleasant association ever since. "The Heart of the Artichoke" was "noticed" and has been reprinted many times. I can encourage every writer's secret conviction of the undivine origin of literary authority by reporting that two editors whose magazines had rejected the story, later wrote to ask if I would be sure to show them any story I write "like 'The Heart of the Artichoke.'" Having been judged favorably by others, it turned out to be the commodity they had always sought.

"Susanna at the Beach" (*The Atlantic,* 1954) was written while I was living once again in Lakewood, Ohio, but now I was a paterfamilias with a job, a house, and that spasmodic impulse which grips the short story writer—find the truth by finding the meaning of childhood. (The novelist is usually less gripped by dreamy nostalgia; he insists on his projection against a possibly mastered future.) I recalled summers on the municipal beaches nearby and worried about some idealistic girls I had known. I finished the story in an air-conditioned ice cream parlor near Lakewood High School to which I had fled on a brutal September afternoon. The manager asked if I could do my homework elsewhere; he needed the table; "you kids buy a shake and think you own the place." Sure enough, I discovered my face in the mirror looking rather haggard but too young. The skin of my face has since managed to catch up with my age.

"A Celebration for Joe" (*Antioch Review,* 1954) was a by-blow of the novel, *The Prospect Before Us,* which I was then thinking through. That book was an enthusiastic elegy for an oldcountry individualist who got in terrible trouble because he insisted on following his stubborn personal morality in business in America. Joe in this story is a spiritual cousin to Harry Bowers in the novel. Progress sometimes occurs, but the skinny sons of these thick men are not always improvements on their fathers.

"The Burglars and the Boy" (*Discovery*, 1954) tells about honoring one's fellow man, tells about duty to society, and comes out halfway for the first against the second. A man on leave from a rest home for tired alcoholics in Sarasota, Florida, telephoned me one morning to say he liked my story. I was worried about what the call was costing his family and tried to cut the visit short, but then yielded to his will to have a comfortable chat about the Meaning of Life. I'm not sure what I'd have done if he had telephoned again, collect. (This doubt could provide a sequel to "The Burglars and the Boy.")

"Ti-Moune" (*The New Yorker*, 1955) and "Encounter in Haiti" (*Midstream*, 1956) were both written in Haiti during a pause for breath in the writing of a novel, *The Man Who Was Not With It*. For many American writers, we are told, their work is their way of pursuing health. (This seems much too simple.) These two stories were certainly less than crucial to my survival. I simply wanted to understand a strange society and incurably put my understanding to myself in the form of stories. Writing stories about where I was provided a breath of the safe and sane and *real* while I gathered my strength to wrestle again with the carnival extremity of the novel.

"Paris and Cleveland Are Voyages" (*Hudson Review*, 1957) provided a return to short fiction after coming up from *The Man Who Was Not With It*. With dread I was noting the futility of "the life of Art" as an escape from everyday sorrows and a substitute for everyday joys. The story was partly conceived as a warning to myself. I believe that the hero would probably be less gullible if he were really capable of creating a poem, but in his invincible nostalgic misery he might still be incapable of protecting himself from a cleverly predatory child. I like to think that this is a satire, something like "Frankenstein."

The remainder of these stories was written while I was struggling with the matter of an unruly novel, *The Optimist*. "Aristotle and the Hired Thugs" (*Commentary*, 1957) is partly a tribute to my real father, partly an urging upon myself of the necessity to survive in a time of personal shipwreck, partly another retreat to childhood to find what I can learn from it and thus give over to mastery as an adult. We ransom the present with booty illicitly carried from an imaginary past. I regret the brutal crudeness of the story, which has been attacked for its criticism of the Jewish tradition of non-violence, but I would regret even more being destroyed as were six million other Jews. "The Panic Button" (*Vogue*, 1958) is rather critical of a certain sort of woman. I felt that way at the time, and still do. Later I confronted more directly the American men discovered by such women. They feed each other turpentine. "Sello" (*The Dial*, 1959) just retells that permanent story about Americans connecting and disconnecting in Europe. It's a familiar subject, but like putting on galoshes, every traveller does it in a way which tells his own story.

"What's Become of Your Creature?" (*Playboy*, 1959) examines the bitter yearning of a pleasure-loving, esthetic man for a hip, beat, cool, and frantic girl. The story represents my most recent wrestling with a theme also occurring in "Paris and Cleveland Are Voyages" and other stories not reprinted here. The air of certain times, certain places, the look of certain girls are continually refreshing this story for me. Although suffering trepidations, *Playboy* decided to print the story because, in the words of its publisher, "sheer quality should be a large measure of correctness for us." I was delighted to see the story in this magazine, which has been hospitable to a number of serious writers, both because of the money involved—writers have to be sure of meeting the rent and the alimony in order to survive as writers—and also because it is exciting to have one's best work presented to an American mass audience.

Of course, comment on the hip and the beat has become a minor American industry, but a writer does not invent the terms of his commitments. It has been a part of my time and age. However, if I can ever find the main office of The Beat Generation, I plan to hand in my resignation.

"Love and Like" (*Hudson Review,* 1959) was written while I was fighting the crucial issues in *The Optimist.* After turning away from the novel to write this story, I was able to face the book again with a sense of growth. The lines of connection between this story and other stories and novels are obvious. Does the theme have some personal significance? It does, Herr Doktor. The story has been reprinted a number of times and I am constantly surprised by the assumption of readers that it is autobiographical. Fortunately, I can remember my own life rather clearly, and so remind myself that it is not really like this. Dan Shaper is cautionary, not historical. However, the writing of any story unleashes personal energies and passions upon fantastical events. Here is another application to Marianne Moore's famous line about the job of poetry—to depict "real toads in imaginary gardens." Sometimes the reader finds the warts on the toad—and the jewel in its forehead—so vivid that he forgets that the garden does not exist. And often, of course, writers are like readers.

"A Tale of Two Husbands" was written while travelling a freighter through the Mediterranean from Marseilles to Haifa. "Jim the Man" was written upon my return to New York. Both these stories isolate themes embedded in *The Optimist,* of which I had finally finished a first draft. The unheroic isolation of the bachelor seems to me to be an emblem of the unheroic isolation of various esthetes, hedonists, Platonists—lonely and ambitious and failed and reduced to brutal egotism. In the first story, the failure is that of erotic frivolity; in the other, Jim is a cracked idealist, a cousin to Susanna, wanting to make more than mortal man can make of life on this earth.

These opposite solitudes come to the same thing. The mere fact of isolation usually dominates the cause for isolation or the justifications of it. The man who masters his isolation—comes through joyfully and sternly—will be the great hero of our time.

None of these remarks gets to the root of any story. If they did, the story would be superfluous. A story is first of all what follows when someone holds us near the fire by saying, "Here is what happened and it's important."

But sometimes when we care about someone, *if* we care, we want to know more than the pertinent self which the friend presents to us. We want mere history and gossip, too. And so perhaps these gossipaceous comments about my own work can be justified on the ground that to air is human. To forgive is the domain of readers.

—HERBERT GOLD

MERIDIAN BOOKS

published by The World Publishing Company
2231 West 110 Street, Cleveland 2, Ohio

MERIDIAN FICTION